Deadly Spirits

Deadly Spirits

Philip Marchand

Copyright © 1994 by Philip Marchand

All rights reserved. No part of this publication may be reproduced or transmitted in any form or by any means, electronic or mechanical, including photocopying, recording, or any information storage and retrieval system, without permission in writing from the publisher.

Published in 1994 by
Stoddart Publishing Co. Limited
34 Lesmill Road
Toronto, Canada
M3B 2T6
(416) 445-3333

Canadian Cataloguing in Publication Data

Marchand, Philip, 1946–
Deadly spirits

ISBN 0-7737-5641-8

I. Title.

PS8576.A74D4 1994   C813'.54   C94-930050-0
PR9199.3.M374D4 1994

Cover Design: Brant Cowie/ArtPlus Limited
Cover Concept: Angel Guerra
Typesetting: Tony Gordon Ltd.
Printed and bound in Canada

All the events and characters in this book are fictitious, and any resemblance to actual events or actual persons living or dead is purely coincidental.

Stoddart Publishing gratefully acknowledges the support of the Canada Council, the Ontario Ministry of Culture, Tourism, and Recreation, Ontario Arts Council, and Ontario Publishing Centre in the development of writing and publishing in Canada.

For William H. Ellis and Veronica Ellis

1

SOME MEN, when they start getting into trouble, secrete certain hormones that draw more trouble to them. It's a mysterious process, like the way animals communicate in mating season, and I don't really know how to account for it, but I do know that in a period of my life when I was deeply in trouble I seemed to attract, with an unhealthy charm, certain individuals who could do nothing but cause me problems. That is the only reason I can think of for my getting involved in the life of Charles LeRoy, who carried desperation like a tumor. You could never see it, but you could always sense it, feeding off his healthy blood cells.

Of course, I knew a lot of desperate people when I met LeRoy, and maybe there's no reason, in particular, that I should have foreseen the catastrophe that awaited him. We were both at a clinic for alcoholics in Toronto called Willow Crest. The staff wanted us to feel we weren't at a hospital, but at a haven, a retreat with the serenity of a golf course. It was at the end of a cul-de-sac and was surrounded on three sides by a wooded ravine. Nobody just driving around could see the place. You had to come down that one street, all the way to the end, to find it, and that made a lot of the patients at the clinic vaguely happy.

I knew it made Charles LeRoy happy. LeRoy and I had become friends at the clinic. Among other things, he enjoyed teasing me about the fact that I was an alcoholic reporter. One night we watched a movie on television with Jimmy Cagney as a newspaper reporter. The first scene showed him staggering into the newsroom after five days of alcoholic oblivion.

LeRoy nudged me with his elbow. "That like your paper?"

"They don't have typewriters anymore. The newsroom's a lot quieter."

"So tell me about life on the Toronto *Clarion*."

What could I tell him? That our aging and venerable managing editor, one Emil Hardaker, had all the charm of those old Soviet politicians who used to stand over Red Square reviewing May Day parades? That he set a miserable tone for the paper as a whole? I told LeRoy about my friend Dalzell — gentle Pete Dalzell — who sweat blood for that paper every day of his working life, and was finally rewarded by being named features editor, only his superiors made him pay for his promotion by devising various torments for him. It was the day they refused to run a series of articles he had thought up, had worked closely with a couple of reporters on, had imagined were sure National Newspaper Award material, that Pete Dalzell fell off the wagon. I know, because I spent the night drinking with him. A couple of hours after I left him, he was dead of a heart attack.

Not long after that I was fired. The occasion was a liquid lunch I had with a drinking buddy on the paper, a veteran reporter named Bob Le Gros. Bob was in great form as he told me his theory about Hardaker: how the man kept making life miserable for his underlings because he had never done the right thing for someone in his position and gotten a mistress who could teach him about good wines and trips to Paris and convince him to take early retirement. Hardaker was a millionaire a couple of times over, thanks to the real estate boom of the 1980s, and could afford all those things. Somehow we got from that topic to the idea of doing the definitive story on Charles and Di, and I managed to obtain, from the newspaper's travel agency, two plane tickets for a flight that very night to London. We took it, landed at Heathrow, spent a day pub-crawling in London, and returned. Bob was severely reprimanded. I was fired.

Yes, I was fired, despite the fact I had been doing quite well at the newspaper, reporting on the mighty of Toronto. In retrospect, I realized the big problem wasn't that we had gone to London without permission, or that we hadn't even made an attempt to come back with a story, but that we hadn't booked airfare two weeks in advance for our debauch and gotten a cheap rate for this gross waste of the paper's money. Somebody had to be punished, so why not me?

But I didn't mind. I was actually relieved, in fact. I could gaze upon the ghost of Pete Dalzell with equanimity. Pete Dalzell, whose ravaged heart I had failed to soothe the night he died. Of course, I know how inaccessible that organ is now.

But I also had a beautiful, burning injustice to nurse, and I got down to it. For two weeks I didn't draw a sober breath. And then I checked into Willow Crest to dry out. To dry out and maybe get cured. I was admitting, you see, that I had a Problem. I couldn't get through a normal day without seven or eight stiff ones. Part of myself — a big part — told me not to worry about it. I remember Myrna Tostiak, our food writer — always in the *Clarion*'s kitchen testing recipes for busy career moms when she wasn't flirting with the boys in the mail room, some of whom were beefy lads indeed — assuring me that I was a charming drunk.

Ah, lovely blonde Myrna was a superb flirt. I received my share of her attentions, and I must confess it gave me ideas, but a wise part of me knew that I shouldn't ruin the wonderful mental picture I had of Myrna and myself in the throes of passion by trying to turn it into a reality. With Myrna, I got the idea the picture would always be better than the reality. That same wise part of me knew I was in trouble despite the fact that the flesh on the tip of my nose still had the right shape and color, and there was, as yet, no sign of a drinker's belly on me. I knew it was a bad sign to take a little shot from the vodka bottle in the desk drawer at 11:00 in the morning when you were working on a bitch of a story and no one was returning your phone calls and your temples felt as if they would swell up and burst if you didn't have that drink.

And then there was the small matter of my ruined marriage. My wife and I, who had started out with a genuine love for each other, split after several years of my not coming home until late in the evening — usually around my favorite pub's closing time, as a matter of fact. Of course, there were periods when I reformed, when I dutifully came home more or less on time, but it wasn't long before my resolve weakened. To my horror, I discovered I had my father's irresistible tendency to prefer the public house, and the company of drinking buddies, to domestic bliss. The acorn, as they say, doesn't fall far from the tree. Naturally my wife got tired of this and found someone else.

If I wasn't desperate now, in ten years I would be. That much I knew. And then — the question of my nose and stomach aside — I wouldn't be so charming. There is no such thing as a charming drunk over the age of forty.

So I signed myself in for four weeks of emotional and physical health, the specialty of Willow Crest. And that's where I first met Charles LeRoy. We were both being shaken down before being admitted. A nurse went through LeRoy's suitcase, pulled out a Sanka coffee jar, opened the top, and poured out the contents — a few dozen pills. LeRoy shrugged. He looked modest and polite, a young man with a future in middle management, with his nice brown suit that was neat and presentable, even if it didn't fit perfectly, and his brown wing tip shoes. His hazel eyes gave no hint of expression behind his horn-rimmed glasses.

It was a week before we started talking to each other. That first week was kind of a wake-up week for the forty or so patients in our group. We all sat around waiting for the fog to lift, the brain and central nervous system to start functioning normally again. Occasionally the sitting around would be interrupted by a film or videotape carefully demonstrating what irreplaceable brain tissue we were killing off with our drinking.

Then the cure began. We got up at 7:30 each morning, had a nutritious breakfast, and did exercises in a gym. After that we lay on mats while a woman told us, "Your feet are getting heavy now. Your ankles are relaxing and feeling heavy . . ." And some guy would start snoring and she would poke him, and then it was lunchtime. More nutritious food. Gallons of fruit juices. Afternoons we had group therapy, which took us to nutritious dinnertime, and then evenings full of card games and bingo and TV. At 10:30 we lined up for our Antabuse and vitamins, and then went to our rooms for lights-out.

That was just about it. Except I always looked forward to late-night talks with LeRoy. We had adjoining rooms connected by a bathroom. After 10:30 LeRoy would usually walk through the bathroom into my room and sit down for an hour or so. He'd always wear a Southern planter's straw hat that was bent out of shape. It was his lucky hat, he'd told me, and he'd worn it for years. Once he was settled, we'd talk. A few times the night nurse — she was a tough old babe who did things like pull the plug on the TV set when we were all watching a Jays game and wanted to stay up past our bedtime — would open the door, pin us with her flashlight beam, and tell LeRoy to get back to his room. It was all part of the fun.

LeRoy, it turned out, was a great sketcher, and his pencil portraits of staff and patients, usually done on the sly, were a delight. They were close to being caricatures — the night nurse looked like Jimmy Hoffa — but they captured something real in the subject.

He would show me his latest, and then we'd talk about patients. LeRoy would say, "You know that guy with the thick hair who's always coughing? He's been on the skids, all right. He's got wino eyes. You can shave, you can shower, you can cover your wino stink with Old Spice, but you can't hide wino eyes. I give that guy six months before he's back on the street."

And then we'd talk about our groups. We weren't supposed to talk about groups outside of the group, but I was fascinated by LeRoy's shrewd comments. He simply wouldn't volunteer any of these comments in the actual groups. There were patients like LeRoy who would never say more than they had to, just as there were people who would break down and confess to anything — twisted sexual fantasies involving the night nurse, anything. Of the two, I preferred the silent kind. But then I also had the feeling that the confessions of a man like LeRoy would stay in your brain much longer than you wanted.

He had been a street kid, for one thing, a boy raised in foster homes in New Brunswick who had run away to the big city, Toronto, at the age of fifteen. He had an endless fund of anecdotes about his years on Yonge Street when he lived off scams of one sort or another. Some of them were childish, like the occasions he would take a couple of sheets of typing paper, tear them into strips, and sell them on the street as strips of white blotter acid. Other scams, when he got older, were more complex, mostly heavy drug deals. He was proud of two things from his street past. First, he had never been a boy hooker. Anytime a man picked him up, he assured me, he thumped him first and took his wallet. "Fags deserve it," he insisted, "especially the kind that wear gold chains."

He was also proud that he was genuinely streetwise — not just "institution wise." Most kids in his situation, kids from bad homes or no homes at all, tried the street life for a while but couldn't hack it. Unpleasant things could happen to you on the street. It was easier to con people at the Children's Village or wherever Family Court sent you. LeRoy, however, could con anyone, anywhere. That's what he told me. I believed him, even though I knew he was conning me, too, a little.

On "graduation day" LeRoy gave me the number where he worked as a clerk in the city's Department of Public Health. We would meet occasionally for lunch after that, reminisce about Willow Crest, and talk about our jobs — I was now a freelance journalist, writing for magazines. LeRoy wanted me to meet his girlfriend, Theresa Hagedorn, another clerk at his office.

One day when we met for lunch, LeRoy picked through his reuben sandwich and barely said a word. I asked him how he was doing.

"Terrific."

"Be honest, Charles. That's not what your face is telling me."

LeRoy laughed loudly, as if this were the first time he had been amused in a long time. "I forgot all about Dr. Glinsk's favorite phrase." He shook his head. "Listen, Hal, if you hadn't been at Willow Crest, I don't know. I give you all the credit for my staying there four weeks without going nuts."

"So what's eating you?"

"I've got big news, my boy. I'm going to move to Vancouver. I'm going to the coast to get my head together, just like the hippies used to do. Why don't you come along? You're freelance. You don't have to stay here."

"Vancouver?"

"That's right, Vancouver. The Pacific Ocean, the Rocky Mountains, you'll love it."

"It's the Coastal Range, not the Rockies. Anyway, I don't think so."

"You should get out while you can, Hal. Toronto has a bad effect on sensitive people like you. Sooner or later it starts to make you feel like a loser. Before you know it, you are a loser. The first sign is you get all upset about the Maple Leafs, and then you keep talking about what you're going to do when you win the lottery, and then you're lost." LeRoy shifted in his chair and looked around the restaurant. "Just one lousy shot of rye, that's all I want. One shot of Canadian Club. So what do you think?"

"No thanks."

"Think it over. I can see a lot of growth potential in you, as Dr. Glinsk would say." He leaned across the table. "I need somebody with your strength of character, Hal. You give me hope for better things."

A waitress dropped a plate on the floor, and LeRoy jumped.

"Charlie, something's eating you, all right. You're not going to Vancouver because you're in trouble?"

"Hell, no. Everything's terrific."

He lifted his reuben sandwich as if to take a bite and then put it down again. "Once in a while I do think somebody's following me around."

"Are you serious? Who?"

He shrugged. "I don't know. Maybe it's just an old street kid's antennae working overtime."

"Some people call it paranoia."

"Paranoia can be your best friend on the street."

"You're not on the street anymore."

"No. Some of my old buddies are, though."

"You think there are people out there looking for you?"

"I haven't been involved in anything bad for almost two years, but that's not so long. People who get burned don't need refresher courses. They remember who did it."

"But you don't know?"

"No, I don't know. Anyway, that's not the reason I'm going to Vancouver. I just want to start over."

As the weeks passed, LeRoy became more serious about moving. One day he called up to say he'd found a place in Vancouver, he was moving in a week's time, and he wanted me to come over Friday evening for a nonalcoholic drink with him and Theresa and Theresa's girlfriend. A little farewell-to-Toronto drink. So Friday evening I walked over to his place in the Yonge/Davisville area of Toronto, only a couple of blocks from where I lived. It was an area of numerous high-rise apartment buildings, all of which looked as if they had been designed by Stalin's favorite architect.

When I arrived at his apartment and he let me in, I could see almost everything had already been packed in cardboard boxes. LeRoy, who had on his lucky hat, invited me into his kitchen, sat me down, and asked what I wanted to drink.

"Got some orange juice?"

"Hal, if you want orange juice at seven at night, go back to Willow Crest, will you? They'll give you a medal. Here, have a can of 7Up."

Like all alcoholics, we had to drink something. One man I know, a pillar of strength to his Alcoholics Anonymous group, goes through the year wired on thirty cups of black coffee a day. LeRoy told me he went through two cases of 7Up a week. Myself, I liked orange juice. He handed me a 7Up with one hand and a rectangular object in brown wrapping paper in the other.

"What's this?"

"Open it."

It was a framed pencil portrait of myself that LeRoy had sketched a few months before. Seeing it again reminded me of how taken aback I had been when he had first shown it to me. It was my face, all right, and yet it wasn't me, either. Something about the set of the mouth suggested more determination than I possessed. It was the face of a man who, if pressed, might display a little courage. Courage was a commodity all of us at Willow Crest desperately lacked and desperately needed.

I was pleased beyond measure at the gift and, as usual in such cases, could barely manage to say thank-you.

"The Bill Murray of Willow Crest," LeRoy said.

It was true that if you squinted and caught my face at a certain angle, you could say I looked a little bit like the actor. I grinned at LeRoy and banged my forehead against his kitchen wall, the way Bill Murray would when having a fit.

"Thought I'd get it framed before I left Toronto," he said. "Something to remember me by."

"Charles, I —"

"By the way, could you give me a hand before we meet the girls? I'd like to carry a footlocker down to the basement storage."

"Sure."

"It's in the living room. It's not heavy, just a few things in it."

"Where we meeting the girls?"

"The Red Lantern. Do you know it?"

"Singles bar, isn't it?"

"Everybody gets into the suds and has a real good time. That's where I met Terri, as a matter of fact. She was working for an insurance company. I introduced her to the joys of life in the civil service."

"How she feel about your leaving?"

"I told her I'd get in touch after I settled in, and she could maybe join me." He shrugged. "If she wants to."

"Are you serious?"

"No. I'm tired of her. Come on, don't look so shocked. That girl's been around the block a few times. She knows what's what. Besides, she's got a kid."

He paused for a moment, then sighed. "She's all right. In fact, I'd say she's pretty decent. But she's . . ." He looked up at the clock. "Better drink up. We're already a few minutes late. Hal, don't feel you have to make a big impression on this girl. A lot of Terri's friends look as if they've been brought up on Ken-L-Rations."

A half hour later we were walking into the Red Lantern, looking for our friends. The red lights were dimmed, and the place was filled with children. Eighteen-year-olds, twenty-year-olds, who had gone to high schools that had condom dispensers in the washrooms. Twenty-five and you were pushing the outer limits of age at the Red Lantern. The walls were barnboard and the tables were cable spools, covered by red-and-white-checked tablecloths. Every seat looked like a keg of nails. Obviously the idea was that you came here and left the office behind or the classroom or wherever it was you spent the daylight hours eating shit.

Theresa turned out to be a good-looking brunette in her early twenties. Her friend, who seemed the same age, was one of those red-haired women who always look as if they've just been crying. She might have been pretty if it hadn't been for the expression on her face, one of a girl waiting for a long-overdue bus after a hard day's work.

Charles introduced me to Theresa, who gave me a good, firm handshake. Then she inhaled deeply on her cigarette. I hadn't seen anybody inhale so deeply since watching children in a swimming class taking deep breaths before plunging into the water. Then Charles introduced me to her friend Sue Spurdle. Sue didn't change her expression. I might as well have been one more stranger come to wait for the bus with her. It made me tired just to take in that look.

At a table near ours four young women suddenly burst out singing "Happy Birthday" to a fifth over a bottle of Chianti Ruffino and a birthday cake.

"Hal, take a look at the cuffs," Charles said. "Not bad, eh? A farewell present from the gang at the office. We had lunch at Sai Woo's today."

Theresa took another drag from her cigarette. "You know something, Charles, I don't think Sandra appreciated that little joke you made."

"What joke?"

Theresa gave him a disgusted look.

"You don't mean the joke about the tonsils, do you? This girl at the office," he went on, turning to me, "I read her fortune cookie. It said, 'You will go to a doctor soon and have your tonsils removed.'"

"Sandra's having an abortion tomorrow," Theresa informed me.

"Okay. Bad taste. I'm sorry. What the hell? It's just an abortion."

"You think abortion is a big joke?"

"No, but it's not open-heart surgery, for Christ's sake. Hey, look — entertainment."

A young man wearing a Montreal Canadiens sweater and carrying a guitar stepped onto a tiny stage. He began singing the Beach Boys' "California Girls," only when it came time for the verse "I wish they all could be California girls," he substituted the words "I wish they all could be Mississauga girls," referring to a Toronto suburb. The girls at the table with the Chianti Ruffino let out a faint cheer. Mississauga girls, no doubt. I began to feel quite gloomy.

As the evening progressed, Sue and Theresa had several beers. The more Theresa drank, the more interesting she seemed to find me. At one point she asked me how Charles and I enjoyed our stay at Willow Crest. "Charles tells me there was a lot of romance going on those four weeks."

"I suppose so."

"A lot of sleeping around?"

"It's hard to sleep with somebody when the nurse checks your room every hour with a flashlight. Maybe some people did it in the ravine. I don't know. Basically a clinic for drunks is not my idea of Club Med."

"They say you have to hit rock bottom before you can really stop . . . you know, drinking."

"That's right, Hal," Charles said. "You'll be sitting in the public library with a rope around your pants for a belt, and an empty bottle of Lysol in your coat pocket. No one will come within a radius of ten feet of your body because of the smell, and then you'll decide maybe you should stop drinking."

An hour later we were back at his apartment, sitting in his barren living room while he poured Scotch for the girls and 7Up for the two of us. He put some music on, a bouncy rock group with a relentless drummer. The drumbeats insisted we should get excited, but nobody in the room, I noticed, was responding. We all seemed to have something on our minds.

"I really think it's great your going to Willow . . . your trying to stop drinking," Theresa said to me. "I know it's not easy. My dad was a drinker."

A brief picture flashed through my mind of my own father, rye on this breath, crying and telling us kids how much he loved us. I said nothing. She meant the compliment sincerely, but I didn't like hearing it. I didn't know how much longer I would deserve it.

Not long after that, she asked Charles to get her pack of cigarettes in the kitchen. When he left the room, she walked over to me, placed her hands on my shoulders, and gave me a kiss. A long, wet one.

"Way to make our guest feel at home, Terri," LeRoy said from the kitchen doorway. He took off his straw hat and tossed it onto a cardboard box in a corner of the room. "Entertain him with some foreplay while I get your cigarettes. What's next? The Congress of the Monkey from the *Kama Sutra?*" He handed her the pack of cigarettes with an exaggerated smile, as if he were an obsequious maître d' handing over a dropped glove. "Don't get the wrong idea, Hal. She doesn't do this for every guest. You have to rate."

"Shut up, Charles."

"Hag, why in hell did we ever get involved? Let's look at it objectively. It's true I'm not the worst guy in the world. I don't ask you to iron my underwear, like some husbands I know. I don't ask you to do anything . . . naughty when we're in bed. I mean very naughty. But why'd we ever start this in the first place?" He sighed. "Anyway, I think the party's over."

"What about you, Terri?" Sue asked after a moment of silence. "You going home?"

"Yeah, let's go home."

"You don't have to go," LeRoy said. "Stay here if you want. Seriously. My bedroom has a lock on the door. Think of me as an Eskimo who shares his wife with his pals."

"I'll take Theresa home," I said.

"Suit yourself."

He and Sue got up and walked over to the front hallway. "I don't want to go home just yet," Theresa murmured when they walked out of the room. "My little girl . . ."

Out of the corner of my eye I caught a glimpse of LeRoy and Sue by the front door. Sue had her arms around LeRoy and was nibbling away at his throat, rubbing her knee against his leg. This put a new light on the situation. Evidently he had his own plans for the evening.

After they left, I walked over to the glass door in front of the balcony, slid it open, and went out. It was a mild September night, and a humid calm, heavy with pollution, lay over the city. It didn't take long for me to make a decision. I would escort Theresa home, shake her hand politely, and go back to my own place. Not that I was suffering an attack of morals, but I didn't really know what she was after. I wasn't vain enough to assume it was the pleasures of my body. It's still a good body, I'm happy to report. Standing just under six feet, I'm still reasonably slim — with a trace of love handles, to be sure. But I have all my teeth and most of my hair, and my Irish ancestors bequeathed me the face that in a dim light bears a distinct resemblance to Bill Murray's. Still, that's not what was giving her the itch. I don't like it when somebody wants something from me and I don't know what it is.

Of course, there were a few clues floating around. I have heard, after all, of the "so who needs you?" approach to ending relationships. But if Theresa was trying to pull that, she had definitely made a mistake. You couldn't beat LeRoy at that game. Not in a thousand years.

Suddenly I became aware that Theresa was standing behind me. I turned around, and she moved closer until her body was almost touching mine. She made no move. She just looked at me as if she had made her own decision and nothing on earth, certainly not a man's scruples, would stand in her way.

In that split second I had to make my decision all over again. The split second passed. I put my arms around her and we kissed. In my case, the part of the brain that we share with reptiles became very insistent all of a sudden. And something else, a voice inside said, *You've given up booze, your little friend who always stood by to help you when you needed it, so why deny yourself a roll in the hay? It's not as if women are breaking your door down these days.* It was the voice of bitterness and, as usual, bitterness turned out to be an extremely bad adviser.

Charles's room was empty like the rest of the apartment, except for a double bed and the cardboard boxes. Theresa sat on the bed and undressed, and then it became very easy to forgive the reptilian part of my brain. We made love seriously, like a pair of lethargic but dogged wrestlers. It was okay. No moans of ecstasy, or outbursts out of *La Traviata,* but she was obviously hungry for affection and a loving touch, and I tried to oblige, and she did, too.

Neither of us wanted to stick around afterward, and we got dressed and left the bedroom before we fell asleep. Surprise. Charles was alone in the kitchen, drinking coffee. Neither he nor Theresa looked at each other. "Hello, Charles," I mumbled.

"Taking Terri home?"

"Yes."

He was chewing a fingernail as he spoke. I saw a thread of blood running from the nail to his knuckle.

"Where's Sue?" Theresa asked.

"Home alone. I wasn't in the mood. I told her I was host to some microscopic organisms she didn't want to know about, so her feelings wouldn't be hurt."

We were a silent for a moment, and I asked LeRoy if there was something the matter. He didn't answer me, but spoke to Theresa as he licked the blood off his finger.

"Terri, I'm going to do something I've rarely done in my life, and never to a lady friend, and that is to apologize. I'm sorry. Whether because I'm missing a gene somewhere, or my little infant psyche was permanently bent out of shape, I am not capable of loving you, or anyone else. All the therapy groups in the world won't change that."

There was another moment of silence, and then LeRoy stood up and kissed her on the cheek. Theresa didn't move. He sat down again and put the tip of his bleeding finger back into his mouth while he spoke.

"You never tried to fuck me over, Terri, mentally speaking, except maybe tonight a little bit. Many of your predecessors weren't so considerate. No sirree. They tried to be — what was it Glinsk called it? — controlling. But they didn't succeed, though they gave it a good shot. You'd be surprised, Hal, what lies under the surface of many lovely ladies. Or maybe you wouldn't. Anyway, let's part on a note of relative good feeling, Terri. Take her home, Hal."

I turned to Theresa. She nodded.

"I seem to be losing it, Hal," LeRoy said. "Losing it. It scares the hell out of me."

"Losing what, Charlie?"

He shook his head. For a moment I thought he was going to cry. Was this a con of some unbelievably devious sort coming on? If so, he deserved an Oscar.

"Can I do something for you, Charlie?"

"Maybe. I don't know. I'll give you a call. I'm afraid that in the Friends of Charles LeRoy department, Hal, you're it. Ain't nobody else. Don't split on me."

"I won't."

He took the tip of his finger out of his mouth, wiped it off with a tea towel, and shook my hand. And then we left.

At Theresa's doorstep I kissed her good-night. Her eyes, too, were wet with tears.

"Do you want to talk about it?" I asked.

She shook her head as she fumbled in her purse for her key. When she found it, she looked at me. "Thanks for the evening."

"Thank you."

"You were nice. You know what I really liked?"

"What?"

"When we first met, I could tell you had good manners. You were very polite. You weren't trying to come on to me. Guys don't have good manners anymore."

She opened the door wide enough for me to catch a glimpse of a framed portrait, done in pencil, on the wall of her apartment. It was a good resemblance of her, only with a hint of innocent, childlike mischief in her eyes that I would never have guessed, from tonight's experience, that she possessed. The drawing was done by someone who must have loved her enough to see that fading quality in her.

"Good night, Theresa."

"Could you do me a favor?"

"Sure."

"I've got the keys to his place. Could you give them back for me? Since he doesn't want to see me anymore?"

That night, in my own bed, I had a nightmare. I dreamed that somebody was staring at me through my bedroom window. I woke up, turned on the light, and noted that the curtains on that window were drawn and nobody was looking through it. And then I suddenly thought of LeRoy, and a terrible chill went through me. I knew he was in trouble, serious trouble, at this very moment, and when he asked me not to turn my back on him, he meant now, he needed me now.

I couldn't shake the feeling. The longer I sat up in bed, the stronger it became until I thought, *What the hell? Even if it is four in the morning, I'll pay him a call.* So I got dressed and walked over to his apartment. I knocked on his door several times and then opened it with Theresa's key. Inside, the lights were still on in the kitchen, but everything else was dark. "Charles," I called out softly. No answer. Then I noticed light under his bedroom door. I walked up to it and knocked lightly. Again no answer. I pushed the door open. Charles was lying face-up, on his bed, staring with sightless eyes at the ceiling. The room looked as if an abstract expressionist had exploded into a frenzy, throwing splotches of dark paint on the walls and the floor and on LeRoy's chest.

2

AFTER CALLING the police, I spent several hours at Fifty-three Division, sleeping on and off in a room used as a first-aid station. At one point they took my clothes to look for bloodstains, and I had to call a friend, Bernie De Luca at the *Clarion,* to fetch me some new ones. He didn't miss a beat when I made the request, or gave Fifty-three Division as my address of the moment.

"Carlo told me last night you were, uh, giving information to the cops about some homicide," he said.

"Carlo in the penalty box last night?"

"Yeah. He's been pissing off Emil again."

The penalty box was the room where reporters worked off the police radio. Most reporters hated the assignment because ninety-five percent of the stuff that came over the radio was trivia, and it was tedious waiting for the other five percent. There was a persistent belief, in fact, that the higher-ups used the assignment as a punishment for bad behavior, which might be true in the case of Carlo, who fancied himself the last of the crusading reporters in a newspaper now run, he said, by corporate stooges.

"Anything I can do to help?" Bernie added in a tone of voice that let me know he knew there were probably more than two pairs of ears involved in this conversation. Bernie was a crime reporter himself, one of the best actually. The more gruesome the murder, the better he was. A body dismembered and scattered all over the province brought out the best in him. The odd thing was, there wasn't the least thing morbid about him personally. He had one of the sunniest dispositions of anyone I've ever met. We were partners in a rotisserie league in the newsroom and we never once fought over draft picks or trades. That's a real test.

"No thanks, Bernie. I'm okay."

"For God's sake, don't handle anything by yourself, Hal. I mean, our cops are tops, as we all know, but . . ."

"Yeah, I get your drift." I did, too. But I'm the kind of person who tells lawyer jokes with one hundred percent conviction, and I just didn't feel like calling one now. I was innocent. Bring on the constabulary, I didn't care.

At noon they did come. Officer number one was F. Wilson Staigue. He was a man in his fifties, with white hair yellowing at the edges, a little heavy in the gut, and built like a good tackle. Not a great tackle — he had the instinct to go for somebody's knees all right, to bring him down hard, but he had too much intelligence to risk his own good health in the process. Officer two was a tall young man named Garfinny, with a narrow innocent face and blue eyes.

After he finished reading his notes, Staigue looked up at me and began beating a tattoo on the surface of the desk with a ballpoint pen. This went on for about a minute and then he stuck the pen into a jar with a let's-get-down-to-business motion. "All right, Mr. Murphy. Let's talk about last night. In which the unfortunate Mr. LeRoy was stabbed in the chest. You met him at his apartment about 7:30 and together walked over to the Red Lantern about half an hour later. That right?"

"That's right. Who told you — Theresa?"

"Yup. You met Theresa and the other girl Spurdle at the Red Lantern. Spurdle and Hagedorn had several drinks, but you and LeRoy were stone sober."

"We were both on the wagon, Inspector."

"Yes. You and him were at Willow Crest."

"What else did Theresa tell you?"

"That the four of you went back to LeRoy's apartment and you and her ended up in the sack. In LeRoy's sack, no less. Nice guy."

"Okay, that wasn't the smartest thing I ever did, but it didn't seem to bother LeRoy particularly. He and Theresa had just about had it."

"That's not what she told us."

For a moment I was stunned. Then I remembered I was talking to an officer of the law and not somebody who'd taken a Boy Scout pledge never to tell a fib.

"I repeat. They were finished."

"And that's why you felt free to charm your way into her pants."

"*Charm* isn't the right word, Inspector. The girl has a mind of her own."

"Yes, but she was drunk and you were sober. That changes things." He suddenly changed his tack and gave me a melancholy smile. "Happens all the time, of course."

I knew why he said that. He wanted me to feel that he understood me, and that he would understand my confession when it finally came pouring out. It would be easy, and such a relief for everyone. I looked at my fingernails. He grabbed his pen out of the jar, leaned back in his chair, and gnawed on the pen.

"After you took the girl home, you went back to LeRoy's apartment. Why?"

"I was worried about him."

"Were you?"

"Yes, I was. After I went back to my place, I woke up with a . . . I was worried. He wasn't himself that night. He was very upset. Not about me and Theresa. About . . . I don't know."

Staigue nodded as if to encourage me to continue, and I knew I shouldn't have said a word. Staigue had it all figured out, and everything I was trying to say probably underlined his conclusion. I had come back to the apartment and was confronted by an angry LeRoy. Perhaps I had even taunted him. A guy like me, who'd seduce his friend's girl right before his eyes, would do a thing like that. We got into a fight and I settled it with a carving knife. Things like that happened all the time in the city. Romantic triangles — the biggest cause of homicide among the degenerate classes. LeRoy and I were both members of the degenerate classes. Willow Crest was proof of that.

Staigue and I stared at each other. He wasn't righteous or angry. He just wanted to put me in jail for a few years. That's all. It was probably the best solution to this mess for all concerned — except me, of course. And as for the truth, well, Staigue could always use Pontius Pilate's famous line. What is truth? It is expedient one man should go to the slammer for the people, lest the people get upset, and it is better to send the wrong man to the slammer than no man at all. That was cop logic, and there's a lot to be said for it. Of course, the cops had to make a deal with people. They could send me to the slammer as long as they gave the crown attorney a halfway decent script for the benefit of a jury. That wasn't so hard. I had a motive for the killing, and I was there alone roughly at the time of the murder. They just needed a little bit more evidence. Maybe not even a little bit more.

"So you went back when?"

"About four o'clock."

"Your friend normally up that late?"

"I don't suppose so. But, like I said, he was upset and I thought he might still be up."

"Find out why he was upset when you got there?"

"When I got there, he was dead."

"Take a cab over? We could find the driver."

"I walked. It's just a few blocks."

"Meet up with anybody on the way? Anybody you can produce as a witness?"

"Is this a way of saying I'm your chief suspect?"

"Well, let's see. We got two and a half hours between the time you left LeRoy alive and well, according to Miss Hagedorn, and the time you discovered his body." Staigue smiled. "Time enough for anybody to wander in and take a whack at him, eh?"

"I do believe you're being ironical, Inspector. For your information, LeRoy did have enemies."

"Who?"

"You know his background as well as I do. A couple of weeks ago we had lunch and he told me he was afraid somebody was after him. He wasn't specific, but it could have been a lot of people he used to know on the street. People he'd given little surprises to that weren't nice."

"Why did he think somebody was 'after him'?"

"I have no idea. It was enough to make him want to move, though."

Staigue let that register, more or less. "What about the blood on your shirt? It's LeRoy's, I believe."

"I may have touched him, or something else covered with his blood."

"Now you're a newspaper . . . *ex*-newspaper reporter. Reporters are supposed to be smarter than that."

"Look, Inspector, I came into the room. I saw LeRoy bleeding all over the walls. I was shocked. I was stunned. I wasn't thinking about what I touched, particularly."

"Nice to see you can be cool about this, Murphy. While you're at it try murder one for size. Twenty-five years, no possibility of parole."

Staigue started to beat another tattoo on his desk with his ballpoint pen. I reached over and grabbed the pen out of his hand. Staigue looked at me, startled. It took him a second to recover, by which time I had also grabbed a pad of paper from his desk and had started to write a phone number on the top sheet.

"You want to ask me any more questions, call my lawyer."

Staigue looked at the sheet of paper I shoved at him as if it had come from a tile floor underneath a urinal. Then he looked up at me, with an expression of extreme annoyance. "All right, Murphy, we won't keep you. But I'd call that lawyer if I were you."

"We'll be meeting again, I take it."

"You bet. Just don't try to disappear on us, will you? Because if you do, that will get me very upset, and we'll have to put you behind the pipes right away. And don't try to see Miss Hagedorn, either, because that will get me very upset, too. I might suspect you're trying to jerk around a witness."

Walking out of the division, I began to see just how excellent a suspect I was. If someone better didn't show up for the part, and soon, they would go for me. I knew Staigue was smart enough to have doubts about my guilt. Real murderers try to make up better stories than I just did. More to the point, I was neither drunk nor under the influence of any drugs when the police first arrived at the scene. That fact probably weighed more heavily with Staigue than anything else. Most human beings can't bring themselves to murder another human being without the aid of some mood-altering substance. That's a simple fact of life. Staigue knew it very well. So he had to have his inner doubts, and the inner doubts were obviously strong enough so that he didn't want to get involved with lawyers just yet. But his inner doubts would never stand in the way of cop logic for long.

I took the subway home to my own apartment, a modest one-bedroom in a building called Grosvenor Mansions. Built around the turn of the century, the Mansions had lots of "character." That meant nothing more than a trickle of water ever came out of the hot and cold water taps, electrical outlets were scarce, and the radiators leaked. It was home, however. Naturally my friends the police had been there before me, looking for evidence of some sort. They had been nice enough. They had put everything back. Sort of. The mattress was back on the box springs, for example, but the sheets and the bedspread lay on that mattress like the clothes of a woman who had been raped.

I hadn't been home for fifteen minutes when someone knocked on the door. It was my neighbor Gord, a lanky man in his early forties. He sported a Fu Manchu and long, stringy hair that dangled limply from his balding dome. Gord had come to Canada more than two decades ago as a draft dodger from Fitchburg, Massachusetts. He had hung out in Toronto ever since, keeping a sharp eye out for FBI and RCMP agents, although he was long past the age any army would be interested in him. Otherwise, he played his guitar, smoked dope, and worked at carpentry jobs for people who wanted home renovations done real cheap.

"Hal, what's happening?" he asked. "A cop was nosing around about you."

I must have looked queasy, because he started to assure me he hadn't told them anything. I invited him in.

"Sorry I can't offer you a beer, Gord. How about some orange juice?"

He accepted a glass, sank into an armchair, and smiled benignly at me, waiting for me to tell him why I was now a person of interest to the police. I saw no reason not to. I was too tired to come up with some bullshit explanation. When I was finished, he commiserated with me and started to tell a story about a friend of his, a dope dealer, who'd been stabbed to death. I cut him off.

"Who was the cop?"

"Some odd name. I forget."

"Young guy, blue eyes, baby face?"

"Yeah. Looked like the kind of kid who was into model railroads in grade nine."

"Garfinny?"

"Yeah, that's it. Wanted to know if I'd heard you come in last night."

"What did you tell him?"

Gord suddenly looked sheepish. I assured him it didn't matter.

"I said I heard you come in about two. Hope that's okay."

"Sure. Anything else? C'mon, Gord, don't feel bad. I've got nothing to hide."

"I said I heard you leave a couple of hours later."

"Well, Gord, I owe you one. You corroborated my story."

Now it was his turn to breathe a sigh of relief, and then to flash a big grin. He was delighted to consider me in his debt.

"Didn't know you were such a light sleeper, Gord," I said.

He looked mysterious. "I wasn't sleeping."

I decided not to inquire further. Instead, I let him finish the story about his dope dealer friend, then we talked about homicides and police in general for a while. Finally I told him I had stuff to do. When he left, I tried to get more sleep, but it was impossible. For one thing, Garfinny's visit to Gord — despite Gord's partial confirmation of my story — was an unpleasant reminder of my status as chief suspect, something that didn't make sleep any easier. Neither did my memory of LeRoy's last moments. That he had reached out to me as perhaps the one friend he could count on was an unbearable thought.

I got up instead and bought the final edition of the *Clarion*. They had buried the story, which was only three or four paragraphs long, in the city section. The unspectacular murder of a nobody like Charles LeRoy didn't rate any more space. Not in the Toronto of the nineties. And much to my relief, my name wasn't included. "Police are holding for questioning the man who discovered LeRoy's body, a friend who had partied with the slain man earlier in the evening. Two women present on that occasion are also being questioned."

As soon as it was evening, I called Theresa Hagedorn. Action diminishes fear, they say. Maybe it could also help appease the shade of poor LeRoy. There was no answer. Then I looked up Spurdle, S. in the phone book and called Sue.

"Hello," she said.

"Sue? This is Hal Murphy."

There was silence for a moment. "I thought the police were —"

"Holding me?"

"Yeah."

"They were. They let me go."

"Oh."

"Where's Terri, Sue?"

Another moment of silence. "How should I know where she is?"

"I thought you were a friend of hers."

"I don't know."

This girl was such a bad liar that for a moment I felt a pang of sympathy for her. Serious lying is like anything else. You need the training and experience to do it well and, unless you have natural talent for it, it really should be left to the pros.

"Look," I continued, "I didn't kill Theresa's boyfriend, in case that thought had crossed your mind. You're a smart girl. You know the cops wouldn't let me go if they had any reason to believe I killed him. All I want to do is ask Theresa some questions. I'd sort of like to find out more about my friend's murder."

"You're going to be a detective?"

"For the time being. I have this nervous reaction, Susan, when I see a mangled body. I want to know how it got mangled. Especially when it used to be a friend."

"Terri's moved out of her apartment. She's living with her mother. She made me promise not to tell anyone where she's living."

Sue hung up. I looked through the phone book for more Hagedorns, but none panned out. That was all right. I knew where she worked.

My first call Sunday morning, however, was to Dr. Saul Glinsk, my psychiatrist at Willow Crest, who usually worked weekends. Glinsk, a short, slender man in slacks and a polo short, liked me. I had never displayed "resistance" or a "negative transference" to him in his group. In fact, I was downright helpful to him at times. When a few members of the group were defensive, I was one of the ones who pushed the attack and got them to express their real feelings. I discovered I had a flair for that kind of thing, God help me. Of course, neither I, nor anyone else, ever tried it with LeRoy. He was too cool even to be defensive.

After I pressured Glinsk on the phone, he admitted he had twenty minutes free that morning. I took a cab ride out to the clinic, and found him in his office. He smiled as he rose behind his desk to shake hands with me, but throughout the twenty minutes remained safely behind it.

"I understand what you're getting at, Heywood. LeRoy probably had lots of enemies on the street. But, as you know, he wasn't a talker."

"I'm not asking for professional confidences, Doctor, but could you give me some factual stuff on him — like his background?"

"Are you sure you want to get involved with this?"

I covered my eyes with my hand. "This thing has ripped the hell out of me. I think I could maybe accept what happened better if I wasn't passive about it. Know what I mean? If I could just help the police with the investigation even a little bit. I'm a reporter, which means I know how to dig around a bit."

He opened a manila folder on his desk and started reading. "Charles Albert LeRoy, born December 10, 1957. Father died when LeRoy was three years old, driving a milk truck into a utility pole while suffering an epileptic seizure." Glinsk giggled. "I'm sorry," he apologized. "It sounds bizarre, but it's true." He continued reading. "Mother worked as waitress, admitted to hospital on numerous occasions for beatings given by two of her common-law husbands. Died three years ago from complications arising from cirrhosis of the liver. No other immediate relatives. LeRoy left New Brunswick in the summer of 1972 and hitchhiked to Toronto where he has lived since. Served six months suspended sentence for assisting a breaking and entering, 1973. Acquitted on technicality of trafficking, 1978. Had no fixed address until he obtained his first permanent job with the Department of Public Health, City of Toronto, six months ago. Given leave of absence and urged to take four-week course at Willow Crest by same department."

Glinsk looked up and gave me a small, cheerless smile. "Not a lot of information, is it? It gives you an idea, though."

"An idea of what?"

"Well, I shouldn't —"

"Look, if I knew LeRoy, he wouldn't give a damn about anything you said about him right now. And you can be one hundred percent sure I'll never quote you."

"In my opinion LeRoy was a complete sociopath. As such," Glinsk continued, shrugging, "he was difficult if not impossible to treat. Sociopaths are very hard to crack, Mr. Murphy. They don't come any harder."

"What do you think he did between the time he arrived here in '72 and the time he got a job with the city last year? That's over twenty years."

"You'd know as well as I do."

What I didn't know, I certainly could imagine. LeRoy was proud that he had never stood on cold winter nights on the sidewalks of the chicken run, waiting for a car to pull up and a man to roll down the window. But he had never said anything about being a long-term companion to some nice man with a nice apartment. As well, no doubt, he had been on the road for months and years at a time. He had often talked about mining camps and construction camps in the north.

"Thanks, Doctor."

"I'm sorry about LeRoy, you know. I would have liked to have helped him, but he didn't seem to want it."

No, he didn't seem to want it, except the last time I saw him alive. And then I had failed him. There was no use in remorse, however, or getting annoyed at Glinsk because he didn't have a clue, either. The doctor had done his best. If there was an empty look in his eyes, it was no doubt because at one point he had actually given his all trying to reach people like LeRoy, and then one day he realized he would never succeed. It happened to a lot of people in Glinsk's profession.

The next day I paid City Hall a visit. One of Theresa's fellow employees pointed out her cubicle. She was on the phone when I saw her, facing a partition with a poster on it of surf pounding rocks, with something inspiring written underneath. She turned around while she was still on the phone, and the instant she spotted me, her mouth collapsed. "I told you. I'll get them tomorrow . . . this afternoon. Okay . . . yes, Gerry, thank you very much. Goodbye."

"May I sit down?" I asked her as she replaced the receiver.

"Please get out of my office." Her voice was low because of everybody around her.

I sat down, anyway. "Theresa, let's have a talk," I suggested, also in a low voice.

She closed her eyes and shook her head like a child throwing a tantrum.

"Theresa, that night I left you I went back to Charles's place and discovered his body. Think about that for a while." I paused for a second to let her do so. "I haven't slept much since then. It's the kind of memory that gives you unpleasant dreams. It's also the kind of experience that can get you into trouble with the police." She continued to stare at her desktop. "I'm asking you to help me," I continued. "Not help me a lot, help me a little. Talk to me about LeRoy, who he saw, who he talked about. Anything might be helpful. I can't trust the cops to find out who killed him. They might get lazy and settle for the nearest candidate. That's me, Theresa."

"Please get out of my office." Still she didn't raise her head.

"What is this, Terri? I'm a nonperson all of a sudden? You had a different attitude last time we met, as I recall." Now she looked up at me, furious. I smiled. "Hey, eye contact. That's what they liked at Willow Crest." I stopped smiling. "Come on, Terri, you can't really believe I killed Charles. You must have thought I was at least a decent human being when we went to bed. So why not act on that notion? It'll spare you unnecessary grief. You've got enough of the other kind now."

"Why should I trust you? Why should I trust anybody?" She swallowed hard, a lump of pain in her throat.

"Good question. There's no reason for you to trust me particularly. I guess it's more like faith I'm asking for."

"Going out with Charles was an education. He taught me all

about 'faith.'" Her voice sounded like that of a woman reporter I once knew, fifty years old and bitter for so long she nursed her bile like an old, sick, beloved cat. Terri swallowed again and got up. "Let's get out of here. Have lunch or something." We went down to the cafeteria, grabbed a couple of sandwiches and, because it was a warm, sunny day, went out to eat on the grass next to City Hall.

"How did Charles teach you about faith?" I asked her when we sat down.

Theresa stared at the fountains in front of City Hall for a moment. In the sunlight, studying her features, I was reminded of Pete Dalzell's face the night he died. Her skin looked as if the blood were drying up in the veins beneath it. There was a dark, unhealthy hue on her cheeks.

"It was hard. I knew Charlie was going out with other women, but I was never sure who or why. He didn't tell me, of course. I didn't ask him. I just knew."

"You never had suspicions about particular women?"

Theresa shook her head.

"What about your friend Susan? Was Friday night the first time they contemplated intimate relations?"

She looked at me and then turned away. "Who knows?"

"Did they know each other very well?"

"Not really. I think Friday night was about the second or third time they met, as far as I know."

"Well, Charles was a fast worker. Why did you tell the cops you and he were still together?"

"I didn't say that. I mean, I didn't tell the cops we were breaking up or anything. I just said we were, I don't know, thinking things over. Charlie asked me if I wanted to come with him. I thought about it, but I knew it was just talk."

This was interesting. Theresa, of course, might be lying to me. She might have handed Staigue a line about how close she and LeRoy were. More likely Staigue had lied. Standard interrogation technique.

I unwrapped the cellophane from my roast beef sandwich and,

unwisely, took a look at the thin gray slice of meat on top of the lettuce. Whatever animal this meat had come from must have died after a prolonged illness.

"You really going to try to find Charles's murderer?" Theresa asked me.

"I'm going to give it a good shot. Let me ask you something. Did you really think, after you heard the news, that I killed Charles?"

"I said to myself, 'Terri, don't think *anything*. He didn't kill him. You're a bad judge of character, but not that bad. Please, God, not *that* bad.'"

She looked at the grass by her feet for a moment and then at the people walking by. I had the feeling these people had suddenly become, for her, a different species, talking a different language, sending and receiving messages through a different kind of nervous system than the one she owned. "You thought it was tough finding his body. Try living with what I did." She was silent for another moment and then said, "Please, I don't want to talk anymore. Really. I'm going for a walk. Sorry I can't help you."

We rose together. "Before you go," I said, "I have to ask one thing. A couple of weeks before the murder, Charles told me he was worried somebody was onto him. Did he talk to you about it? Was that why he wanted to move?"

Theresa looked genuinely puzzled. "No. It wasn't like Charlie to be scared. He told me he was tired of Toronto. I could believe that a lot more than he was scared of somebody."

"Did he ever mention any names to you of people he'd known on the street? Anybody at all?"

She actually seemed to think about it.

"Well, there's Anna."

"Anna?"

"This sounds so classic, I'm embarrassed. A couple of nights he mentioned her name in his sleep. When I asked him who she was, he told me it was some girl he knew. Anna Lightfoot. An Indian girl, fifteen or so. Hooker. Typical of his buddies."

31

"That's the only name he ever mentioned to you from that period of his life?"

"'Fraid so. Even that, by the way, I wouldn't take for cash. Charlie sometimes made things up. It was a habit with him."

"Well, it's a name, anyway. Thanks, Theresa."

She took her sandwiches, still in their cellophane wrapping, and slowly, as if greatly fatigued, walked over to a trash can. She threw them in and headed across the plaza, off to the crowds on Queen Street. She didn't look back.

She was a loser, no doubt about it, but she also seemed like a decent sort. Charlie, in his unpleasant way, had paid her a genuine compliment the night of his death. She wasn't manipulative or deceitful. But then I remembered that in Dr. Glinsk's group the one class of patient I had never been able to get a read on was the class known as females. It was possible I wasn't reading Theresa very well, either. She could be a lot more complicated, tragically so, than I gave her credit for. Was she enraged that she hadn't gotten the slightest rise out of Charlie by sleeping with me? Was that rage further stoked, in some way I couldn't understand, by Charles's singular apology to her? I didn't want to bet my life that I knew the answers to those questions.

That night I met a friend of mine, a social worker named Chris Lang, at a bar on Yonge Street. On the first floor an Axl Rose clone was inflicting irreparable hearing damage on his audience; the second floor, with a few pool tables and pinball machines, was quieter. With his bushy beard, wire-rimmed glasses, and farmer's overalls, Chris looked as if he should have been handing out bags of granola in a health food store. But he knew the young LeRoy's world better than most.

"How's it going?" I asked.

"Looking for a runaway."

"Kid from a foster home?"

"Right. Boy, fourteen, slim build, brown hair, last seen wearing jeans and a denim jacket. You should see the files in the Youth

Bureau down at Fifty-two Division, all the missing juveniles. Every one has brown hair and jeans. With a slender build. I wish one of these days I'd have a runaway who was a fat redhead, or favored the preppie look."

"Cops ever find 'em?"

"Usually. By accident. This kid has friends, though. Some very nasty friends. That's what I'm worried about."

The waiter appeared, gray hair over a thin red face, so thin it looked as if time had burnt most of the flesh off it, leaving a layer of skin stretched tight over the hollows and bony surfaces. Chris ordered two more drafts for himself. I asked the waiter if they had soda water.

"On the wagon, Hal?" Chris asked.

"Just finished a four-week course in health and sobriety at Willow Crest."

"You been at Willow Crest?" the waiter asked incredulously. "How old are you?"

"As old as I look."

"You can't be more than thirty-five, then. Hell, those were my best drinking years."

I knew what he was talking about. He meant that when he was thirty-five he could drink anybody under the table, and it wasn't until fifty that he lost all control and had to give the booze up, and compared to him us younger folks just didn't have it. I said nothing. It doesn't matter to me where people get their self-esteem.

"What's up, Hal?" Chris asked when the waiter left.

"A friend of mine's been murdered. Somebody stabbed him in his apartment. I had the misfortune to discover his body."

"You're kidding. Who?"

"A guy named Charles LeRoy. You might have known him. He was on the streets for a while. About my age, my build, brown hair . . ."

"An adult street kid."

"Yeah, that's right."

Chris thought for a moment. "Yeah, I remember a guy named LeRoy. Hasn't been around for a couple of years."

"He went straight. Got a job at City Hall."

"You mean he didn't become a youth worker? That's what most of those 'reformed' street kids want to become — youth workers. Was he a good friend of yours?"

"We were friends. I met him at Willow Crest."

"Who did him in?"

"Don't know. He did tell me a couple of weeks before he died that someone out of his past — somebody he hadn't done favors for — might be after him. Did you know any of his friends from the past?"

"Sorry, Hal. Hardly knew him, really. He was pretty much of a loner. I've met a hell of a lot of guys like him in the couple of years since I last saw him. After a while, they all merge into this blob of brown hair and denim jackets."

"You ever heard of Anna Lightfoot?"

"Was she a friend of LeRoy's?"

"Supposed to be."

"I don't recall seeing them together, but that doesn't mean anything. She's an Indian girl. Ojibway, I think, from Manitoulin Island. She'd be about sixteen now. I haven't seen her in a year, Hal. Nobody has. Nobody I know, anyway."

"Was she a hooker?"

"She worked the streets with the best of them. Until about a year ago, like I said. Then she disappeared from Toronto."

"Disappeared?"

"That's right. A lot of her friends were very upset, girls who knew her."

"Anybody have any idea why she split?"

"Nope. I assumed she'd just gone back to her reserve. Indian kids will do that — bounce back and forth between the reserve and the city like Ping Pong balls. They get in trouble here, they just hitchhike north, back to their aunt or grandmother or whatever. But the kids were into all kinds of rumors, like she'd been wasted by a pimp, or one of her customers."

"Did she have a pimp?"

"Skinny little guy named Walrath. Not much to look at, but don't let that fool you. If he wants to cause you problems, he'll make sure they're major ones."

"A Toronto boy?"

"He's told everybody he's from Detroit. Actually, I heard he's from Fenelon Falls, north of here, where his old man runs a gas station. By the way, you don't want to talk to him. He won't tell you a thing. Unless you pay him, and then I wouldn't guarantee what you'd get for your money. Anyway, the girls were upset, I think, because another girl disappeared a few weeks before Anna, a friend of hers named Debbie . . . Debbie somebody, I forget. No one's seen her, either."

"She's an Indian?"

"White girl. I don't know if there's a connection or not. I mean, even if there were . . . they could have just gone north together, or out west. Or hell, even to Florida. They could have found some guy in a Winnebago, and the next thing you know, they're rolling down I-75 to Tampa Bay. Enjoying the Southern climate, just like all the other snowbirds. Listen, Hal, if you really want to find out more about Lightfoot, I'll tell you who to see. There's a guy named Malcolm Kelly who works for a group called Pathfinders. They work with native kids, and he knows every Indian in the goddamn city. Really. If anybody in Toronto knows where Anna Lightfoot is, it's him."

"Where can I find him?"

"Right now, the Silver Dollar. Ask around. He'll be there."

"Terrific."

"Hal, a word of advice. Leave the detective work to the cops. Looking for people like Lightfoot and Walrath is like looking for AIDS. It doesn't do your health or your peace of mind any good."

"Thanks, Chris. I'll remember that."

The Silver Dollar was a country and western bar frequented by numerous Toronto Indians. Musicians I knew who played there called it the Silver Toilet. They disliked it because the audience tended to ignore them. On average nights the audience started out depressed and ended, thanks to the mood-altering properties of beer, hysterically miserable.

A short ride on a streetcar got me there by 8:30, just in time to watch the band wind up their set with a reasonably emotive rendition of "Blue Eyes Crying in the Rain." The joint was packed. In a corner of the room, near the bandstand and the dance floor, was an area where the Indians sat. I headed there and asked somebody walking to the washroom if Malcolm Kelly was around. The man looked stunned by the question, so I repeated it. He made an effort to figure out who I was, gave up, and pointed to a table with two men. One was about six feet, with high cheekbones and deep-set dark eyes. He wore jeans and a khaki work shirt. The other was the same height but thinner. He was dressed in a black T-shirt and a cowhide vest, while his black hair was braided on either side of his head with leather thongs. The only remarkable thing about him, however, was the expression on his face. He looked as if he were the only guy in the place actually enjoying himself. He appeared tremendously amused by everything happening around him.

I walked over to their table and, taking a guess, addressed the man in the khaki shirt as Mr. Kelly. I was right. He looked up at me, stared hard in exactly the same way the first man had, and asked, "Yes?"

"Can I talk to you for a minute?"

"Sure. What's on your mind?"

"Name's Heywood Murphy. A friend of mine, Chris Lang, said you might be able to help me."

Kelly raised a puzzled eyebrow.

"He's a social worker. Children's Aid."

Kelly still looked puzzled.

"Anyway, it doesn't matter. I'm looking for a girl named Anna Lightfoot."

When I mentioned Anna's name, a tiny muscle in his face jerked, and I knew in that split second that I had his full attention. Another moment passed, and Kelly sat back in his chair, doing a good impression of a stone-faced Indian.

"I had a friend named Charles LeRoy," I said with a note, I'm sure, of desperation entering my voice. "A few nights ago I walked into his apartment and found his corpse. Somebody stabbed him through the heart. Nobody knows who."

"Our highly trained police force will no doubt clear up the mystery very soon."

"The cops think I did it. They're proceeding on that theory, anyway. I want to point out a better alternative to them."

"Good luck."

"Thank you. LeRoy used to be a hustler. I figure somebody he once knew on the street killed him." As I spoke, I was aware of how fatuous, as well as desperate, I must have sounded, as if this were all a preposterous and guilty story I was making up. Still, I took a deep breath and continued. "Lightfoot might have a line on that. Lang told me she's out of town."

"He's right. And she didn't leave a forwarding address. Poof, she disappeared. Can't help you."

"You must have some idea where she might be."

"Why me?"

"Okay, forget it. If you could tell me somebody else who might be able to help me find her, I'd appreciate it."

"Hey, Kelly . . ."

A man's voice tore through the babble of the room, a big voice with an edge to it that jolted the system. It was the kind of jolt you feel when you slip on a step coming down a staircase. Instantly I spotted him. He was a man about Kelly's height, but probably with fifty pounds more to him, and it didn't look like fatty tissue. He was the kind of man who makes his living moving refrigerators around a warehouse. Tonight he was wearing his good-time clothes — peach-colored shirt, cowboy hat, and an evil pair of shades. As he came closer to our table, I noticed he was weighed down by a few pounds of silver-and-turquoise jewelry, including a bracelet that looked heavy enough to shackle the leg of one of the galley slaves in *Ben-Hur*.

"I hear you kicked my little brother out of a healing ceremony at the Lodge," he said, pointing a finger at Kelly. The Lodge was a center for native people.

"Your brother was drunk, Jerome. He was loud and he was showing no respect."

The two launched into a bitter argument about Jerome's brother that veered off into other issues I didn't understand, but which I gathered had to do with local politics of the nastiest sort. At one point Jerome flashed a grin that he meant to be intimidating — it succeeded with me, anyway — stuck his finger in Kelly's glass of beer, shook a few drops in Kelly's face, and then wiped it on his ample thigh. Kelly stared at him. If he was angry or frightened, it was hard to tell. Enunciating each syllable as if he were talking to a deaf mute, he made a highly insulting remark. I think it had something to do with Jerome's habitual copulation with his own grandmother.

Jerome kept on grinning. "One of these days, Kelly, you and I are going to have it out like men. One of these days." He turned to me. "How's it going, white boy? Looking for an easy lay?" He glanced at a nearby table where three women sat. Two of them, indeed, looked as if they didn't care greatly what anybody did to them as long as they didn't have to be too conscious while it lasted.

"I was having a private conversation with Mr. Kelly."

He put his hand on my shoulder. Close up, it looked as big as a pot roast. "Lend me ten bucks for a few beers, will ya? You look like you can afford it."

"No."

I looked at the hand on my shoulder. He removed it, made a fist with it and, in slow motion, raised it to about an eighth of an inch from my nose. "See you later, you cheap asshole."

"See you later."

It was a pleasant sensation to see this man turn around and walk away.

"Malcolm, let's ask the gentleman to sit down," Kelly's friend said. The invitation made me feel rather grateful, coming as it did at that precise moment. I took a chair.

"Sounds like you're having some bad luck," Kelly said.

"Yes, I am."

"Hope it don't rub off on us poor Indians. We got enough of it." A waiter appeared. Kelly looked at me, and I shook my head — not for want of desire, however. I don't think I ever wanted a glass of beer so much in my life.

The friend also shook his head. "Got to keep in shape."

"Well, I'm gonna have to replace one, anyway," Kelly sighed, and ordered one more.

His friend introduced himself as Wolf.

"What's this about staying in shape?" I asked.

"Wolf's a dancer," Kelly said. "With Av Bernstein's group."

I could have kicked myself for not reading our dance critic's columns more often. I didn't have a clue who Av Bernstein's group was. Perhaps to enlighten me, Wolf stretched his arms as if he were Mikhail Baryshnikov floating across a stage.

"So who's this LeRoy character?" Wolf asked.

I told them about LeRoy, and Theresa, and the last night we spent together. I was surprised at how much effort it took for me to do this in a reasonably coherent fashion. I had already told the same story, more or less, to other people, but perhaps because I felt, for the first time, a hint of intelligent friendliness in my listeners, the horror of it began to emerge. As a result, I could hardly pronounce words or put sentences together or link things in the simplest chronological sequence. I felt like a six-year-old trying to tell his mommy about some terrible event at school.

"Don't know the guy," Kelly murmured after I finished. "And you say you never met Lightfoot?"

"Never. But you know her, don't you?"

"Very well. You might say she's a little sister. A little sister who's had a very bad time of it, and we wouldn't think kindly of anyone who brought trouble on her."

At that moment the angry voice called out Kelly's name a second time, and we saw Jerome lurching toward us. This time his mouth was open and he looked as if he were hyperventilating. Clearly in the twenty minutes or so since our last encounter, he had stepped over some thin line in his psyche. As we rose from our chairs, I obeyed my nervous system and quickly moved out of Jerome's path.

I'm not exactly sure what happened in the seconds that followed. There was a flurry of arms as Jerome flailed at Kelly. Somebody shoved me hard from behind, and when I turned around, two other people, who had their hands on each other's shirt, fell at my feet. Several people started screaming. My eyes met the blank stare of a man sitting at a table next to ours. I had the sudden impression he had been sitting in that same chair for years, that he had never once left it, and that he would continue sitting there for many more years. He lifted a dark brown hand and rubbed one of his eyes lazily.

Somebody nudged me. It was Wolf, anxious, it seemed, to direct my attention somewhere. He pointed to the floor where Jerome sat on top of Kelly and was digging into the big man's face with both hands, which Kelly was strenuously attempting to remove. I looked at Wolf.

"We'd better do something," he said almost cheerfully.

I thought about it. In the one and only fight I ever had, at a bar in Moses Lake, Washington, I was beaten up. I was drunk and it didn't hurt too much at the time, but it hurt later. Still, these two guys had been friendly to me, and I knew I would feel worse afterward if I did nothing.

I stepped behind Jerome, grabbed his hair with both hands, and pulled hard. His body seemed to lift a fraction of an inch and then remained inert for a second. Suddenly I was no longer pulling, because the body had decided to rise by itself and I could feel a tremendous burst of energy under its scalp. I knew then that in one second I would be face-to-face with Jerome and in deep trouble, so I let go of his hair, stepped back, and grabbed a chair to put between me and him. This wasn't a particularly smart move. Jerome snatched the chair away from me and held it up in the air, and I'm not sure what would have happened next if Kelly, who had managed to get to his feet, as well, hadn't shouted at Jerome from behind.

Jerome threw the chair across the room and turned to face Kelly, and while he was turning, Kelly landed a superb punch. He must have hit the old solar plexus, the peritoneal cavity where the nerves cross, because Jerome instantly bent in agony and gasped for air. From behind him a fat Indian woman pounded his shoulder blades with a furious windmill motion, but I don't think he noticed.

Once again Wolf nudged me. This time he pointed at three policemen who were charging through the doorway of the Silver Dollar. I must have visibly paled.

"Scared of the gendarmes?" Wolf asked.

The police, in fact, had never particularly bothered me before. On the rare occasions when they did stop me in the street for drunk-and-disorderly conduct, I felt like a college kid caught in the commission of a harmless prank. *Yes, Officer, despite this temporary excess I am basically a nice guy, an upstanding member of the public of which you are a servant.* Now, for the first time, I had a full grasp of their function and powers. They could punish people. "Yes," I said to Wolf.

"Here, try this. It makes you invisible." He gave me his "don't worry, be happy" wink, unzipped a leather pouch, took out a small cellophane bag full of red powder, and smeared a tiny bit on my face. Then he did the same to himself. An instant or two later the police brushed by us. As we turned and walked out, I noticed that they had grabbed the Indian woman who was trying to beat up Jerome.

Outside, Kelly and Wolf invited me to "take a stroll." We walked a couple of blocks to the University of Toronto campus where the Neo-Romanesque and Gothic Revival buildings sat comfortably in the darkness, a little shabby but still dignified, relics of an older and better time. Pity that the students they now served were familiar with jogging suits and abortion clinics. But the buildings and the lawns around them created one of the few zones of calm in the heart of the city, especially at night.

We sat down on a knoll next to an empty flagpole. "Wolf," I asked, "what was that powder?"

He didn't respond immediately, as if he had to think it over. "Ancestral lore of the Ojibway," he said finally.

"It really makes you invisible?"

"Well, actually it doesn't. It makes people not notice you. There's a difference."

"Must come in handy. You have lots of trouble with cops?"

"I'm an Indian with no fixed address. That answer your question?"

"And you're a medicine man."

"No." He paused for a moment. "I used to dabble." Another pause. "I'm interested more in Judaism actually. Making your life holy through —" He shrugged. "I like Martin Buber, Fackenheim . . . a lot of contemporary theologians."

Kelly shook his head. Wolf smiled and put a hand on his shoulder. "My friend never did agree with my fooling around with ancestral lore. I don't blame him, either. A lot of it's bullshit. Trouble is, it sometimes works for me. Like your saints work for you, Malcolm." Kelly gave him a weary, sidelong glance. This was clearly part of an ongoing discussion they had had many times before.

"Is it always this exciting at the Silver Dollar?" I asked.

"No," Wolf replied. "Usually it's very boring. But tonight we had you, and then Jerome."

"I wasn't trying to generate excitement. I just wanted to ask about Anna Lightfoot."

"You were all right, Heywood. You were unpredictable. Stay like that and you won't have to worry about the cops. They only catch people who are completely predictable."

"What about the guy who killed my friend? What if he's unpredictable, too?"

"Then you've got a problem."

"Right. I've got a big problem. Any suggestions?"

Kelly and Wolf looked at each other for a moment, and then Wolf grinned. "Malcolm, you slay me. Admit I was right. Come on, admit it."

Kelly turned to me. "Wolf's referring to a prediction he made earlier tonight — that I'd meet somebody who'd help me in my quest."

Wolf closed his eyes and intoned solemnly, "Medicine man see vision. White man sent by spirits, come to Malcolm."

"Shut up."

"Your quest?" I asked.

"Yes, my *quest*. Which I haven't started yet, because I'm a little afraid of what I'm going to find at the end of it. It just so happens I'm looking for Lightfoot myself. She just seems to have disappeared."

"Why are you looking for her?"

"A week ago I found out this fat little white guy was asking around for Lightfoot. Nobody knows who he is, but somebody said he hangs out with her former pimp."

"Jimmy Walrath."

"Yup. If Walrath's after her, she's in big trouble. Owes him money or has something he wants. Anna's a friend of ours, like I told you, and I'll be damned if he finds her before I do."

"So when I showed up, you figured I was with Jimmy, too."

"Unlikely, but you never know."

"I trust I've convinced you I'm telling you the truth."

Wolf laid a hand on my shoulder. "You convinced me, my friend. You'd have to be real smart or real dumb to try to con us with a story like yours. And you look sort of in between."

"Thanks."

He snickered.

"You ask Walrath himself what's up?" I asked Kelly.

Kelly sighed. "That's what I mean when I say I've been slow off the mark. I should start with him, but I hate that guy. Makes me want to kill just thinking about him. Anyway, he seems to be making himself scarce these days."

"Maybe I can ask around."

"Oh, boy. You're out of your depth."

"I'll show him around," Wolf volunteered.

"If you want to take that responsibility, Wolf, be my guest. Maybe this guy is sent for a purpose, like you say. A purpose too mysterious for my little mind to grasp. The big question is —" Kelly turned to face me "— are you going to be more of a help or a hindrance?"

I shrugged. Unless I was mistaken, Kelly was still a bit suspicious of me, or maybe he was just trying to calculate how much trouble and bad luck I was hauling around. He stood, announced he was going home and, for the first time that evening, offered me his hand. "Good luck."

After he left, Wolf suggested the two of us visit Paradise, a club Walrath had been known to frequent. Within walking distance of the campus, it was a well-known Toronto bar on a street full of boutiques and outdoor cafés where you could spend surprising amounts of money on exotic coffee and unsatisfying crepes. In Paradise's heyday the street outside it would be filled every Friday and Saturday night with cruising sports cars. A man in a white suit would sit on top of one car with his feet on the passenger seat, scouting the action while someone else drove. Inside the bar there would be an unheard tinkle in the air, the resonance of men who had the golden touch of successful chiselers. Since those days the bar had switched from disco ball and mirrors to exposed brick wall and fans hanging from the ceiling. Young white men in football jerseys, with bulging pectorals and deltoids, walked around on the balls of their feet, and young women who worked in offices and spent far more money on clothes than they could afford and thought the Red Lantern unsophisticated flocked there.

Outside Paradise we paused before entering. Two young women wearing lipstick in bright concupiscent shades passed us on the sidewalk. Wolf smiled at them. They glanced at us as if we were something just deposited on the steps by a dog. Obviously neither of us looked wonderful. There was a thin line of dried blood trailing from a corner of Wolf's mouth, for one thing. He must have gotten in the way of a stray fist during the hubbub.

"Is our powder still working?" I asked him.

Wolf took a pinch and rubbed our faces with it. Then we entered the vestibule of Paradise and saw a tall, broad-shouldered man wearing a tie, jacket, and running shoes. He had a trim little mustache and hair that knew the daily caress of a blow dryer. At the moment he was saying something in the ear of one of the women who had just passed us, his right hand resting on her buttocks. But he noticed us, all right.

"Sorry. No jeans allowed," he said to Wolf.

"Come on, give us a break," I said.

He kept staring at Wolf and didn't even glance at me. He seemed to find Wolf fascinating, as if he were a midget dressed up in a tuxedo.

"Don't give me a hard time, eh? Take your friend back to his wigwam."

"I see. Redskin not good enough for white man's singles bar."

The man looked at me now, then rubbed the top of his fist with the flat palm of his hand. "You don't know when to give up, do you, dumbo?"

Wolf nudged me. "You've done enough fighting for one night, brother."

Outside, we looked for another entrance in back and found two men sitting in an open doorway leading to the Paradise kitchen. One was short, skinny, and gray-haired, the kind of guy who looked as if he survived through sheer speed, filching goodies from the pantry in the time it took smarter, heavier men to open and close the pantry door. The other was a young man with a case of acne so raw that it looked as if he were in the first week of chicken pox.

"You go through the front door, fellas," the gray-haired man said.

"A nasty man wouldn't let us in," I told him. "We have jeans on."

"Well, it's a high-class joint."

"Is there a way through the kitchen?"

I took out a twenty. The older guy put his face near it as if he were a cat sniffing a bowl of unfamiliar cat chow. Then he stood, looked inside, and waved us by. "See that door? That's where you go through. Hurry up. The chef's buggered off."

"Thanks."

"Tell you what," he added as he took the bill. "Check out a girl named Rhoda in a green-striped dress. She's the Paradise gang bang special. But wear your condoms, boys."

We walked into the kitchen and through the door he had indicated. All the customers were drinking beer and humming like the strings on a viola. A band was playing and a lead singer in a jumpsuit was howling into a microphone until his face turned red and the veins in his neck stood out. Wolf startled me by bounding up to the dance floor and dancing beside the two girls who had ignored us and who were now dancing with each other. He moved like a Michael Jackson with testosterone. It was magnificent. Everyone else looked awkward in comparison with this professional. Never once did he look at the girls, but they certainly looked at him, even when he had left the dance floor and was standing beside me, making a survey of the customers. He was grinning from ear to ear.

I was about to comment on this when he nodded in the direction of a corner table where two women and a man were sitting. "See the girl in the blue dress?" he shouted in my ear. I could hardly miss her. She had short hair dyed the color of a Coke machine, eyeliner so thick it made her eyes look as though they were on the bottom of moon craters, and a dress that was blue on her right side and mauve on her left. "She's a hooker," Wolf said. "Name's Sandra. Used to work for Walrath."

Sandra was staring off in the distance and didn't notice us until we had actually reached their table and Wolf called out her name. The other two had already noticed us. The man, in his late thirties, sported wire-rimmed glasses over pale gray eyes and wore a beige suit. The other woman looked much younger, and almost demure, with a simple skirt and blouse and shoulder-length hair, which was brushed a hundred strokes a day, purged of split ends, and pinned into place neatly above each ear with a barrette.

"Sandra," Wolf said, "I'm looking for Walrath."

Sandra cast her gaze somewhere off into the ozone layer again.

"Walrath? Who's Walrath?" the man in the beige suit asked. The other woman rolled her eyes. "Forget it, Michael."

"What's happening, anyway?" I asked him, to draw attention away from Wolf.

"Boogie oogie dancin' shoes," he said. "You know something? Twelve years ago I spent a couple hundred bucks learning disco on my lunch hour. I can still do a mean L.A. Hustle, can't I, Lois? But where are the discos of yesteryear, I ask you?"

"Jesus Christ, leave me alone," Sandra blurted. She raised her upper lip over her gums, Dracula-style, reached into her mouth, and yanked at her upper teeth. A plate came out. "See that? Six fucking teeth I lost. Him and his pool cue."

Michael tapped my arm and nodded at the woman next to him. "This is my friend Lois." Lois glanced at me. She knew that whatever I was looking for, it wasn't her. That was cool. She was concentrating on what Sandra was saying.

"One night Jimmy and a friend of his come in, and I'm sleeping, right? And Jimmy says, 'Come on, sweetie, there's a couple of slopes want to see you.' So we go down to Chinatown, this pool hall, and we get there and Jimmy starts swinging the cue. That's right, all over my face. I can't see because the blood's running down my eyes, and Jimmy gets me on the pool table and says to these three slopes, 'Whatever you want, boys. It's on me.'"

Michael tapped my arm again and leaned over to say something confidential. "Lois is a hell of a smart cookie. I'm not kidding. She works so she can buy the drugs of her choice. She knows what she's doing."

"Yeah, that's right," Sandra said. "I'm not working for Walrath anymore. I don't know where he is. Go ask Anita over there. Her brother's a good friend of his. *Capiche?*"

"There's nothing wrong with that," Michael shouted in my ear.

Wolf stood. "I'm sorry to hear that."

"Yeah, sorry. See you later, okay? You're interfering with my business."

"I mean, is there anything wrong with that?" Michael shouted again.

"Nothing," I said. "Sounds like she has a very liberated lifestyle."

Wolf asked Sandra about Anna Lightfoot.

"You mean, Pocahontas, the Indian princess? You know what the difference is between an Indian princess and a squaw? Fifteen drinks."

"No, serious," Michael said, tapping my arm a third time.

"Would you please stop tapping my arm?" I felt as if quite enough liberties had already been taken with my person tonight.

Sandra raised a corner of her upper lip in a sneer, but not a big sneer. She didn't want to expose her toothless gums. "Pocahontas isn't going to last too long. You'll probably find her under some railway bridge, jerking off winos."

"You haven't seen her?" Wolf asked.

"No. Not for a year." She turned her head away and tried to fit her dentures back into her mouth. Michael sat back in his chair, looking at nothing in particular. He suddenly seemed quite thoughtful.

Wolf and I walked over to the woman Sandra had pointed out. She was petite, dark-haired, and maybe twenty, with skin that looked well scrubbed with Phisohex, lips delicately polished and buffed with a colorless gloss, and a pleasant little nose. Her companion was a dark, curly-haired young man wearing a white-on-white shirt unbuttoned halfway down his chest. She was swaying her body slightly to the beat of the music; he looked as if he were thinking about how to pass the time tomorrow after he got up around 11:30 and had a late breakfast. When we approached the table, she glanced at us, mildly alarmed.

"Excuse me. Are you Anita?" Wolf asked. He said it in a very serious, polite tone of voice.

She nodded.

"Is your brother around?"

"What do you want with Tony?"

Her companion suddenly leaned across the table in front of her. "You looking for Tony?"

"Yeah, I'm trying to find a guy named Walrath. A lady we talked to said he could help us."

"Tony don't have nothing to do with that pimp."

"He could still help us maybe."

"Tony's probably playing pool tonight at Carafa's," Anita said. Her companion looked at her as if she ought to have known better — broads in general being smart to leave things like this in the hands of guys like him. But he sat back in his chair and looked over in the direction of the dance floor. *Fuck it,* his face declared.

"Where's Carafa's?" Wolf asked.

She gave him an address on St. Clair Avenue West, in an area noted for billiards and espresso rooms, and stores where you could pick up wedding gifts like the Blessed Virgin Mary with organdy flowers in a bell jar. Her companion got up in a slow, bored way and walked over to another table.

"Friend of yours?" I asked.

She shrugged. "He's my cousin. He usually gives me a ride home. The bus takes *hours.*"

"What's your brother's last name?" Wolf asked.

"Barzula."

"Thank you very much."

"Don't mention my name, please. He hates me enough already."

I started to walk toward the front entrance, but Wolf tapped the side of my arm and nodded in the direction of the kitchen. We looked inside. A fat man in a chef's uniform was putting something in a microwave. When he saw us, he looked extremely annoyed. "What do you guys want?"

"Mind if we go out this way? There's some guys waiting for us out front."

"Assholes." The way he said it, it wasn't clear who he was referring to — us, the guys supposedly waiting for us, or the customers of the disco in general. He jerked his head in the direction of the outside door.

"Why'd you want to go back out through the front door?" Wolf asked when we were outside.

"I wouldn't mind walking by our friend at the door."

"Want to get into another fight tonight?" Before the last word was out Wolf stopped and threw a punch aimed directly at my own solar plexus. He was quick, all right — dancing had obviously done good things for his coordination. If he hadn't pulled the punch in the last second before it landed, I would have been sprawling on the ground that instant with my eyes halfway out of their sockets.

"Listen to your friend, the wise old Ojibway medicine man. What you're trying to do is blow off steam. That's dangerous."

"Dangerous?"

We emerged from the alley on to the sidewalk. Wolf smiled at another girl walking into Paradise, with the same results as before.

"While you're doing it, you feel terrific," he continued. "The adrenaline's spurting through you, you feel ready to tear people apart. But it's no good. One, the other people might tear you apart first. Two, even if you get away with it, you just feel drained afterward, weaker and smaller than you were before. You know what I mean?"

"I'm listening."

"Besides that, you'd be getting those two guys in back of Paradise in trouble." He gave a tremendous yawn. "That fight in the bar kind of tired me out. But let's find this guy Barzula before we quit tonight."

We found the poolroom easily enough, although it involved a tedious ride on the subway and on a streetcar. There were fifty guys in there, shooting pool or playing tabletop soccer, and enough secondhand cigarette smoke to make your throat raw. I went up to the counterman. "Anita Barzula asked me to give her brother a message. She said you could point him out to me." He gave Wolf a funny look, but seemed to find me unexceptionable, and nodded at a bare-chested man playing a pinball machine.

"Tony Barzula?" I asked him. He looked at me with fear in his eyes that came and went so fast I began to doubt I'd seen it, especially when the fear was replaced by a look of indifference worthy of one of the guys who sell tokens and tickets in the subway. He was a tall, wiry man in his early twenties, with a smooth, hairless chest — but one with sufficiently enlarged pectoral muscles so that he obviously enjoyed not wearing a shirt in public. He had a tattoo of a dagger and a rose on his right bicep, which was also of considerable size for a wiry man.

As soon as I addressed him, he turned around, leaned with one arm against the machine and, with his free hand, played with a key chain hanging from his belt. It looked as if he had about forty keys on that chain.

"Yeah, that's me. Do I know you?"

"No, you don't. The name's Heywood Murphy. This is my friend Wolf."

Barzula looked Wolf over. "Wolf," he muttered. "Awooooooo."

"We're looking for a girl named Anna Lightfoot."

Barzula turned back to his machine. "Get outta here. You want a hooker, ask a cabbie."

"How about her friend Walrath? They say the two of you are pals."

"Who says that? I don't know no Walrath."

"Sandra says that. For one."

Barzula stopped playing. "What do you guys want?"

"Anna Lightfoot. Short of that we wouldn't mind talking to your friend Walrath."

"I told you, he's not my friend."

"You know him, though."

"Maybe."

"What is this, a guessing game? We have to guess whether you know him? I'm not a mind reader, Barzula. I just go on what people tell me."

"Who sent you guys?"

"Charles LeRoy."

"Am I supposed to know him, too? Tell LeRoy, whoever he is, I can't help him. Sorry to disappoint."

"I wouldn't worry about that. He's lying in a morgue right now and he's not feeling big disappointments anymore."

"How'd he get there?"

"He ran into somebody's knife. Nobody knows whose. Anna was LeRoy's friend. One of the few he had, besides myself, actually. That's why I'm looking for her. Just want to have a little chat."

"Oh, I get it. Junior detective time. Sorry. Still can't help."

"The cops, by the way, have no idea LeRoy knew Anna. I imagine they might be interested in that fact. Maybe talk to Anna's friends while they're at it."

He thought that over for a moment. "I'm going for a burger. You can come along if you want."

The three of us walked up the street to a diner. We went inside, sat down at a table, and a short, bald man at the grill shouted, "Hey, what's the idea with no shirt?"

Barzula groaned. "Where's this, the Royal York?"

"It ain't the swimming pool, Barzula."

"Come on, Freddie, don't give me a hard time. You'll probably get a few girls coming in if I sit by the window."

Two other customers, men in their forties with watery eyes and thick fingers that were familiar with pneumatic drills and shovel handles, grinned. Freddie turned away and began scraping the grill with a metal spatula. "What do you guys want?"

"Cheeseburger." Barzula looked at the two of us. We both shook our heads. "Coffee, too." He leaned back in his seat and played with the salt and pepper shakers. "Look, guys, I have to be careful, you know? I got a rep as being a friend of Jimmy's, so everybody who gets burned by Walrath comes to me. Assholes. Jimmy never cons anybody who doesn't ask for it. Can you imagine some guy who's stupid enough to give Jimmy fifty bucks and Jimmy tells him, 'Go to room, you know, room 415 at the St. Leonard and she'll be waiting for you'? And the guy goes?" Barzula shook his head. "Anyway, I haven't seen Jimmy for months. I'm sorry to tell you that, but what can I do?"

"You know him, though," I said.

"Sure, I used to hang out with him. He's a funny guy. But you don't fool with him. I've seen him go after guys with a hammer, you know the claw end of a hammer, and tear skin off them. Me, I don't go for that."

"He sounds like a lot of laughs all right. Where's he now?"

Barzula looked at Wolf. "How come you Indian guys never say nothing?"

I glanced at Wolf, too. He was kind of irritating playing the Silent Oracle. Then he smiled ever so slightly, but still didn't say anything.

"When he has something to contribute to the conversation, he'll let you know."

"Yeah, well, quit staring at me, will you? I don't know where Jimmy is. I stopped hanging around with him months ago, like I said. But I hear he's off the streets. He's got a new scam."

"Oh?"

"I don't know what he's doing, but he's playing with big boys now. Crack or something. That's what I hear, anyway. You won't find him taking fifty bucks from guys coming off the afternoon shift anymore."

"What about Lightfoot?"

"She's gone, man. She ripped Jimmy off for a couple of grand and split. Probably to Vancouver. If I were her, I'd go to fucking Hong Kong. You don't do that to old Jimbo."

"When was that?"

"Geez, that was a year ago."

I sat back in my seat and let out a sigh. Freddie came over with the cheeseburger, put it in front of Tony as if it were a hundred-dollar bill he owed him from a bad night of poker, and walked off. Wolf and I looked at each other.

"Thanks, Tony," Wolf said, rising. "We'll see you around."

"Hey, the cigar store Indian talks. I was beginning to think I might have to use sign language."

"See you later, Tony," I said.

"Good luck. If you do see Walrath, tell him I scored 850,000 points playing Terminator 2, will you? We used to have a thing going, you know, a competition."

"Yeah, I'll tell him."

Outside, Wolf and I agreed to call it a night and meet sometime tomorrow at the Lodge. For a few minutes I watched him walk away, reflecting with pleasure on the fact that this man seemed to be on my side. I was beginning to feel, since LeRoy's death, the way I had felt as a small child when there were powers I couldn't understand and I was much closer to all the fathomless terrors of life. I knew then how hard it was to survive without somebody on your side. It was no different now. LeRoy, I realized suddenly, had assumed he could make it without anybody on his side. He assumed he could make it by himself. He should have known better.

3

THE NEXT MORNING I remembered I still had Theresa Hagedorn's set of keys, which prompted the question of why Terri had given them to me. Maybe she really was so angry and disgusted with LeRoy that she had wanted to get rid of them that instant when we said good-night. On the other hand, maybe she was setting me up. But if so, how could she have known I would have gone back that night? I couldn't think my way around that objection. But part of me couldn't shake the feeling that she knew what she was doing when she handed them over to me.

In any case, there they were, and I might as well make use of them. Of course, I couldn't get back into his apartment with these keys. The apartment might still be guarded by a policeman. But there was the trunk we had taken down to the storage area, and another key opened the trunk. LeRoy might have left something in the trunk, a small indication of what had turned sour and dangerous in his life.

When I got to the basement of LeRoy's building, I found his footlocker where we left it. I pulled it out and opened it with one of the keys. Inside, covering almost the entire length and width of the footlocker, was a box with a picture of an American navy warship, circa 1800. *Build a decorative masterpiece that will last for years.* I opened the box. I was aware, of course, that by so doing I was tampering with evidence, as Staigue might say. But I was smart. I had brought gloves with me, and made sure I touched nothing without them. Years of watching cop shows on television had taught me at least that much.

The plastic parts were all there, in cellophane bags. Everything looked undisturbed, as if the box had just recently come off the shelf of the toy department. Below that box were three bundles wrapped in tissue paper. A sixteenth-century Spanish galleon, a Yankee clipper ship, and an American cruiser from the Second World War. Three decorative masterpieces.

That was it, except for three other small items. One was a photocopied sheet of paper. The top left-hand corner of the sheet had been torn slightly, as if it had been pulled out of a number of sheets stapled together. I read what was on it:

> including the current revival of interest in education of our young people for Total Observance. Have you noticed, just for one little example, or not so little example, how many families are now sending articles of clothing, supposedly "all wool" garments, for laboratory analysis, to find out for sure if these are really all wool? So they're not unwittingly going against

> Deuteronomy 22:11? We've noticed.

> These are people who might have been content, a few years ago, to teach their children some "Bible stories," or an outline of "Jewish history." Some of these same people are now sending their children to schools like Beth Yehuda Yeshiva. All the more reason, then, to honor those who have made Beth Yehuda Yeshiva possible. The ones who have been innovators and leaders all the way.

Below these paragraphs was a list of names. Beside the list somebody had written phone numbers in pencil.

The second item was another sheet of paper in an envelope. The sheet of paper looked like a photocopy of a photograph, but so light almost no details of the picture could be made out. You could see the photograph was of a man and a woman, and that was about it.

The third item was a ring wrapped inside wads of tissue paper. A gold ring, with a bright blue stone in the center, perhaps a sapphire. I slipped the ring, the first sheet of paper, and the photograph into my pocket, then put everything else back into the trunk, closed the footlocker, and shoved it back into its compartment.

After I left the building, I went to a phone booth and checked the phone numbers of the people on the photocopied list. Everybody had a phone number different from the number somebody, presumably LeRoy, had written down beside that list. Everyone except Solomon and Lydia Rothbard. That last name every reader of the business section of the *Clarion* was familiar with — Sol Rothbard was a major developer in the city. Retail space, I think was his specialty. Solomon and Lydia weren't listed at all in the phone book, so I took out a quarter and punched out the number written in pencil. Two rings, and a woman answered.

"Could I speak to Jack Birnbaum, please?" I asked, picking out a name from the list at random.

"Jack Birnbaum?" she repeated. "Sorry, you've got the wrong number."

Whoever the lady was, her voice was as soothing as someone's gentle fingers rubbing my temples after a hard day at the newsroom.

"Oh, I see. I've mixed the numbers up. This must be the Rothbard residence."

"That's right. Who's speaking?"

"I'm a friend of Jack's. I have his number here from a list of Beth Yehuda sponsors."

"What list?"

"Just a personal list he made out."

"Oh."

"Sorry about that."

"Quite all right."

I was sorry, in fact, our conversation was over so quickly. But I had the information I needed, and that information told me I would be having more conversations with this marvelous voice before long.

So I hung up and called the office of an old friend of mine, a lawyer named Shelley Rheingold. If you were Jewish, and you lived in Toronto, and Shelley didn't know you, you weren't worth knowing. No answer. Then I remembered it was Rosh Hoshanah and called her apartment. No answer. I called her parents' home.

Her eighty-year-old grandmother answered. She had heart trouble and several other organs were at different stages of collapse. She was one of those old people who should long ago have been clinically dead but who manage to keep going on the strength of some curious passion. In her case I think it was a passion to tempt her granddaughter into obesity with various baked goods. She spoke over the phone in a voice that sounded as if somebody had his hands around her windpipe and was squeezing hard.

"Hello. Who is this?"

"Can I speak to Shelley please?"

"Who? Who is this?"

"Can I speak to your granddaughter?" I shouted.

"You want to speak to Shelley?"

"Yes, please."

"Shelley is having dinner now. Goodbye."

Just as she was about to hang up, I heard a muffled exchange on the other end, and then Shelley came on. "I thought that was you, Hal." She laughed. "What's up?"

"Have you run into Lydia and Solomon Rothbard lately?"

"Solomon *Roth*bard? Are you writing a story on him?"

"No. I can't explain it all now. It's very complicated."

"I'll be very interested to hear your explanation, Heywood. And, no, I haven't run into him lately."

"He does shopping centers, doesn't he?"

"They don't call him the Monarch of Malls for nothing. He started out with eight shoe stores he inherited from his dad and then switched to malls. All over North America. I mean, *all* over."

"What's he got to do with Beth Yehuda Yeshiva?"

"The Yeshiva? Hal, what is this about?"

"Just curious."

"I bet you're just curious. The Yeshiva is one of his many interests, if you want to know. Along with such things as his collection of Russian and Soviet avant-garde painters, reputed to be the world's finest. Apparently he got interested in that kind of art when he was a university student and a rabid Trotskyite. Then he got into the shopping mall business because he figured it's all part of the Late Capitalist phase of history. He ain't your ordinary mall magnate, that's for sure."

"Shelley, you're losing me. What's this got to do with Beth Yehuda?"

"Well, the latest is he's made a complete turnaround and is now part of the 'We want Messiah now' crowd. In other words, a total religious nut. Beth Yehuda would fit into that. It's a Hebrew School for kids that's really, really Orthodox. The last month or so he's been heading a big fund-raising drive for the school. If I'm not mistaken, tonight's one of the parties he's holding for supporters. Get this, even Cardinal Moone and the mayor might be there. Or maybe that was last week's party."

"Since when does Cardinal Moone help with Hebrew schools?"

"I'm not saying he actually gave money, Hal. But he likes to give moral support, I guess, for political reasons too various to mention."

"Where does Rothbard live?"

"Sixty-five Ratherwood. I know because my family lived across the street when I was a little girl. So when do I get my explanation?"

"I'll call you this week, Shelley. Promise."

After that I took the subway to the Lodge, a three-story brick building that used to be a Bible college. It had a cafeteria, a gym, and a series of rooms that were now offices, complete with reconditioned Underwood manual typewriters and plaster walls painted the color of rancid mayonnaise. They were now used by native court workers, native drug abuse and alcoholism counselors, and native employment counselors. I walked into the reception room where a girl sat behind a switchboard. Three or four other adolescents sat in chairs and on top of a table, looking at me with mild but not unfriendly curiosity. That is, it was much more friendly than if I had been a policeman, and considerably less friendly than if I had been a stray dog. "Is Wolf around?" I asked the girl behind the switchboard.

"He's sleeping in the gym," another girl said, grinning. "Come on, I'll show you."

She bounced off the table and walked down a long corridor to the gym. In one corner I could see Wolf contorting his body. Dancing exercises, I assumed.

"Somebody here wants to see you, Wolf."

Wolf straightened, looked at me, and grinned. "June, meet the man who helped to lay low the great Jerome."

June gave him the look, perfected by teenage girls, of bottomless disgust. "Get outta here, you liar." Then she grabbed a basketball and ran off dribbling it. "Goodbye, Wolf," she called out as she made a wildly unsuccessful shot at the hoop.

"What's been happening?" Wolf asked.

I explained to him what I had done in the morning and showed him the list of names, the photocopied picture, and the ring. He barely looked at the list and the blurry photo, but turned the ring over in his fingers.

"Let's go," he said, pocketing the ring and giving the other items back to me. "I want to get something."

We got into a Volkswagen beetle he said he had borrowed from a friend and drove to his uncle's house, a semidetached brick house in a neighborhood the renovators had overlooked in the 1980s. During the drive, I wasn't favored with an explanation of what he was fetching. When we arrived at the house, Wolf unlocked the front door and walked in.

"Uncle Mose?"

"Come on in, Wolf. No Mountie hiding behind the door." The voice came from a room at the end of a hallway. We walked down the hallway, which was covered with a roll of linoleum full of holes, to a kitchen. Two men sat at a table. One was beefy and red-faced and wore steel-toed work boots, green work pants, a T-shirt, and a baseball cap. His friend, in jeans and a mustard-yellow sport shirt, was thinner — a sad-eyed, friendly-looking Indian who wore his gray hair in a brush cut. He smiled on seeing us. Half his teeth were gone, and the surviving bits of bone sticking out looked as if they'd soon follow.

Wolf introduced me. The bigger fellow was his Uncle Mose and the smaller was a man named Antoine.

"How you doing, Mose?"

"Not bad. Not bad at all."

"I want to use my pipe, Uncle. Tonight."

"Thought you swore off that, boy."

"No . . . not yet. Not completely."

Mose shook his head. "I told you. You can't screw around with it. Take it seriously, or leave it alone."

"I know, Uncle."

Mose looked at me. "This boy's pretty spooky. He's what you might call real A-1 medicine man material. If he wants to be." He nudged Wolf with his elbow. "Can't do anything else. Never seen anybody so allergic to work."

"He dances beautiful, Mose," Antoine said. "He's a beautiful dancer."

"Where's the pouch, Uncle?"

"Same place you left it."

Wolf got up and left the kitchen. I looked at the wall covered with little placards. "Your criticism is sincerely appreciated. Thank you very much and fuck you," one read. The whole wall was covered with these humorous messages. Before I'd read half of them Wolf was back in the kitchen with a leather pouch.

"Thanks, Mose," he said.

Mose shrugged. "You ought to think about going home, Wolf. People on Manitoulin miss you. You know there's a game there tomorrow with the Union of Ontario Indians? I was thinking of going if I could pitch."

"Don't believe I will, Mose. Thanks again."

"Call me up if you change your mind. I'll get us a ride."

I eyed the pouch as we left the house. "Wolf, I get the idea this pipe is like a Ouija board or something. Am I right?"

"Don't be cynical."

"Sorry. Occupational hazard of the newsroom."

"Heywood, can I ask you something? I grew up in a tent in the woods. A tent. That's where I lived, summer and winter. But that wasn't bad. What's bad is that even living in the woods you meet an awful lot of white people who think you're dog shit. Now that's hard to take. That's a big disadvantage in life. So what I want to know is how come you're cynical and I'm not?"

"I don't know, Wolf."

"Okay, we'll skip it. Now listen to me. I'll tell you what this is about and I won't bullshit you. Not that I'd ever succeed with a Canadian reporter. The smoke of the pipe is a bridge between the material and the spiritual worlds. It's like ordinary smoke — you can see something solid, a piece of wood, turn into smoke and then vanish, turn into something else. The smoke is the bridge. You see what I mean?"

"I think so."

"So I'm going to talk to the pipe. And I want to have LeRoy's ring with me, because it's the only personal thing of his you have, and it's probably soaked through with whatever spirit or soul he had, and the grandfathers might have something to say about it. Don't make a face, Heywood. I goddamn well know what I'm talking about."

I enjoy spooky stuff as much as the next man, but I don't place a whole lot of faith in it and I get irritated when it spills over into serious matters. Still, this could be an interesting spectacle.

"You're psychic, are you? What your uncle called being A-1 medicine man material."

"Yes, as a matter of fact I am psychic. I'm what every granola head wants to be." He gave me a very angry look, which I knew had nothing to do with me. "Ever since I was fourteen I knew I had this — whatever. I would dream things in great detail and they would happen. Somebody would break a leg in a car accident. Somebody would die. Somebody would get a job in the city. I foretold all. And why anybody would think this is a wonderful talent to possess is beyond me."

"So why do you use this pipe?"

"I don't know. A rabbi I know, a good friend of mine, tells me he believes two things about my pipe. One, that it works. And two, that it's evil. I know the first part is right, and sometimes I think the second part is right, too."

"Well, don't compromise yourself on my behalf."

"What else have we got to go on?"

"Nothing."

"Right. So let's meet later tonight. You know the Rosehill Reservoir?"

I knew the Rosehill Reservoir. It was a small grassy area in the city adjacent to a wooded ravine that was also a city park. It had some local notoriety as a spot where gentlemen liked to get to know each other very quickly in the days before AIDS.

Wolf was waiting for me when I got there, sitting on some concrete steps that led up a grass embankment near the reservoir. I noticed he had tied the ring to a thong and was wearing it around his neck. He said nothing by way of greeting, but stood when he saw me, immediately climbed the stairs, and started walking across the flat area of the reservoir. A few men were pacing around with the wordless intensity of prisoners in an exercise yard. Somebody ran by us in a jogging suit. Wolf didn't seem to notice. He barely seemed to see me. I had the sense that he was looking through things, that he was thinking very hard about something. It was a sense I had at least once before when I met a man who had gone insane and was wandering the streets of

Toronto, looking as if he were desperately trying to remember something.

Wolf walked to the edge of the ravine and then started down a path to a creek running through its center. We followed the creek until we came to a clump of trees. Wolf walked behind a couple of them, vanished from sight, and then reappeared a moment later.

"This looks all right," he said. "I'm going to smoke my pipe in there. You wait here."

"Wolf, are you sure you're all right? You're in a funny mood."

"I'm all right. Just make sure no one interrupts."

Then he disappeared again behind the trees. I sat down by the creek and tried to relax, but the only thing I could think of was a glass of beer. Every tissue in my body was craving a cold swallow of Labatt 50. I tried desperately to think of other things, and hardly noticed someone walking along the path toward me until he was about ten yards away. His shuffling along the path in the darkness reminded me for an instant of the zombies in *Night of the Living Dead*. There was the same heaviness in the footfalls, the same suggestion of a being animated by some unintelligent purpose.

He tripped over something on the path and fell. I stood to help him, but he rose quickly and was up before I reached him.

"Fucking path. You have to watch every step you take with these fucking tree roots." He wiped his hands on his pant legs and then looked at me. In the darkness I could make out the features of a man of about fifty, with thinning hair meticulously combed. There was a very hungry feeling to this person.

"Got a light?" he asked.

I produced some matches and lit his cigarette for him. He lightly touched my hand, the one holding the match, with his own.

"What's up?" he asked.

"A friend of mine's in the bushes, talking to his pipe. I'm making sure no one disturbs him."

"Talking to his pipe? What *pipe*?"

"His prayer pipe. He's an Indian."

"Yeah. Tell him he can suck on my prayer pipe. Is he really an Indian?"

"That's what I said."

"That I gotta see. I didn't think any Indians were gay. I thought it's a white man's sickness." He said all this in the boundless sincerity of his Canadian innocence.

"Who said he's gay?"

The man stared at me for a moment and then shook his head. "It's a crazy world. It doesn't seem that long ago this place was full of —" He smiled wanly. "Kids. Nice kids, good-looking kids. They'd look at me and say things like, 'I'd love to climb the hill with you, dear, but aren't you afraid of a heart attack?' You know, 'cause I was in my forties and I looked it. I'm your hard-working average Joe and not a pretty boy. And how many of these kids now are still alive, I wonder?"

He looked at me as if he actually expected an answer. Then he cleared his throat. "Some of them used to say, 'Well, it's too late now to worry about AIDS. You know, I've been a slut for so long.' But I figured that was a stupid attitude. I always carry condoms now."

The last sentence ended in a note of appeal.

"Good for you," I said. "Best of luck to you."

"I'm really curious what you're up to. Mind letting me in on the secret?"

"I did. See you later."

He shrugged and wandered off, his head lowered to keep an eye out for tree roots.

I looked over at the trees, but there was still no sign of Wolf. I waited for another ten minutes, drifting off into a reverie of my own when I was startled by a laugh. Something told me to make myself immediately inconspicuous, and I squatted behind the nearest sizable bush. My instincts were never better. From the trail up ahead four young men came sauntering by, one idly slashing the foliage by the path with a long stick. Three of them, who must have pumped iron, were built like the rear end of an Econoline van. They walked as if they had basketballs between their thighs. The fourth, with the stick, was of normal size, but in their company he looked skinny. He had a nose and eyes like a weasel's, and shoulders and arms that showed he was working out with weights, too. The three big ones looked as if they might show mercy after they had broken several of your bones, but I knew the fourth, once he had somebody helpless, would never stop. I could only pray they didn't meet up with the man I had just talked to. He was exactly who they were looking for. I also prayed Wolf didn't choose this moment to emerge from behind the clump of trees.

My second prayer was answered. The four men continued on their way until they disappeared, and Wolf still was nowhere to be seen. The Labatt 50 reappeared in my mind's eye, as radiant as a beer bottle lit up in a TV commercial. And then I heard a soft rustling in the trees where Wolf had gone. A dog jumped over a log in front of them. A large, lean dog with yellow eyes. It stood there looking at me, its mouth open, its tongue hanging out. I'm not usually afraid of dogs, but I could feel my heart pumping blood at an alarming rate. The animal eyed me for a moment, then jumped back into the trees out of sight.

I went back and sat down by the stream and waited. I'm not sure how long I waited. I just know that at one point I looked up and Wolf was standing beside me. He was motionless, and eyeing the stream, too.

"Finished with your pipe?"

"I didn't light it. There are funny feelings in this place."

"I don't doubt it. Since you left I've had to deal with an amorous gentleman and hide behind this tree from four gay bashers. This is no place for communion with the spirit world."

"Well, I thought all that was a thing of the past, around here, anyway. My mistake. Let's go someplace else."

"Fine with me. Especially as I just saw a very mean-looking dog. He had big teeth and big, furry ears, Wolf. Was he a friend of yours? Or what?"

"Come on, let's go. I'll talk about it later."

That meant he would never talk about it, but I didn't complain. We went to another park, much larger, north of the ravine. No lonesome nighttime strollers were in this area, thank God. Wolf and I hiked for a while until he found a grassy spot near a row of trees. "This is all right," he said. He opened his pouch after sitting cross-legged and fished around in it. I could see he had a knife in it, among other odds and ends. He took out a small bag and a braid of sweetgrass. Then he unwrapped the pipe. It was a long, thin pipe, almost two feet long, carved out of wood with four black feathers dangling from the end of the stem. He laid the pipe on the cloth for a few minutes and sat motionless with his eyes closed.

"This place is all right," he said finally. He lit the braid of sweetgrass and passed it underneath the pipe so that the pipe was covered with its smoke. While doing this he began a soft chant in a language I assumed to be Ojibway. He continued this for about ten minutes until he allowed the spark in the sweetgrass to die out and the last wisp of smoke to disappear. Then he placed the pipe gently on the cloth again and filled the bowl of the pipe with a few pinches of a tobacco mixture he took from the bag. He resumed his chanting and lit the bowl with a match. After a few seconds, a thin tendril of smoke rose steadily from the bowl. Wolf continued to chant, raising the pipe in the air, lowering it, and then pointing it in the four directions.

Afterward he smoked the pipe slowly, and with every puff seemed to drift more deeply into a reverie. Eventually he placed the pipe on his lap, the mixture in the bowl almost consumed, and simply sat and stared in front of him. The only part of his body that moved was his diaphragm, expanding and contracting slowly. I had the feeling I shouldn't have been sitting there, as if I was intruding on something intimate and private. Gradually, in any case, I began to feel drowsy. Wolf sitting there so still, like a thin, hungry Buddha, and the faint scent of the burning tobacco, worked like a tranquilizer. My eyelids drooped, I nodded, and I was asleep. Sometime later I was awoken by Wolf's hand on my shoulder.

"Heywood, do me a favor," he said. "Take your ring back." I yawned a couple of times, reached over, slipped the ring over his head, and put it in my pocket. Wolf smiled. He uncrossed his legs, wiggled his outstretched feet, stood, and stretched himself luxuriously. He seemed much happier now than he was when I fell asleep.

"Feel like having a bite to eat?" he asked.

"There was a party I wanted to crash tonight, if it's not too late. Mr. and Mrs. Solomon Rothbard. I wanted to ask them what their private phone number was doing on a piece of paper I found with LeRoy's ring."

"Who are Mr. and Mrs. Rothbard?"

"Wealthy people, Mr. Wolf. Very wealthy."

"Can I come? I won't embarrass you. I'll change my clothes and everything."

"It would certainly help if you didn't look as if you'd spent last month in a canoe with a load of beaver pelts."

I knew at that moment that it would be a big mistake bringing Wolf with me to the party. But I was still drowsy and I didn't have the energy to say no.

"What did the pipe tell you?"

"I saw some things. I saw a white hen spattered with blood. It was lying on the ground surrounded by feathers and pools of blood. I think it had its throat cut."

"What?"

"It was very clear. The hen was lying on the ground in front of a heap of stones. It could have been an altar of some kind. There was a cross on top of it. A sort of cross, anyway. The edges were all bent in a funny way. I couldn't recognize the shape."

"Did you see anything else?"

"Nothing."

"So what's that mean?"

"I don't know. I just see things. Usually they don't make any sense, like that. Somebody else has to make sense of them."

"Well, I can't."

"Not now. Maybe later."

"Are you going to talk to your pipe some more?"

He looked at his pouch for a while, holding it as if it were a keepsake from a lover. "I just might consult my friend the rabbi. I just might give this up for good." He looked at me. "The thought makes me feel curiously . . . exhilarated." He sighed. "Keep that ring. I don't want to see it again. There's something nasty about it. Seriously, Heywood."

I arranged to meet Wolf in an hour at my place and then proceed to the Rothbards' house. I had hopes of receiving information there of a less cryptic nature than what the pipe had conveyed. News bulletins from the spirit world were fine, but nothing beat hearing something from the lips of living human beings standing in front of you, in ordinary contact with other living human beings. Such beings might not owe much allegiance to truth, God knows, but they could never run that far away from it, or escape truth completely. The nerves in their flesh wouldn't allow it.

4

THE FIRST THING I did when I arrived back at my apartment was to phone Bernie De Luca. His friendly voice in my ear was pure balm to my own nervous system.

"Is Carlo doing any follow-up on the LeRoy story?" I asked him.

"Nope. It's been handed over to me," De Luca said. "Sort of. We won't run anything unless they make an arrest. I'm sorry to say your friend's murder has to compete for space in the paper with a lot more interesting mayhem."

"Poor Charlie. Not that he'd mind much. I suppose tongues in the newsroom are wagging."

De Luca's only response to that was a hearty chuckle.

"Emil say anything? Like about how this proves he was right all along to fire me?"

"Well, you know his style. He doesn't say anything, just shakes his head sadly."

"In case anyone asks your opinion, Bernie, you won't be wrong if you tell them I had nothing to do with it."

"Nobody's said otherwise. Even your friend Cheryl Greenbaum, who knows what evil lurks inside the hearts of us men, hasn't raised a word against you."

Cheryl Greenbaum, the *Clarion*'s fearless champion of oppressed women everywhere. She'd never forgiven me after I'd gotten tight at a *Clarion* Christmas party and carried on with Myrna Tostiak in what I thought was a rather playful and debonair fashion. Unfortunately the two of us were seated at the same table as the unamused Greenbaum.

"That's not so surprising. We're only dealing with some guy getting stabbed to death. If I was involved in something serious, like telling a sexist joke, it'd be a different story."

"She'd have devoted a whole column to you. Then you'd really be in trouble. Anyway, everybody's curious, Heywood, but nobody's jumped to conclusions. And don't forget. Anything I can do."

"Thanks, Bernie."

I changed into my best clothes and waited for Wolf. It was hard because I had the fidgets. I thought about nibbling on something and opened the refrigerator, but there was nothing in there except for four plastic jugs of orange juice, a head of lettuce with lots of brown spots on it, six rubbery carrots, and jars of ketchup, mustard, mayonnaise, and blue cheese salad dressing. I glanced up at the cupboard above the stove where I used to keep my liquor. I had poured the contents of all the bottles down the sink the morning I left for Willow Crest, but the thought occurred to me that I wasn't one hundred percent certain absolutely every single bottle had been emptied and thrown out. It would be interesting to check that out, I told myself, just see if I remembered correctly. If I was wrong, if there was still some booze left, I wouldn't succumb to temptation. Really, I wouldn't. I opened the cupboard door. It was empty.

I wandered into the living room and picked a book off a table. A history of the War of 1812 by some university professor in North Carolina. I read three sentences and then put it down. Apart from drinking, my worst vice was buying books. I had long ago run out of space for them, even though two walls in my living room were devoted to bookshelves. Now books were stacked on the floors, on tables, even in the bathroom beside the toilet.

When Wolf finally dropped by, he was a sight to behold. He was wearing evening dress — a black swallow-tailed coat, a white vest, stiff white shirtfront, black tie. He had obtained this ensemble, he told me, from his "theater connections." The odd thing was that he looked great.

We drove off in his friend's Volkswagen to Ratherwood, a leafy avenue with old, impressive houses — Tudor affairs with circular driveways in front. Houses for successful lawyers, stockbrokers, kidney and gallbladder specialists, and the fabulously wealthy Rothbards. A block away from the address I told Wolf to pull over and park the car. When he turned off the engine, I just sat there. My hands were shaking.

"It's no use, Wolf," I finally said. "My nerves are shot. I can't go into that place without a drink."

He put his hand on my wrist. "Yes, you can. You were fine last night. You'll be okay now. I'm backing you up."

I shook my head.

"Come on," Wolf insisted, "let's get out and see the house, anyway."

We climbed out of the car and walked down the block until we were almost at the Rothbards' house. Just before we got there, two cars arrived and eight people, one of them Cardinal Moone, ended up going to the front door. When the door was opened to admit them, we could hear the faint sounds of people's voices. Clearly there was a huge crowd inside. This realization bolstered my courage.

I took a deep breath and stuck my hands in my pockets. "Okay, Wolf, don't forget who you are." He was supposed to be, if anyone asked, a representative of the Almighty Voice Survival School, where native culture was taught along with algebra and chemistry. I, meanwhile, was a friend of Sol Rothbard, unless I met Sol himself. Then I'd have to tell him straight out why I'd come: to ask him why his personal phone number — his wife's, that is — was in the possession of my late friend, the former hustler, cross-addicted alcoholic, and man-about-town Charles LeRoy.

A woman wearing an apron answered the door. She seemed

stunned at the sight of Wolf. I smiled but said nothing, merely gesturing as if to step inside the door. After all, she certainly hadn't demanded that Cardinal Moone's party give their names and state the reason why they had just rung the doorbell. It worked. Slightly flustered, she gave us directions to the room where the party was in full swing.

It was a large room with candles and dim lighting and, yes, it was packed. I could pick out a few well-known faces at a glance, however — an anchorwoman for CBC's *Prime Time News*, and the cardinal himself, Francis Moone, tall, hearty, with an Irish slab of a face. There was Paul Hornak, an executive assistant to the premier of our province, a little fellow still obviously delighted by the fact that he ate at the tables and sipped the wine of the great. There was His Honor, the mayor of Toronto. His Honor was blessed with no great intelligence, grace, or physical presence of any sort. As a boy in school, he was mediocre in his studies, laughable as an athlete. His teachers predicted for him a not completely grim future as a diligent furniture salesman, or something of the kind. But he had shown them all. Not only had he actually graduated from university, but he had landed a junior executive-type job and gotten himself elected to City Council a few years later. He worked like ten men. He was nice to everybody, including the secretaries — especially the secretaries.

He hung around council meetings constantly before his first election. It was discovered that he had a gift for sniffing out the real and hidden agendas of upcoming meetings, for knowing who was going to stroke whom — or conversely, who was going to stick it to whom — before these events happened in council chambers. With such gifts, and the knack of articulating the wishes of the people he lived among — the families who owned John Deere tractor lawn mowers — he had seized the top political post in the City of Toronto.

There he stood now in the living room, wearing aviator glasses and his trademark knowing smile. Across the room, near the archway where Wolf and I stood, was his mother, nibbling on some pâté.

"Wolf, there's somebody I want to talk to."

"Just do your thing, Heywood. I'm okay."

"Stay out of trouble?"

"See that girl with the hors d'oeuvres tray on the other side of the room? I'm going to stalk her and get me some free supper."

I walked over to the mayor's mom and said hello. Her smile was warm and enthusiastic, and her eyes were cold and suspicious. She had a knack of arranging her face that way.

"I'm Heywood Murphy. I met you at the reception for Cardinal Moone last year. Just after he got his new red hat."

"Oh, yes, *Hey*wood. How are you?"

"Not bad. Is our host about?"

"He's off somewhere, talking to some people from Beth Yehuda. Lydia, I don't know. She doesn't like parties."

"Not even her own?"

"She's indisposed tonight, according to Sol."

"How disappointing."

"Disappointing is an understatement, if you ask me. That girl's a powerhouse in the community, but you never hear about it in the newspapers. The Rothbards want publicity like you and I want heart trouble."

"Quite a place they got."

Indeed it was. Honey-colored oak paneling gleamed in the candlelight. Gorgeous mahogany and rosewood furniture, very Louis Quatorzey, lay about in corners and alcoves of the room. By contrast, a framed oil painting dominated the main wall, all circles and rhomboids in bilious shades of green and yellow. "Look at that," she said after spreading more pâté on a piece of bread and noticing the direction of my gaze. "They got it from some Russian refugee in Chicago. They say it's worth a fortune now."

Before I answered she was distracted by a hand on her shoulder. She turned to face Albert Batt, senior alderman from Rothbard's ward, and introduced us. It was clear he didn't remember who I was, although I had interviewed him at least twice — a lapse of memory strange in a politician. Then again it might help explain how he managed to lose two campaigns for mayor of Toronto.

"Paul Hornak's told me your boy's said no again, Hannah," Batt said to her.

"Why would he say yes?" she asked. "Is what they offered as good as being mayor?"

"He doesn't want to be mayor forever."

She smiled, grandmotherly malice in her eyes. "Anxious for another campaign, Bert?"

Bert guffawed. "I've learned my lesson, I'll tell ya. Ah, Mr. Hornak. Speak of the devil. Come to get the power behind the throne on side?"

Hornak, in a dark blue suit, a grin splashed from ear to ear on his round baby face, ignored Batt and squeezed Hannah's hand. He looked like the apple of some neurotic mother's eye. "Well, don't you look healthy with that marvelous tan. Been to Las Vegas with Hizzoner?"

"He's been trying to get me to go, but no way. I tell him, you go by yourself and blow a little steam. You don't want your mother hanging around. I got the tan at Myrtle Beach, Paul."

Hornak turned his smile on me. "Murphy, how are you doing? Freelancing these days?"

I nodded.

"I didn't know you were friends with Sol. He's not exactly chummy with the press."

"You'd be surprised at the people he knows."

Hornak looked at me suspiciously, which I expected, but also with a hint of alarm, which I definitely hadn't expected, because Hornak made it his business never, under any circumstances, to show anything resembling alarm. That look changed in a second to his more habitual expression, one that implied we were co-conspirators in a rather amusing intrigue.

"You're a talented man, Heywood. Hope it works out for you." He smiled at the three of us. "Gotta be going, folks. Heavy schedule tomorrow. Take care of yourself, Hannah."

A few minutes after he left, a tall heavyset man walked up to us. "Bert, do you know who the hell that Indian is?"

All of us looked across the room. Wolf, who evidently had been sidetracked on his quest for hors d'oeuvres, was demonstrating some highly athletic dance steps in front of a group of women who were screaming with laughter. He looked like the bird in a cuckoo clock on amphetamines.

"Geez, don't ask me," he said. "Putting on quite a show, isn't he?"

"He came with you, didn't he, Mr. Murphy?" His Honor's mother asked.

"He came the same time I did. I think he has something to do with that Indian school in Toronto."

"I think I'll talk to that fellow," the tall man said. "Last week somebody crashed the party here and made off with a pair of silver candlesticks."

"Where is Rothbard, anyway?" I asked Batt.

"I thought the two of you were friends," the mayor's mother interjected. "I mean, the way you came in together. You looked like you knew each other."

Why the hell did I bring Wolf with me? I thought ruefully. Ignoring the woman, I looked around the room quickly. The other exit was in the corner where Wolf was doing his routine. As I walked by, I could hear one of the women marveling, "Talent like that, you should be on TV." I just kept walking out of the room, and into the hall. A stairway was at the far end of the hall, and I took it.

I peered into the first room off the hallway on the second floor: there was a TV in a wall cabinet, a set of *Encyclopaedia Britannica,* and on one wall a huge framed color photograph of four or five people looking like tourists in a Mediterranean country. Something in the way one of the men was posing for the photograph caught my attention. I was about to look at it more closely when I heard the crack of a billiard ball.

A second crack, and then a third. I followed the sound to a room with a pool table in the middle. A woman was standing over the table, examining the green felt. Then she banked a shot off the side, hitting the brown ball and causing it to roll majestically into a corner pocket.

"Very nice," I said. The lady straightened and looked at me. Her eyes were a glittering brown in a pale face framed by auburn hair. She was a slender woman, in her early thirties, with a cream sweater and a long burgundy wool skirt. She grimaced slightly at my compliment, as if to confess it was all a fluke.

"One of our guests, I presume?" she asked.

"I'm sorry. What did you say?"

"One of our guests . . . I *presume?*"

I'd heard her the first time. I was just taken aback by her voice. It was the same soothing tones that had come to me over the wires of Bell Canada earlier today.

"No, I crashed the party," I answered.

"That's not funny."

"You must be Mrs. Rothbard. I'm Heywood Murphy."

"Murphy?" She thought for a moment. "You *weren't* invited, were you?"

"That's what I said. I'm surprised to find a powerhouse of the community playing pool, by the way, instead of mingling with your distinguished guests."

"Powerhouse of the community?"

"In the words of our mayor's mom."

"Well, you've got a very trustworthy source of information. I'm sure there's nothing I do that escapes the notice of that woman's canasta club."

"Not only that, she's downstairs right now appraising your art collection."

Mrs. Rothbard let out a small groan.

"Shelley Rheingold told me about your party. But I didn't come for the party, actually. I came to see you."

"Why?"

"I wanted some information."

Her back stiffened. "Excuse me, but I really don't like being accosted in my own house by a total stranger. I find it very disturbing, in fact."

"Understandably. If this didn't involve somebody's murder, I would never be so bold. I'm basically an extremely shy man."

She stared at me. I could tell one thing from that stare. A single word she didn't like the sound of, the slightest tone in my voice that rang false, and I'd be out on my ear.

"I wanted to ask if you knew somebody named Charles LeRoy."

"Never heard of him."

"You sure?"

"Yes, I'm sure. It's not the kind of name that pops up in my social circles, if you know what I mean."

"Too Gentile."

"Exactly."

"Then how did he get hold of this?" I took out the photocopied list from a jacket pocket and handed it to her.

"This was put out by the local committee for Beth Yehuda," she said. "And this LeRoy person had it?"

"In his possession when he died."

"A victim of murder?"

"Somebody stabbed him to death last Friday night. He was a friend of mine."

"You're serious, aren't you?"

"I didn't come here to get the mayor's autograph, Mrs. Rothbard."

"Well, let's talk then," she said, putting the list on a chair. "Grab a cue while you're at it. I don't get to play with people very often. You'll find I'm much better at playing pool, Mr. Murphy, than I am at mingling with guests."

"I certainly hope so."

"What are you complaining about? You weren't even invited."

We reached into the pockets and retrieved the balls. Mrs. Rothbard racked them, chalked her cue, leaned over, and got off a hard, satisfying shot, scattering the balls around the table.

"Who was Charles LeRoy?" she asked.

"He worked for the city's Department of Public Health. When I met him, he was on a leave of absence — improving his work attitudes by learning how not to destroy half his brain cells with drugs and alcohol. We were both at a clinic."

"A clinic?"

"Shit! I should have made that." I handed the cue to Mrs. Rothbard. "Willow Crest. Yes, Mrs. Rothbard, you see before you a reformed alcoholic."

"And why was LeRoy stabbed to death?"

"I don't know. And neither do the police. Mind you, LeRoy used to be a petty criminal, and that category of citizen is more familiar with violence than you or I. But that's all I know. And despite his failings I rather liked him. It upsets me that somebody killed him. I think that the person who did it should be found out and made to pay for it."

"The job of our police force."

"Well, I hope so. But this case seems . . . difficult. Cops are basically civil servants, and they don't always rise to the occasion."

"You're going to help them out?"

I shrugged.

"I can't understand why he'd have my number," she said. "Or that sheet of paper."

"I don't, either. It bothers me a lot that I don't."

"You really have no idea why your friend was killed?"

"Like I say, he was a petty criminal, and when you're a petty criminal, you hurt people. It's part of the job. Sometimes people try to hurt you back. Maybe somebody got carried away. Who knows? But that phone number is curious."

"Very curious. We know very few people who are not extremely rich or observant Jews, or both. I'm not bragging, or complaining. It's just a fact."

Mrs. Rothbard sank another ball. She was damn good at this game. I put the list back in my pocket, the same pocket that held the ring and the photograph. I took the ring out and showed it to her, and could hardly believe it when I saw a look of alarm on her face. I seemed to be having that effect on quite a few people tonight.

"You are full of surprises, aren't you, Mr. Murphy? This belongs to Ivan Lusk."

"Ivan *Lusk*?"

She nodded again. "He had a ring just like this. And his initials — see by the stone there?"

"You know Ivan Lusk?"

"His family knew mine. He used to come around a lot before I got married."

At that instant we both heard footsteps running up the stairway. Several footsteps. Mrs. Rothbard looked out into the hall. "Sol, what's happening?"

"We're looking for somebody. A young man —"

"Wearing a green corduroy jacket? And a lousy pool player?"

Mrs. Rothbard was suddenly surrounded by people staring at me through the doorway as I reached for the chalk to rub on the tip of my cue. Foremost among them was a man I knew immediately to be Solomon Rothbard. He wore a white shirt, and a dark blue tie and suit on a slender, six-foot-plus frame. His face was lean, made leaner by a trim black beard and the dark eyes of a very cool player. He looked like the kind of man who could instantly calculate the odds of drawing an inside straight in a game with a dozen wild cards. I've played with guys like that. They usually have very engaging smiles when they keep raising you.

"This man wasn't invited here tonight," he said to his wife.

He said it not as a complaint but as a melancholy statement of the facts, in a voice that was low and curiously gentlemanlike, as if his voice box had been aged in fine port. If happy marriages were the result of happy vocal cords, these two were in heaven.

"I've just invited him. We're having a game of pool."

Solomon looked at his wife briefly, then at me. I could tell there was nothing in the world he hated more than somebody in his house who had no good reason to be there. A familiar female voice made itself heard in the hallway.

"He's probably here to write a story and sell it to some editor."

The progeny of that female now stepped into the room beside Rothbard, his knowing smile intact. "Are you freelancing these days, Mr. Murphy?" the mayor said. "How's the market for fired reporters? By the way, your friend's down below. The two of you can leave in the same police cruiser."

"So you got him. Your mom wrestle him to the ground?" I shouldn't have said that. It wasn't exactly a witty remark. At this moment, though, I hated this smug mother-and-son duo with a burning, irrational hatred. I would have loved it if he had taken a swing at me and we got into a nice punch-up. I had already forgotten Wolf's sage advice of last night. Fortunately His Honor wasn't one for punch-ups.

"Don't you talk about my mother."

"She's a formidable woman. I'm sorry to say, you pale by comparison."

"You're scum, Murphy. You're a —"

"That's enough of that," Rothbard said sharply. The aged-in-port voice had quite a bite to it when the man was aroused. "I'll handle this, gentlemen. You'd all do me a great favor if you went downstairs."

The mayor continued to give me a death glare, but he and the others backed out of the room. Rothbard closed the door behind him.

"I appreciate I'm breaking up a game of pool," he said. "But you will leave immediately. I did not invite you. I don't know why you came. If you are here to write something —"

"The lady was guessing. She's not even close."

Rothbard looked a bit relieved. Perhaps he'd be spared a newspaper article describing his lovely home, after all. "Well, I'm thankful for small mercies. Anyway, I still don't know why you're here."

"I know," Mrs. Rothbard said softly.

The two of them looked at each other for a moment. Rothbard's face was so controlled I had no idea whether he was suppressing anger, or hurt, or just strong curiosity.

"Then you can explain to your husband, Mrs. Rothbard," I said. "I won't trouble either of you any longer. May I have the ring back?"

She gave a tiny smile and handed it over. "Goodbye, Mr. Murphy."

"Goodbye, Mrs. Rothbard."

"I'll take you downstairs," Rothbard said.

"Have you called the police?"

"That was the mayor's suggestion. I don't believe I need their assistance."

"Of course you don't. We wouldn't dream of staying where we're not wanted."

We marched down to the front door. Standing there was Wolf, guarded by the tall man, who had his arms folded over his chest like a cop in a silent movie. Meanwhile Wolf smiled happily, like a kid who had just gotten off a terrific ride in the amusement park.

"Is this your bouncer?" I asked Rothbard.

The tall man looked secretly pleased at being called a bouncer, but Rothbard gave me a frosty look — very frosty.

"Did they get nasty with you?" I asked Wolf after we left.

"One man kept demanding what I was doing there. I told him he should ask you because you knew more than I did. He was so rude. Poor Cardinal Moone was very embarrassed."

"Did this man have a woman with him who seemed like his mother?"

"Yes."

"Well, my friend, you were just interrogated by His Honor the mayor. And we narrowly escaped a visit to the slammer. Did you really have to make a spectacle of yourself?"

Wolf grinned.

"I'm not taking any more chances," I continued. "I'm going to see Ivan Lusk alone."

"Who's Ivan Lusk?"

"You've never heard of Ivan Lusk? Or Chronos Corporation?"

"No."

"You've been too busy talking to your pipe to learn about the great financial monuments of the white man's civilization. Chronos Corporation is a well-known conglomerate controlled by Mr. Lusk, who is supposed to be a very smart man. He is also, according to Mrs. Rothbard, the owner of that ring you find so repulsive. How lucky for me they're family friends. So I'm going to return it tomorrow and ask him how it ended up in LeRoy's trunk. Charles certainly picked up some curious artifacts in his brief career."

The next morning I phoned another colleague on the paper, a business reporter, and got Lusk's address, which turned out to be in the heart of a wealthy but not the most fashionable neighborhood; it was slightly nouveau. Lusk's dad, I recalled, made his fortune marketing a product for upset stomachs in the United States. In Canada this didn't quite give his son the cachet of other wealthy men whose grandfathers had built department stores or made fortunes pushing bootleg whiskey in the States during prohibition.

I went out to look for a cab to hail. Like most reporters, I'd gotten used to taking cabs everywhere. My only problem now was that I had to pay the driver with cash instead of *Clarion* taxi chits. Unfortunately Lusk's neighborhood, like Willow Crest, was out of the way of Toronto Transit routes, so I had little choice this morning.

While waiting for a cab to appear, I noticed a car drive by slowly. The man in the passenger seat gave me a good once-over. An unmarked police car. They're easy to spot when your nervous system is tuned that way. Chrome parts are missing, and there's a well-worn look to them. They just have that cop car look. Anyway, it went on by, made a turn at the next intersection, and disappeared. That was it. The suspect, me, had had an eye kept on him. At least I knew there wasn't a warrant out for me yet.

The taxi driver I ended up with found Lusk's house easily enough. It was a two-story Georgian mansion, painted a blueish-gray, and set about two hundred feet back from the road, with two or three enormous weeping willows and some noble-looking fir trees on the front lawn. To the left and right of Lusk's home were houses that looked as if they were custom-designed for Mafia kingpins. They had fountains with statues in the front yard, and lots of arches and balconies, but Lusk's place was faultless.

Five minutes after I pushed the doorbell, the front door opened. A woman appeared with brilliant green eyes and short, honey-colored hair. She wore a plaid shirtdress, unbuttoned a good way up from the hem. It was a casual dress, of the kind that can't be purchased with a casual amount of money. I figured it was the butler's day off.

"Is Ivan in?"

"Can I tell him who's here?" she asked in a tone of voice that clearly informed me I better have a damn good reason for ringing her doorbell. I showed her the ring.

"Tell him Heywood Murphy has an item that belongs to him."

She reached for the ring, but I pulled my hand away.

"If you don't mind, I'd rather show it to him personally. It's not that I don't trust you, but, well, for the sake of my peace of mind, I'd just like to keep my hands on this."

She stared at it for a second, and then gave me a look as if I were a salesman trying to unload shoddy goods on her.

"I've been assured it does belong to your husband."

"Where did you get it then?"

"I'll be glad to tell your husband, Mrs. Lusk. I'd tell you, too, but I hate having to repeat myself."

"Would you mind waiting outside?"

She shut the door in my face, and I waited for what seemed like a very long time. Perhaps she had consulted with her husband and he had told her to phone the police. That wasn't a nice thought. I wanted to satisfy my own curiosity, not waste time satisfying the curiosity of the police. But Mrs. Lusk eventually opened the door. "Ivan's in the backyard," she said. "You can go around the side of the house."

Out back was a patio and another hundred feet of lawn, which ended in a row of trees. On this lawn were two men playing croquet, one dressed in a dark gray three-piece suit and the other in clerical black. As I approached the two, the cleric looked up. It was Wolf's friend, the cardinal. His opponent, with his back turned to me, hit an orange ball six feet into a green ball. "Sorry, Eminence," the opponent said. "I believe this means you've lost the game." He turned and faced me. "Murphy?" he asked.

"That's right."

"We're about to finish a game here, if you don't mind. I'll be with you in a minute."

He put his left foot, shod in a mahogany-colored loafer, on top of the orange ball and took a sudden, vicious crack at it with his mallet. The green ball shot off several feet. Lusk looked up at the cardinal with a little smile.

"Go ahead, Ivan. Don't prolong the agony," the cardinal said in a hearty, good-loser voice. Lusk hit the orange ball through a wicket. In three more moves he won the game. Lusk looked as if he still had his baby fat, and not much physical coordination to go with it, but he sure could wield a mean croquet mallet.

"I should have known better playing one more game," the cardinal said. "I'm no competition for you."

"On the contrary, your game is quite . . . strong. A trifle *eager*, perhaps," Lusk replied. "Shall we have lunch?" Lusk turned to me and gave me an odd smile. Odd, at least, in the sense that it conveyed not the faintest idea of pleasure or amusement on the part of its owner. He was a tall man with a face as smooth as an eleven-year-old's, but a peculiarly melancholy eleven-year-old. His eyes were sad, and when his smile faded, you could tell the corners of his mouth were turned slightly down in a permanent pout.

"It's refreshing," I said, "to find you so accessible, I must say."

The cardinal shook his head. "You should have more security, Ivan. You're too well-known not to have some in this day and age."

Lusk gritted his teeth and raised his mallet in the air. "Any interlopers will be met with croquet mallets. I am armed and ready." He lowered his mallet and gave me a look I can only describe as baleful. "As a matter of fact, I do have security, but they know when to make their presence felt. Now, Murphy, what is this business with a ring?"

I took it out and gave it to him. He frowned and turned it over in his hand, obviously deep in thought. "Where'd you find it?"

"Among the personal effects of a late friend of mine. Charles LeRoy."

"LeRoy . . . LeRoy . . . don't recall the name. Should I?"

"Not necessarily. Unless you had friends in the clerical staff of the Department of Public Health at City Hall. Or with hookers, B and E men, drug pushers, and other members of our criminal subclass. Or, I suppose, with the staff and patients of Willow Crest. LeRoy's name is known in those three circles."

"Sounds like an unfortunate man," the cardinal said.

"Very. Somebody stabbed him to death last Friday."

"Somebody from the circles you mentioned?" Lusk asked.

"Probably. Nobody knows yet."

"I see. How did you know him, Murphy? Which circle were you involved in?"

"I'm not a criminal and I'm not a civil servant."

"Oh, yes. Willow Crest. Of course."

"Of course? What do you mean, of course? Have rumors of my

alcoholism been noised about in Chronos Corporation? How flattering."

"I recall the episode of your . . . trip to London. I told Emil at the time not to make a big deal out of it. There are other ways of disciplining wayward employees than outright dismissal. Especially employees with a . . . problem. But Emil can be very hard-nosed, as you know."

"Yes, I know." I shouldn't have been surprised Lusk knew Hardaker — or even me, for that matter. Lusk was famous as one of the rare members of the Canadian financial establishment who had buddies in the press.

"So that's your ring, is it?" I repeated.

"Looks like my old fraternity ring."

"Fraternity?"

"Alpha Sigma Chi, McGill University chapter."

"Valuable, is it?" Moone asked.

"Hardly. My ring was filled gold with a lapis lazuli."

"Was?" I asked. "Isn't that yours? I mean, how many Alpha Sigma Chi rings have the initials I.L. engraved on them?"

"Yes, of course." Lusk put the ring in his pocket. "I suppose I ought to thank you for finding it, but I must say I'm still nonplussed about the whole thing. I have no idea how it ended up where you say it did."

"I was hoping you could enlighten me on that very question."

Lusk sighed. "Well, I'll think about it. In the meantime, we're about to have lunch. You may join us, if you like. Paul Hornak's dropping by. I believe you know him."

I had never received a less enthusiastic luncheon invitation in my life. Clearly Lusk felt obliged to be somewhat nice to me — I had, after all, returned his property to him — but it was also clear he hoped I'd decline. No such luck. I wasn't finished with Lusk and this ring business by a long shot.

The cardinal whistled sharply. "Come on, Alec, come on," he shouted as a beagle came running from the trees. The dog leaped around His Eminence's ankles while Moone bent down and tickled one of his ears. Then Moone straightened, and we walked to the house with the dog beside us.

Moone and I sat down on the patio at the back of the house at some white, wrought-iron, glass-topped tables, while Lusk pushed open a sliding glass door and walked into the house.

"Since Mr. Lusk neglected to do the honors, allow me to introduce myself," I said. "Heywood Murphy. You must be Cardinal Moone. I saw you at the Rothbards' last night."

The cardinal looked blank. Then he frowned. "Were you the fellow with the native person there?"

"That's right. We were both thrown out."

"Good gracious. What was that all about?"

"We weren't invited."

The cardinal looked horrified. "Don't tell me you crashed his party?"

"'Fraid so."

"The Rothbards are so private," he groaned.

The sliding glass door opened, and Lusk came out in the company of Paul Hornak, now casually dressed in blue slacks and a salmon sport shirt. "Lunch will be here presently," Lusk announced. "Paul, you know Heywood Murphy?"

For the second time in two days I could detect an uncharacteristic look of alarm on Hornak's face as our eyes met. Again the look quickly vanished. "Indeed I do. We saw each other last night, as a matter of fact."

"You just missed a croquet massacre, Paul," Moone said.

Hornak smiled. "Ivan's a wizard. We all know that. You should challenge him to tennis. That's your game, isn't it, Eminence?"

Lusk reached over to pet Alec, who was settled comfortably in the cardinal's lap. Alec's eyeballs rose in his sockets as Lusk's hand descended on his head. The dog was panting heavily.

"Alec, you're all tired out, aren't you, boy? Aren't you?" the cardinal said. "Look at his fur, Ivan. Isn't it shiny? That's a real sign of a healthy dog."

"Well, Murphy, I think I know the answer to our little mystery," Lusk said.

"Do tell."

"We had a maid with the habit of stealing little valuables. When my wife discovered it a month ago, we dismissed her. I'm almost certain she took the ring. Probably sold it to somebody in your criminal subclass. Maybe to your friend LeRoy. How'd you know the ring was mine, Murphy?"

"Mrs. Rothbard identified it."

Lusk stared for a second. "You know Lydia?"

I shook my head. "Casual acquaintance."

"The Rothbards don't *have* casual acquaintances."

"What was your maid's name, Mr. Lusk? I'd like to talk to her."

"You have money for the plane fare to Manila?"

"The Philippines?"

"Yes. Turns out she told the immigration officials at the airport she was here in Canada for three weeks to visit her brother and see Niagara Falls. After she got in, she forgot about Niagara Falls. The immigration boys sent her back a few weeks ago."

"What was her name?"

"Nina Roxas. R-O-X-A-S."

"Was she staying with her brother?"

"I believe so. They had an apartment out on Curtin Avenue, I think. Nina used to tell me they had some trouble in their building. Told me somebody smashed in the windshield of her brother's Nissan one night in the underground parking lot. Under the impression, I gather, that he was a Pakistani, or some such thing. There are a great many East Indians living in that area."

"It's a serious problem," the cardinal observed. "Some people in our diocese have made a study —"

"Westview Apartments, that's it," Lusk interjected. "That was the name."

"Thanks. I'll look them up."

The glass door slid open and out walked Mrs. Lusk with a trayful of cucumber sandwiches and deviled eggs. A black maid followed with an ice bucket.

"Thank you, sweetheart," Lusk said.

"I hope you gentlemen enjoy your lunch. Do you like the wine, Ivan?"

Lusk turned a bottle around in the ice bucket so he could read the label, and then mumbled something vaguely affirmative.

"Ivan told me you're going to renovate, Mrs. Lusk," the cardinal said.

"Pretty soon. There's so much wasted space I'd like to put in some really good Italian furniture."

"My wife is an enthusiast for contemporary Milanese design," Lusk said dryly.

Mrs. Luck tisked and playfully squeezed his round shoulders. "You like it, too, Ivan. You know darn well."

"Are you going to put in a Jacuzzi, Cynthia?" Hornak said. "I hear you're quite fond of them."

For some reason Cynthia didn't seem to hear the question. "Enjoy your lunch, everybody," she said, and then whisked herself back into the house.

"Did Cynthia make these sandwiches?" the cardinal inquired, already attacking one.

Lusk shook his head. "She's too busy looking at furniture catalogs. Have some, Murphy?"

"No, Alec," Moone suddenly barked. "No. *No.*"

The beagle was sniffing with canine enthusiasm at the sandwiches on Moone's plate. The cardinal picked up the dog from his lap and put him on the ground, where he started a piteous whine.

"A glass of Montrachet everybody?" Lusk asked.

I smiled. "Willow Crest, remember?"

"Sorry. Forgot about your . . . difficulty." He poured tall glasses for the cardinal and Hornak.

"Who was that Indian with you at the Rothbards' last night, Mr. Murphy?" Moone asked. "Alec, be quiet."

"His name is Wolf. He's an Ojibway. A medicine man."

"A medicine man. Very curious. I was talking with him at the party after he was taken into custody, so to speak. He knows some of the band chiefs I met at a native land claims conference a few years ago."

"He's helping me out. I have an interest in knowing who killed Charles LeRoy, since I discovered his body. We're on the case, so to speak."

"Does he employ psychic powers?" Lusk asked with a slight smirk on his face.

"As a matter of fact, Mr. Lusk, I had him go over that ring of yours. You'd be surprised what he came up with."

"Really? I can't say I'm terribly interested. Mysterious visions from the unknown don't usually excite me. I get enough of that reading economic forecasts."

"Don't be so cynical, Ivan," Hornak said gaily. "Let's hear it. Sounds fascinating."

Lusk groaned with disdain that bordered on the theatrical.

"I won't be offended if you tell me to shut up, Mr. Lusk. I know people in your position, as a rule, don't have to listen to anything they feel might possibly bore them."

"No, no. If Paul insists."

"All right. I'll tell you briefly what Wolf saw when he handled your ring. This is all by way of the smoke from his pipe, incidentally. His, uh, prayer pipe. It's sort of a conduit to the spiritual realm. You can call it hocus-pocus, or whatever you want, but the information's free of charge, so what the hell? He saw a white hen with her throat cut and her feathers scattered around. In front of a stone altar, or a mound, with something iron on top of it, like a cross bent out of shape."

Lusk, Moone, and Hornak stared at me.

"Is that it?" Lusk asked.

"That's it," I said.

Lusk leaned back in his chair and absentmindedly reached for another deviled egg. "I'm glad you said this information was free of charge."

"What do you make of it, Eminence?" Hornak asked. He sounded as if he were enjoying himself hugely.

"Sounds like umbanda."

"Voodoo?"

"The Brazilian version. The white hen with her throat cut sounds very much like it. Also, the stone altar with the iron on top of it. Devotees of umbanda often construct something like that in worship of Leba, who's a kind of demon, I guess, a devil. You worship Leba if you want to satisfy evil wishes."

"As a matter of fact, Wolf felt something very nasty about your ring, Lusk," I said.

"Umbanda can be quite nasty," Moone agreed. "I don't mean to cast any aspersions on anyone's culture, but umbanda has its dark side."

"You can't be serious, Murphy? Is there anything else you have to tell us?"

"Your ring ever been to Brazil?"

"Not on *my* fingers." Lusk shook his head. He took another sip of wine and then leaned back in his chair and gave the ever-grateful Alec a pat on the head. "I have had thoughts of visiting Rio, though. To see Corcovado and the beaches. I suppose I wouldn't mind seeing some of those umbanda rites. I'm sure they really do it up for the tourists. Is that your last question? Really, ask anything you want. Consider my patience as unlimited."

"It's a tempting offer. But there's nothing more I can ask."

"I hope you're going to ask Heywood to stay for dessert, Ivan," Hornak said. "The missus told me it's lemon soufflé. Your cook has a real gift for things like that."

"Thanks. I'd rather be going."

"Very well," Lusk said. Then he seemed to think something over. "Call my office if you want anything else. They'll give me the message."

That was nice of Lusk. It would have been nicer if he'd actually told me something useful about LeRoy, but at this point I was beginning to despair if anyone would ever tell me anything useful about LeRoy. So, after the maid called a cab for me, I said goodbye to the businessman and the politician and the cardinal and the cardinal's dog, and decided I would pay a visit to the brother of Nina Roxas. At home I checked a phone book and discovered Lusk had been right. Someone by the name of Roxas — F. Roxas — did live on Curtin Avenue, which was in the west end of Toronto in an area where high-rise apartment buildings had appeared like surprising and unwelcome growths in the Ontario soil. The area was rapidly becoming an extensive suburban slum, and it was depressing just to take the bus out there.

Westview Apartments was on a side street where kids stood on the sidewalk, fitfully taking turns on their skateboards and looking fully capable of smashing in the windshield of somebody's Nissan. The directory in the building listed an F. Roxas on the first floor, apartment 112. I pressed the button. No one answered. I pressed again. A few seconds passed and I heard a "Hello."

I took a guess. "Fernando!" I shouted.

There was a silence, followed by a barely audible "Yes."

"My name is Heywood Murphy!" I shouted again. "I'm a friend of Nina's."

"Who?"

"Nina's!"

"Who is speaking?"

"I'm Heywood Murphy. I'm a friend of *Nina's*."

Another few seconds passed. Finally I heard a click, opened the door, and made my way to Roxas's apartment. A tiny man in khaki shorts and an undershirt opened the door on my second knock.

"Mr. Roxas? Fernando? Could I talk to you for a moment?"

Roxas looked me over. He had the air of a man who feared trouble the way men who have had heart attacks fear the sensations in their chests. I was probably trouble.

"I'm not from the police, or a collection agency, or the immigration department," I said. "I just want to talk to you for a few minutes."

Roxas opened the door all the way, and I stepped in. He led me to a living room with a deep purple sofa, a TV table, and a walnut console. Those were the only furnishings, except for a picture of a lake in a tropical sunset — the kind of picture that hangs in Chinese restaurants.

We sat on the sofa. "You know Nina?" he asked.

"Actually, not all that well. I wanted to ask you if she knew somebody named Charles LeRoy."

Roxas shook his head with a brisk, almost convulsive motion. "Nobody named LeRoy."

"Are you sure? She never mentioned a name like that?"

Roxas shook his head again.

"Fernando, why did Nina stop working for Ivan Lusk?"

"What do you want to know for?"

"I'm trying to find somebody Nina might have known. It's very important. It has nothing to do with Nina herself, or you, or —"

"Somebody told on her. Somebody called up the immigration department. Nobody has to tell me, I know. I know damn well. I said to those men, first of all, she's my sister, she should be here, no problems. But it took fourteen months for them to interview her back home. Three times they interviewed her, *three times,* and each time she had to take the bus 500 miles to the consulate in Manila —"

"Wait a minute, Fernando. Slow down."

"*Three times*. And then she turns twenty-one, and they say, 'Sorry, you can't come now.' I say to them, 'What the hell are you doing? You don't want my sister to come? What's going on? Somebody tell me. What's going on?' So she comes as a tourist. She works hard, she stays out of trouble, and I can name you a dozen other people who came as tourists and they're getting into all kinds of mischief in the eyes of the law and the immigration people don't touch them. No way. I say to them, look —"

"Fernando, was there something about a ring? Somebody stole a ring from Lusk?"

Roxas shrugged. "She never said nothing about that. You ask Mr. Lusk. He'll tell you. She was the best maid they had. A good worker. A good girl. She doesn't take welfare, she doesn't get in trouble, she's a *good* girl. I don't know." Roxas shook his head, his eyes moist, his voice thick with grief. I could understand his feelings. Nina Roxas shouldn't have been sent back. Illegal immigrants working as domestics were a sought-after commodity among the affluent classes of Toronto. Unlike other domestics, they never just quit on you. If they had to leave, they always gave you notice and, best of all, supplied you with a replacement, another illegal immigrant.

"You know Nina?" he asked again.

"No, not really."

"Somebody said get a lawyer. But what can they do? Nina's gone. And she was smart, too. She's got brains. She was going to take a computer course. If you're good, IBM pays everything."

"I'm sorry, Fernando." I stood up. "Thanks for talking to me."

"If you want to help Nina, she could use some money. She's got no job now and no place to stay. She has to live with her cousins."

"Give me her address and I might send her a check."

Roxas shook his head. "No. She doesn't want to give out her address."

"Sorry. Can't help her then."

Roxas rose and walked me to the door. "Do you know a good course in electronics? I can take classes in the afternoon, because I work the night shift."

"Never thought of it myself."

"I don't want some course where you spend a lot of time and you can't get a job. I had a friend who took a course in upholstering. He spent six months at it and then he found out that's what they teach all the kids in those technical schools. All the stupid kids learn to be upholsterers. Nobody needs upholsterers. It's just crazy, he told me."

"Thanks again, Fernando."

I let myself out of the apartment without further delay. The air was a little too thick with hopelessness for easy breathing. Too much time in an atmosphere like that and your energy level drops. Drastically. With your energy gone, your last hope for a good break goes. That's one thing that living with an alcohol problem teaches you, and teaches you well.

5

As I was fitting my key into my door, somebody called out my name. Two men in their twenties had just entered my apartment building and were walking down the corridor. The one in front looked a little under average height and weight, with short-cropped hair and a mustache like Lech Walesa, but something in his appearance — his rolling walk, the way he stuck his jaw out, the tightness of his T-shirt over his shoulders — telegraphed the message that he was physically dangerous. I never did get a close look at the guy behind him because I was fascinated with his buddy, the way a small rodent is fascinated with a python in front of its path.

When he was a few feet from me, he suddenly twisted his upper body, which was the last clear impression I had of his movements. The next sensation I experienced was of something hard hitting me in a soft part of my body, near the kidneys, and the next instant I was on the floor.

My body, anyway, was on the floor — but right after the blow my body disappeared. It was replaced by a series of pulsations so hot they instantly melted down everything in the universe except my consciousness of agony. Even that was about to be consumed in waves of fire. At one point I felt like fainting, but the point passed, and I heard a voice speaking from somewhere in the universe that, incredibly, still existed outside my sensation of pain. "You were a friend of that scumbag LeRoy, weren't you?" the voice said. "Well, stay away from Theresa, fuckhead, or I'll kill you. Y'unnerstand what I'm saying? Stay away from her." He landed a kick on my rib cage, but it was pro forma, and not very hard. He had done his damage.

I heard the front door of the building close behind them and managed to pull myself up and open my door. I staggered over to the living room couch and lay on it for a half an hour, rubbing the outraged side of my body in an attempt to soothe the lingering pain. It had subsided a little, and I was almost on the verge of being able to think straight when the phone rang. It was Garfinny.

"Just checking to see if you're in," he said. "Got some questions for you."

Ten minutes later he was knocking on my door. I let him in, took some books off a chair, and offered him a seat.

"You read all these books?"

"Most of them."

"What's the matter with your side?"

"Too bad you couldn't have come around a little earlier, Garfinny. Half an hour ago two fellows paid me a visit. One of them punched me out. Right here. Just one hit, but it did the trick. Whoever he was, he trains himself to hurt people."

Garfinny grimaced when I pointed out the spot where the fist had made contact. Obviously he knew about the same technique of inflicting pain as my visitor did.

"Did you identify your assailants?"

I tried to recollect the first man's face, and as I did, the image of his mouth, some slight curve of his lips, gave me a clue. "I think it was Hagedorn's brother. You know, uh . . ."

"Peter Hagedorn?"

"Yeah."

Thank you, Officer Garfinny. Peter Hagedorn. I would remember that name.

"You know this Hagedorn guy?" I asked him.

"He's been in contact with us."

"And?"

"I can't say much more than that."

"Listen, Officer, it would help me if —"

"Do you want to lay a charge against him?"

"Of course I do."

Garfinny took notes while I told him exactly what had happened. Then I asked him again about Hagedorn, but he cut me short.

"The fact is, you saw Miss Hagedorn, even though Inspector Staigue told you clearly not to. We may have to bring you into custody."

"Come on, Officer, Theresa and I are lovers. I wasn't trying to intimidate her or anything. That was the last thing I'd want to do."

"What about this Anna Lightfoot she told you about?"

"A friend of LeRoy's. I was looking for somebody who knew LeRoy, other than me and Theresa, somebody who could shed light on what the hell was going on with him. It's not easy, I'll tell you that much."

"Your job, Mr. Murphy, is to tell us exactly what *you* know. We'll do the rest. Have you seen Miss Lightfoot?"

"I haven't yet had that pleasure, Officer. Probably never will." I then gave him the few details I knew about Lightfoot.

Garfinny put away his notebook. "Miss Hagedorn doesn't wish to encourage any further intimacy. If you see her again, we'll take appropriate action."

"Behind the pipes, eh?"

Garfinny gave me a level glance. Behind the pipes. I wondered what was holding them back from carrying out their threat of "appropriate action" right now. It couldn't be much. "Any breaks in the case?" I asked. What I really wanted to find out was a little more complicated — to wit, were they still working on the hypothesis that I was the killer?

Dumb question. Five days after the murder and they still had no one else. Garfinny just shrugged and got up.

"We'll drop in on Mr. Hagedorn," he said as he headed for the door. "If he committed that assault, he's in serious trouble."

"Thank you."

"In the meantime, you better go to emergency. Do you want a lift?"

"Thanks, Officer, but not right now."

"You better not fool with that. You can be seriously injured. Also, if they prosecute, they'll need a medical report."

"Yeah, I will."

Shortly after he left I went to the bathroom and urinated. Much to my relief there was no blood in the toilet bowl. That, plus the fact I was beginning to feel almost normal again, made me postpone going to the hospital. Intellectually I knew I should get checked out. Practically, when I feel reasonably okay, my capacity for putting off visits to doctors is huge. Instead, I phoned De Luca at the *Clarion*.

"Bernie, can you find out if somebody has a criminal record?"

I had a notion that Hagedorn, who had obviously cultivated his talents as an alley fighter, hadn't gone through life up to now without thumping somebody else.

"It's tough, Hal. I do know a cop who'll punch in a name for me on their computer. But he has to be in the right mood, and these days that ain't too often. If he won't do it, I can always try our computer. There might have been a story if your man was convicted of something. What's the name?"

"Peter Hagedorn," I said, and spelled out the last name.

"This guy have something to do with your dead friend?"

"He's the brother of LeRoy's girlfriend. And a rough customer."

"By the way, you got a lawyer yet?"

"I've spoken with one."

"Terrific. Look, Hal, I'll be glad to do this for you, but promise me one thing. If I do come up with something, for God's sake, don't do anything except on your lawyer's advice."

"Okay, Bernie."

After the phone call, I drew a bath and soaked for about an hour.

It felt good. And, once the ache in my side subsided, it felt good to know that, for the first time, I had an idea of what might have been spooking LeRoy before his death, what might even have made him want to move. Peter Hagedorn. LeRoy was a tough nut and could handle himself pretty well, but if truth be told his best days were probably behind him, as far as street survival was concerned. Hagedorn, who didn't like his sister hanging out with a loser like LeRoy — or who perhaps had other reasons to hate LeRoy — could have been too much for him.

My next move should have been to approach Theresa, but I wasn't about to disregard Garfinny's warning this time around. I didn't want to risk her complaining to the police. The same with her friend Spurdle, who might also know something about Peter Hagedorn and LeRoy. My best move, I concluded, was simply to wait for Bernie to call me back. If he drew a blank, I might have to risk approaching Theresa or Spurdle. Right now, however, I would just put off that decision and relax a bit.

Later I took out the blurry photocopied picture I had found in LeRoy's trunk and examined it. It came more or less with the Rothbards' phone number, but the woman didn't look like Lydia, and the man didn't look like Solomon. Lusk, perchance? Yes, there was a faint resemblance between the smudged male face in the photograph and Lusk's — enough of a resemblance not to rule out the possibility the man was Lusk, but not strong enough to get excited about, either. Had LeRoy, I wondered, tried to work a hustle on either the Rothbards or the Lusks?

These people were way out of his league, but who knows? Perhaps he had a hustle going with Lusk's maid, now sadly deported — the two of them partners in relieving the Lusk household of valuables. Maybe there was even a blackmail angle, which had something to do with this photo. That train of thought was pretty imaginative on my part, but I was at a total loss as to why LeRoy would keep such a document. As far as the Rothbards were concerned, they were raising money; LeRoy, I would bet, would have perked up his ears and sniffed the wind on receiving intelligence of that activity.

I soon got tired of tossing around these speculations and lay on the couch and read a chapter or two from a biography of Barbara Stanwyck. I had put it down and started to snooze when I heard a knock on the door. Startled, I sat up. Another knock. I went to the kitchen and grabbed a monkey wrench from my toolbox — when you live in a rent-controlled apartment, faulty plumbing is your problem — and opened the door. In front of me stood a young man with thick, flowing locks of light brown hair and a face bordering on pretty, spoiled only by two or three pimples.

He smiled. "Hi, my name is Matthias. You Heywood Murphy?"

"Yup."

"Chris Lang told me about you. Nice to meet you."

"Nice to meet you, Matthias. What can I do for you?"

"You know the Bible, Mr. Murphy?"

"A little."

"Do you remember the story in the Gospel of St. Mark, where Jesus cures the man with the evil spirits, you know, and the evil spirits go into the herd of swine and they all run over this cliff into the sea?"

"The Gadarene Swine?"

"Yeah. I'm trying to figure out something. After this guy was healed, he asked Jesus if he could go with him. This is like after he'd been living in tombs, and slashing himself with rocks, and everything. But Jesus said no. 'Howbeit Jesus suffered him not, but saith unto him, Go home to thy friends, and tell them how great things the Lord hath done for thee.' Now why didn't he let the guy come with him?"

"May I ask why I've been singled out for this skill-testing question?"

"No reason."

No reason. I liked that actually. If he'd tried to give me a reason, like any missionary or salesman, I would have shut the door in his face. On the other hand, I wasn't looking for a long talk about the Bible with another of Toronto's lost souls.

"I think Jesus wanted the man to pull himself together first, Matthias. Any more questions?"

"You are a nice guy, aren't you?"

"Chris Lang wouldn't lie to you."

"And you're looking for Anna Lightfoot, aren't you?"

"Thanks for coming to the point. I thought there was a point somewhere, but I wasn't sure. Lang tell you that, too?"

"Yeah. Chris used to be my caseworker."

"Okay. I'm looking for Anna. Where can I find her?"

"Well . . . I told Chris I didn't think she was in the city."

"That seems to be the consensus of opinion."

"I didn't tell him I live with her."

"Oh?"

"With some other people. We're about two hours' drive from here. I'm going there now, Mr. Murphy. You can come if you want."

"Love to, but I'd like to phone somebody first, if you don't mind. A friend of hers named Wolf."

"Sorry, Mr. Murphy." Matthias smiled almost bashfully. "I'm not telling you where we're going."

"It's going to be a big surprise. Well, that's nice. But this person should know where Anna is, too."

"I'm really sorry, Mr. Murphy. We're kind of nervous about people knowing where she is. After you see her, you'll know why."

"He's going to know eventually. Unless you figure I'm taking an oath of secrecy. I don't take oaths of secrecy, Matthias."

"Just see her first before you tell anybody."

"Okay. But I'm going to call him and tell him I'm leaving town. And when we get there I'll tell him as soon as possible where I am."

I phoned the Lodge and left a message for Wolf. I wasn't enthusiastic about going off with this kid but, on the other hand, I sort of owed it to Wolf and Kelly to see Lightfoot and report back to them. And there was still a possibility, however faint it now seemed, that Lightfoot might have some useful information about LeRoy. I could always phone De Luca, of course, when we got to wherever we were going. So I grabbed a duffel bag and some clothes, in case I had to stay for a while, and we went out to his VW van.

"Matthias — that's an unusual name," I said as we climbed in.

"It was the name my brothers and sisters gave me. Remember the Acts of the Apostles?"

"Refresh my memory."

"Matthias was the one who replaced Judas in the Twelve after Jesus ascended to heaven."

"That so? What was your name before that?"

We were halfway up the street in his van before he said quietly, as if confessing a sin of his past, "Jim Sweeney."

"I see. You're not living in a Jesus fre . . . Christian commune by any chance, are you, Matthias?"

"I live with six other people in a house. We try to live according to the Lord's word and the promptings of the Spirit. Sort of like the Apostles. 'And the multitudes of them that believed were of one heart and one soul: neither said any of them that any things he possessed were his own; but they all had things in common.'"

"So who was the Judas you replaced?"

"They had some trouble before I moved in. I'd rather not talk about it."

He then told me we were going to a small town in southern Ontario, about fifty miles from Toronto, called Elliston. To reach it you drove through the pleasant farmlands of southern Ontario dotted with orange-and-yellow brick houses that existed nowhere else in the world except that part of the province. Along the way, Matthias talked about how a Pentecostal minister in Elliston had found the house for the original group of young people who wanted a shelter from the evil mood of the Toronto streets; a house where they could live together, pray together, read the Bible together. He said little about Anna Lightfoot. I did ask him about LeRoy — if he knew Lang he might have known LeRoy — but he couldn't recall the name. It didn't strike me that he was lying.

It was about four in the afternoon when the highway turned into the main street of Elliston. Matthias stopped in front of a three-story frame house in dire need of a paint job, half a mile down a side street. A seven-foot hedge separated it from its neighbor on one side; on the other side was another street.

We went up the front walk, past a Frisbee lying on the grass. As soon as we reached the porch, a tall man with glasses and a thick beard opened the door.

"Ira, this is Mr. Murphy," Matthias said. "Mr. Murphy, Ira Dunmoe."

"Nice to see you, Mr. Murphy. Come on in."

We stepped into a hallway, and Dunmoe pointed to a room on our right. The room had a thin carpet, an upright piano painted white, a new wood-burning stove, and two sofas. Stuffing squeezed out of holes in the sofa.

A young man and woman were playing backgammon on the carpet. The man was tall and thin and wore jeans and a Houston Oilers jersey. His opponent was dressed in jeans and a yellow T-shirt with the ancient Christian symbol of the fish outlined in red across her bosom. In front of the stove sat another young woman, with a skirt down to her ankles and a white-on-white blouse. She shelled peas over an aluminum pot on her lap as I entered, and as she caught sight of me, she gave her head of dark brown hair a little shake. All three greeted me with stares of frank, almost childlike curiosity.

"Have a seat," Dunmoe said. I sat on a sofa beside Matthias. Dunmoe then introduced me to the others — Roy and Joanna, the backgammon players, and Martha with the aluminum pot. Dunmoe sat on the sofa, crossed his legs, folded his arms, and cleared his throat. "Matthias told us you were looking for Anna Lightfoot."

"That's right."

"She's called Sharon Israel now. She took a new name to signify her new life in grace." Dunmoe paused, as if expecting a response from me, but I kept my mouth shut. "Can you give me an idea why you want to see her?"

"Matthias didn't tell you?"

"He said something about a Charles LeRoy. Who is he?"

"Right now an object full of embalming fluid."

"Oh, yes, a victim of murder. I understand. The business of the police."

"LeRoy was a friend. It's my business, too."

"And he said this LeRoy knew Sharon."

The stares of frank curiosity were coming my way, more frankly curious than ever. It was beginning to annoy me.

"How much do you know about Sharon?" Dunmoe continued.

"She's an Indian girl from Manitoulin, and she used to be a hooker from Toronto."

Dunmoe shook his head sadly. "Those are the facts, all right. Until recently."

"And she was acquainted with Charles LeRoy."

"How did he know Sharon?"

"Charles used to hang around the streets a lot. Apparently Anna was his kind of girl."

"May I ask how you met LeRoy?"

"We were pimps together. Come on, Dunmoe, what are you getting at? I'm a respectable journalist, if you want to know, and I met LeRoy when he was a respectable civil servant for the City of Toronto."

"I didn't mean to imply, Mr. Murphy —"

"Sure you didn't. Now I've got a couple of questions for you. One, is Anna Lightfoot — sorry, Sharon Israel — here? Two, if she is, can I say hello?"

Dunmoe cleared his throat again. "Yes, she is here. But she's been sick and she's still pretty weak. She gets upset very easily, Mr. Murphy. I'd appreciate it if you could wait until tomorrow before you talk to her. She's on the mend, but another good night's sleep will make a world of difference."

"What's her problem?"

"Well . . . partly it's a bad depression, which I think is a lingering result of heavy cocaine use. Plus all her other drugs have weakened her resistance to infection, things like pneumonia."

"Sorry to hear that. I'm not going to grill her or anything. I'm just looking for connections. Any I can find."

"You're welcome to stay here. The Lord willing, you can see her tomorrow."

"Fair enough. I appreciate the hospitality, Dunmoe."

"You may have an interest in Sharon," the girl shelling peas remarked, "but you have to realize that we have an interest in her, too."

She smiled, but almost in a melancholy way. "We're Christians, Mr. Murphy. We're obliged to look after other souls."

"That's a heavy obligation, Martha," I replied. "Human souls are dangerous territory."

"Souls aren't dangerous," Dunmoe said. "The world is dangerous."

"Is that why you're living in Elliston?"

"Oh," Dunmoe said, "Elliston can be dangerous enough."

"Yeah," Roy piped up. "Satan, man, he's here, too. I mean, he really is."

With that remark an uneasy silence came over the room.

"Show Mr. Murphy where he's staying, Matthias," Dunmoe said.

Matthias nodded, and I followed him out of the room and down a hallway, which ended in a stairway to the second floor. Underneath the stairway was a bathroom, and kitty-corner to that, the open door of a bedroom. I looked into that room and saw a little sign on the wall that said, "Hello, guest, and howdeedo. This small room belongs to you."

"Your room," Matthias said. "Ira usually sleeps here, but when we have a guest, he takes the sofa in the living room."

"Very Christian of him."

"Come on up and see what Greg's doing in the attic."

I threw my duffel bag onto the bed in the guest room and followed Matthias upstairs. I also noticed a phone near the stairwell, but I realized the switchboard at the Lodge would be closed by now. We went up two flights of stairs to the attic where a wiry young man with a beard was kneeling over a sheet of Gyproc lying on the floor, measuring it with a tape. "Just in time, Matthias," he said without looking up. "I'm ready to nail this sucker."

"This is Heywood Murphy," Matthias said in a way that told me the name wasn't unfamiliar to Greg. Probably Matthias had phoned here after his meeting with Lang to ask Dunmoe permission to bring me home. Perhaps Matthias was told to use his own judgment, see what kind of soul I was before extending the invitation. That could have been the point of Matthias's story from St. Mark. Anything was possible with this household.

For an hour I helped with the Gyproc; it was a good way to ask questions about "Sharon Israel."

"We met her at the Yonge Stop two years ago," Greg volunteered. "Wearing these leather pants." He shook his head. "She hadn't eaten in three days, so we brought her to the house we used to have on Draper Street and gave her a meal."

"She sure didn't want to go at first," Matthias added. "She thought we'd make her sing hymns or something before dinner. But nobody hassled her."

"That was two years ago?" I asked.

"Yeah, two years," Matthias said. "I remember I was on parole then."

"After that first night, we didn't see her for months," Greg continued. "Then she came around and begged us to put her up. She was scared of something. What, she never said. Anyway, we put her up. In those days we put everybody up — junkies, hookers, stray dogs and cats, you name it. That was life in the big city, all right. Well, Sharon stayed a few days, then took off for her reserve up north. A few months later she showed up again, still looking scared.

I guess she's spent most of her time since then either with us or on the reserve. About three months ago she decided to live here all the time."

"She's really accepted Jesus into her life," Matthias said. "It's made a big difference. But she's still running. From a man, or from the devil, I don't know."

At dinner, later that evening, Dunmoe asked Joanna how Sharon was doing. He was sitting at the head of the table, naturally, in papa's chair.

"Oh, much better," Joanna replied. "She's really been getting some rest."

"She must be getting better," Martha said. "I passed by the room an hour ago and I heard you two giggling away like anything."

Both Martha and Joanna shot glances at Dunmoe, but he was buttering every little hill and valley of a huge chunk of bread and seemed not to notice. After a minute or two of silence, he turned to Greg. "How's the work going?"

"Oh, not bad. Matthias and Heywood here helped out before dinner. We got three sheets of Gyproc nailed up."

"That was very kind of our guest to assist you. Mr. Murphy, do you want to tell us a little bit about yourself?"

Once again all eyes were on me. I stirred the spoon in my soup listlessly, eyeing the lentils with resignation. "I was a reporter for the Toronto *Clarion* for five years. Six months ago I left to do freelance work for magazines."

"Can I ask you something personal?" Matthias asked.

"Sure."

"You a drinker?"

"Lang told you that?"

"He sort of hinted it."

"Matthias doesn't mean to embarrass you, Mr. Murphy," Dunmoe replied. "All of us have had to deal with serious problems. All of us have had our particular sin."

"My sin was drugs," Matthias said. "Roy and Joanna, they did drugs, too. Plus, I was a B and E man. Big houses up in Forest Hill — give me a pinch bar and I was off to the races."

"My sin was pride," Greg said. "I was filled with the desire to prove I didn't need anything or anybody. I wanted to live alone and have nothing to do with the Lord, or other people."

There was a moment's silence, then Martha spoke quietly. "My sin was hypocrisy. I called myself a Christian, but I was more interested in finding a boyfriend."

"What was your sin, Dunmoe?" I asked.

"My sin," Dunmoe replied, "was worshiping at the altar of the intellect."

Martha cleared the soup plates and brought on pork chops and her freshly shelled peas. I changed the subject to Anna, but the answers I got to my questions weren't very illuminating. Mostly they confirmed what Greg had told me, and what I already knew: Anna Lightfoot was a frightened ex-prostitute and ex-drug user, the two usually being synonymous, who had been involved with the group on and off for the past few years and who had made a "real" commitment to live with them three months ago. Also, she was "really opening up to the Lord." She "used to get off on some of these rock singers who were singing the devil's tune," I was told. But that was over with now.

After dinner Roy asked me if I wanted to go for a walk with him and Joanna, as he put on an army fatigue coat with a cross drawn in red magic marker on the breast pocket. I said yes, and the three of us stepped out into the cloudless Ontario night. The moon was nearly full. "Let's walk down by the park," Roy suggested. We turned to our left and strolled past more tree-shaded houses.

"I've seen houses like this breathe," he told me. "Back in the days when I was doing acid."

"I remember coming out of this bar on Yonge Street," Joanna said, "after doing some acid, and I saw Jimmy Page walking toward me on the sidewalk. I saw him about three times in one block."

"You both did a lot of acid?"

"Yeah," Roy said. "Then I got into speed. One time I took some speed before I came down from an acid trip. Wow. I spent four months at the Clarke Institute getting over that."

"I suppose that made you seriously reconsider speed."

"Well, actually, I stopped taking it because my stupid hair was falling out."

Joanna slipped her arm into Roy's. "Praise the Lord, Roy. All that's behind us."

We passed a corner with a variety store, and a man coming out with a bag of groceries. "Hey, Roy, how you doing?"

"Fine, thanks."

"How's your little commune? How's sister Sharon?"

"God bless you, brother," Roy mumbled.

"Does he know Sharon?" I asked Roy.

"Naw. He's just seen her around."

We crossed the main street and walked another block until we came to a small park with benches and an old band shell, where we sat down. I asked how life in the commune was going. Roy said it was going a lot better since this guy who was a "real problem" left.

"He didn't want to go to prayer meetings and he didn't want to do this and he didn't want to do that," he explained. "Like, you'd ask him if he was going on a fast and he'd say, no, the Lord didn't lead him that way. Well, sure, that's fine, but all he'd do was spend hours in his room. And nobody knows what he's doing there, right? Well, one night we're praying together, and all of a sudden Ira gets this real pain in his stomach. All of a sudden — bam! — it comes to him, you know, like he *knows* where it's coming from. So he gets up and goes to the kitchen, and there's this guy standing there, and Ira says, 'What were you doing in the bedroom just now?' And so the guy, like, you know, he turns *white,* but he doesn't say nothing. So they were going on like this for about fifteen minutes until all of a sudden Ira yells out, 'I bind thee in the name of Jesus Christ!' Bam! The guy just about collapses on the floor. Remember, Joanna? He was lying there in a fit practically.

"So we went to his room, and there was all sorts of books there on black magic and witchcraft. While we were praying he was conjuring up spirits to confuse us. So we told him he had to get out. But he wouldn't get out. So, like, we took all the stuff in his room and threw it out the door, and he still wouldn't get out. Finally we ended up having to grab him and throw him out and lock the door behind him and then finally he left."

"That was really something," Joanna said.

Later that evening, after everybody had gone to bed, Joanna offered to show me Anna's notebook. We went up to her room on the second floor, a room empty except for a bed, a small desk painted baby blue, and a Mexican blanket on the wall. From the desk she took out a large book with an imitation leather cover, a kind of sketchbook filled with blank white pages. The pages were covered with drawings in black ink, flowers and birds and butterflies and suns peeking out from behind clouds. They were all done with sweet, delicate, flowing lines. In between were sentences written in large, swirly letters, like "Sometimes I think life is very different from what I think it is. Sometimes I think I'm living a dream."

"This is Sharon's notebook," Joanna said. "Isn't she talented?"

"Very. Could I borrow this tonight?"

"She made me promise not to give this to anybody else. When you see her tomorrow, maybe you can ask her."

"Sure. Where's her room, by the way?"

Joanna looked perplexed.

"Is this classified information?" Anna Lightfoot was beginning to take on the mythic proportions of Rochester's wife in *Jane Eyre*.

"Well, I'd rather you ask Ira," she said.

"Does he make all the decisions around here?"

"No, not . . . well, kind of. He's our elder."

"Your elder."

"We all have a voice in things. But he's the most experienced, you know, person. Myself, I'd prefer if we did things like the Hopi

Indians. They had the women in charge of space and men in charge of time. So like the women here would decide who gets the rooms, and how we'd do up the common areas, and the men would do schedules and things. But," she remarked sadly, "that's not in the Bible."

"I guess it isn't. Thanks, anyway, Joanna."

We smiled, and then I took my leave. When I left the room, I saw Roy in the hallway.

"Hi," he said, grinning nervously.

I went down the stairs and heard him knocking very softly on Joanna's door. Then I grabbed the phone near the landing and called De Luca's home number. He answered after a couple of rings, friendly as ever, but with a certain note in his voice I hadn't detected before, a hint of nervousness.

"How'd it go with Hagedorn?" I asked.

"My cop friend wouldn't cooperate, but we scored with our own computer. Found a story dated February 1 of this year. Guy named Scarfoni, owner of several gravel pits in southern Ontario, was badly beaten by two men, one of whom is your friend Hagedorn."

"So he's a pro."

"You bet. Scarfoni stiffed somebody you definitely do not want to stiff."

"Who?"

"He's not mentioned in this story, and I can't remember his name, but I think he was a mobster from Hamilton. Some guy big on drugs and prostitution."

"Prostitution?"

"Yeah. Brought in girls from Third World countries, recruited local runaways — real nasty stuff. Want me to read the whole story? It's only seven paragraphs."

Bernie read the story to me. The part I found most interesting was the sentence that gave Hagedorn's address. It was the address of LeRoy's apartment building.

"Thanks, Bernie. This is very helpful."

"Say, Hal, you're not forgetting what I said about a lawyer, are you?"

"No. But why are you harping on this lawyer business? What's up, Bernie?"

He paused for a moment. "I don't know, Hal, but I think the cops are going for you. You're going to need that lawyer real soon."

"You sure?"

"Can't say anything more. Sorry."

"Okay. Thanks for the tip."

"Hope it works out for you, Hal."

If Bernie was right, it was just as well I was in Elliston right now instead of Toronto. At least I had some breathing space — a little time to reflect on my situation. Not that reflection would do me much good. Bernie's advice about a lawyer looked like the only route left to me. But at least now I had a little more to tell my lawyer when we got down to serious cases. Obviously Hagedorn and the murder victim had more in common than Theresa. It shouldn't be that difficult to find out just what. If I couldn't do it, someone else would have to.

I went to my own room, got into bed, and fell asleep surprisingly quickly, given what I had to think about. At some point in the night, however, I fell into dreams that were restless and unhappy. I dreamed I was riding with Matthias in a van, and suddenly he stopped at a tavern by the highway. As we entered, I realized I was once again inside the Silver Dollar. A young woman dressed in black was sitting at a corner table and sobbing. For a long time I watched this girl, her face covered by her hands, until I realized it was Anna Lightfoot. I wanted to go to her, but somebody else was holding me by the arm.

Something clicked in my brain, like a change of slides in a viewer. The girl dressed in black was sitting on a chair in the darkness, crying. She was wearing a housecoat, either navy or black, and her tears were sliding down a round, delicate, childlike face framed by long black hair. I watched her for a few minutes while my mind drifted through vague, unpleasant spaces, and I didn't know where I was. But gradually my mind stopped drifting, and as I looked again at the girl, I felt a flutter in the valves of my heart. I could recognize the outlines of the guest room and the sign on the wall. I knew now my eyes were open. The instant it dawned on me that I was truly awake, the girl swiftly rose from her chair and noiselessly walked out the door. I jerked my head up as the door closed behind her, and for a few seconds I stared at it, stupefied. Then the last film of sleep passed, my nerves signaled to my brain that my inert muscles were ready to move, and I got out of bed, put on a pair of pants, and walked out of the room.

No one was in the hallway. I glanced to my right and saw the door of the empty bathroom open. I walked quickly down the hall to the living room. That, too, was empty except for Dunmoe, wrapped in a blanket and lying on the sofa like some monstrous woolly larva, snoring heavily. I turned to the dining room, went through it to the kitchen, turned back, returned to the hallway, and then climbed the stairs. I checked both the second and third floors, but every door was shut on the second floor and the third floor was completely empty. The house was utterly still.

There was nothing to do but go back to my room and, since it was only 4:00 a.m., go back to sleep. Three hours later someone knocked on my door. "Breakfast'll be ready in half an hour, Mr. Murphy," Martha announced hesitantly. I got up, more than ready to meet "Sharon Israel." But only the six I had met yesterday showed up in the dining room. After the porridge, toast, and cornflakes were cleared away, Dunmoe invited me to join in morning prayers.

"We have brief prayers, Mr. Murphy. To start our day with the blessings of the Lord."

"Is Sharon going to start her day with the blessings of the Lord, too? I noticed she missed her porridge."

"Unfortunately Martha tells me Sharon spent a very restless night. She's sleeping right now, and she'll probably sleep through the whole morning."

"Okay. I'll skip the prayer circle this morning, thank you."

I stepped out onto the front porch while the others gathered in the living room. Taking in a deep breath, I savored the sensation of being in this rural town, clean and orderly and without any fussy, picturesque qualities, in the sturdy Ontario tradition. This enjoyment was my tribute to the Lord. And, no, I wasn't in any hurry to get back to Toronto.

Fifteen minutes later I saw Greg and Matthias and volunteered to spend the morning helping them. Greg had the day off, he explained, from his job at a local hardware store. So we passed the morning coating ourselves with Gyproc dust and not leaving the devil any idle hands to employ. Matthias had worked before in construction, he told us.

"You know who I thought was a good boss?" he asked. "I used to think the best guy I ever worked for was this contractor who took us out for beers after work. Every day we'd all get pissed together."

I asked no more questions about Anna, except to wonder aloud once if she and Roy had known each other previously. Since both had apparently moved in heavy drug circles, I had linked the two together in my mind. Matthias snorted. "Are you kidding?" he said. "Sharon was a real hustler. Old Roy was just another of your weekend hippies from Mississauga."

At lunch we sat outside on the porch eating sandwiches. Once again Anna was nowhere to be seen. Dunmoe shook his head and told me Anna was awake but feeling quite nauseated, and Martha would probably have to spend the afternoon nursing her. In a way I wasn't too disappointed. I was feeling better than I had in a long time, just working with my hands and feeling the absence of something — heavy air pollutants maybe, or simply the noise, the relentless background of internal combustion engines on the move.

After lunch I called the Lodge in Toronto. Wolf still wasn't in, so I left another message, this time giving the address and phone number of the house in Elliston. While I was on the phone I felt an anxious presence behind me, like a clammy touch on my shoulder blades. I glanced around. Dunmoe stood five feet away from me in the hallway. As soon as I hung up, however, he retreated. I said nothing and followed him to the porch outside, where Matthias was suggesting we all knock off for the afternoon and go swimming. He drove us a couple of miles outside Elliston to a small lake, where a few eleven-year-old boys sat on picnic tables smoking cigarettes. As we got out, Matthias called out to Greg, "We're going to have to fill up soon."

Greg frowned. "There's not much left in the gas fund."

"Let's not worry about it," Roy said. "The Lord will provide."

"Yeah, right. With you that means everybody else will provide."

Roy looked hurt but said nothing. Joanna took his hand, and the two of them ran to the water. Later, when I was sunning myself on a rock, Joanna climbed up beside me.

"Can I ask you something?" she said after a long pause.

"Sure."

"Do you think Roy's a jerk?"

"That doesn't sound like Spirit-prompted language to me."

"Come on. You know what I mean."

"I think Roy has his problems. I wouldn't call him a jerk." I wouldn't, either. In my books a jerk is someone who comes along and automatically your day is less pleasant than it was before he showed up. Roy didn't fall into that category. On the other hand, I wouldn't trust him to do anything real tricky, but that's another story. "What's the matter, Joanna?"

"Greg gets on his back sometimes for not doing anything, But Roy's sensitive. He just gets upset when he thinks he can't get a job, and then Greg starts in on him. I mean, Roy can do things. He makes beautiful jewelry, with silver and you know, semiprecious stones. If he had more silver and stuff, he could practically make his living doing that. But there's no money. So what's he supposed to do? Work in a hardware store like Greg? If he can't do what he's really good at, why should he get some other job? It's not fair."

That's right, I thought. Life is full of injustices. This was also a theme song popular among newsmen, and I knew it well, the tune so many of us dote on. But there was nothing I could say to Joanna except to sympathize with her unhappiness. We chatted for the rest of the afternoon and then went to the Dairy Queen for dinner. When we got home, Dunmoe went straight to Anna's room and had another conference with Martha. Anna was better, he told me when he came down. Tomorrow morning almost certainly she'd be able to talk to me.

So I went to bed early that night. Dreams didn't trouble me this time. I slept reasonably well and woke up naturally. But it wasn't dawn when I woke. It was 3:30 in the morning, according to the glowing digits of my watch. And the girl was back, sitting on the same chair. She was in her housecoat, not crying, not moving, not breathing as far as I could tell. She was just watching me, her gaze as patient as an animal's.

"Anna," I said.

She neither moved nor spoke. I waited for a few minutes and then spoke her name again. She bowed her head and sighed. I thought I heard her whisper something. I called her name, but she was silent again. The silence continued as I lay still myself. It felt as if this bird would fly with any sudden movement. "Anna, did you say something?" I finally asked more loudly.

She lifted her head and stared at me. Then she shook her head slowly and, in a tiny voice barely above a whisper, said, "Anna ain't here. No way. She's gone."

"Anna gone? Where did she go?"

She shook her head again. "You missed her, boy. You missed her by a long time."

And then she sighed and seemed to look down at the floor. I sat up in bed. Suddenly she exclaimed in a petulant voice, "Oh, shit! Reuben, come on, get your clothes on." She rose from her chair and walked over to my bed, kneeling beside it. There was the same delicate round face I had seen last night, the same glossy black hair.

Her dark eyes in the darkness seemed to glitter. "Come on, Reuben," she said, "let's go."

"Where?"

"Come *on*." She pursed her lips as if suppressing a laugh, lowered her head slightly, and gazed up at me almost coyly. "Come on, Reuben, you rotten monster." She poked my side with a hand as cold as a dead woman's. "Get up, you lazy rotten monster."

I asked her to turn around while I picked up my clothes from a chair and dressed. Then I asked her where we were going.

"Let's go outside."

She slipped one of those icy hands into mine and led me out the door and down the hallway to the front door. I could hear Dunmoe snoring from the living room as she opened the door with a quick and, it seemed to me, practiced noiseless motion.

There was a chill in the air from a strong wind, but the girl, who was barefoot and dressed in only her thin navy housecoat, seemed not to mind. She led me around the house to the backyard. Under a sky with no moon, the backyard, which extended about sixty feet from the back of the house, was a dark and private refuge. The hedge protected it on one side; at the back and the side bordering the street, rows of maples and lilac bushes sealed it from the outside. We walked almost to the end of the lot when the girl sat down on the grass and pulled me to her side. She put her arms around my neck and rested her head on my shoulders.

"Reuben," she said after sighing, "I'm so tired. I need a rest. Why can't I stay at your place all the time? Are you ashamed of me?"

"Tell me about Charles LeRoy. Have you seen him lately?"

"*Lee*Roy? That guy from New Brunswick. What are you talking about *Lee*Roy for?"

"He talks about you. In his sleep, I heard."

"Aw, stop kidding me. I never knew that dope."

"I heard somebody killed him. Stabbed him to death."

"In New Brunswick?"

"Toronto."

"Toronto? He's not in Toronto. He went back home."

"When did he go back home?"

"A while ago. I don't know. Come on, Reuben, let's go someplace." She tightened her grip around my neck and put her lips against mine, nibbling at them. I drew my head back to stop her.

"Who might have killed LeRoy? Who didn't like him?"

"Nobody didn't like him. Nobody cares. He just hung around, that's all. I can't even remember what he used to do. You know what I remember? I remember doing it on your little tennis court. On a night just like this. And you said that was my reward for giving you the photograph."

"What photograph?"

"*Mommy's* photograph. You remember. And the time —"

"What was mommy's photograph?"

"And the time you almost punched Jimmy. Remember?" The girl giggled. "You called him little weasel face. Oh, he was mad."

"Understandably. About the photograph, Anna —"

Her face turned serious. "You watch yourself now. You watch out he doesn't get you. He hates you, you know. I mean, really, Reuben."

"Why does he hate me."

"You know why. I just said. How come you never took me to the Park Plaza like Jimmy did?"

"The Park Plaza?"

"Me and Jimmy spent a whole week there. We had a room and we just stayed in bed and watched TV and did some coke and had room service every day and champagne and strawberries for breakfast, and steaks, and everything." She sighed with immense sadness, like an orphan reflecting on her dead parents. "But Jimmy's a tool of the devil. He's Satan's errand boy."

She yawned tremendously and then nestled her head again on my shoulder. Around us the trees fluttered in the wind, which had a sound in it like the winds coming down from the north, sweeping over the landscape of rock and tundra. "I'm your favorite girl, aren't

I, Reuben?" she whispered. "I'm your favorite little girl, you said." She snuggled against me. "You're lonely, too, and you're sad, aren't you? I'll take care of you. Let Anna take care of you," she said in a baby voice. "Honest, I won't let you down, not like those old man-eating bitches." She started to kiss my face lightly and unbutton my shirt. I grabbed her wrist and drew back.

"Anna, don't."

"Come on, let's play," she giggled.

"No. We're grown-up people now and playtime is over." She kissed me on the mouth, her lips open and her tongue prying at my own lips. I gripped her shoulders and pushed her back. "I said no, Anna. You don't even know who the hell you're talking to."

She looked at me as if focusing her eyes on the object in front of her were too difficult. At that instant I heard something snap in the trees by the side of the road. I looked as hard as I could, but it was still too dark to see anything clearly. I turned back to Anna, but her eyes were closed and her mouth was twisted in pain.

"I want to go home," she said. "I want to go home."

"Anna, let's go back to the house."

"I want to go *home*. I want to see my dad."

"All right. I'll help you go home. But the first step is to go back into the house."

"My daddy will take me out to the bush, and we'll check his trap lines and have some fun. I haven't seen him for so long, you know? I bet he doesn't even known where I am." She opened her eyes wide. "Let's go to Wicky."

"Wicky?"

"Wikwemikong. We can hitchhike there."

I heard someone shut the front door of the house. Rising quickly, I pulled Anna up, put my arm around her shoulder, and walked her back to the house. She didn't resist. The will, the life, had suddenly left her body. I felt as if I were gently leading a sleepwalker back to her room. Perhaps I was in a way. When we came around to the front of the house, Dunmoe was standing on the porch.

"Go back to your room, Sharon," he said, not harshly, as we climbed the porch stairs. I took my arm from around her shoulder, and the sleepwalker went inside the house. Dunmoe closed the door behind her.

"Well, you've met her," he said. "That's Anna Lightfoot."

"Why'd you bring me up here, Dunmoe, if that's the state she's in?"

Dunmoe shrugged. "She's been lucid for the past week or so, but she slipped back the day you came. It's been so unpredictable." Dunmoe looked at the street in front of the house for a moment. I suddenly realized why Matthias had dropped by my apartment that day, and why he had driven me to this house: the people in it were lonely. They had lots of joy and inner peace, but they were very lonely.

"Did she talk to you about her dad?" Dunmoe asked.

"Yeah, she did. Is he a trapper up north?"

"Used to be. Right now he's serving a life sentence at Stony Mountain in Manitoba. He killed Anna's mother. Or I should say the woman who conceived her."

"Does she ever talk about a 'Reuben'?"

"Sometimes. I don't know who he is. Some man in her life, I guess."

"And there's lots more where he came from, right?"

"Let's just say her past is a fairly . . . crowded closet. You won't rummage through it in a hurry."

"I was hoping to find LeRoy somewhere in a corner, along with the fellow who killed him."

"We could pray for you, Murphy. I mean that."

"I'm sure you do. Have you noticed anybody watching your house lately?"

"No."

"You don't sound convincing."

"To some people, Mr. Murphy, this house is an object of curiosity. We occasionally notice people gawking at us. I don't think that's what you mean."

"What about Anna? Matthias gave me the impression she was running scared. Is somebody after her?"

"No."

"You still don't sound convincing. Is Anna an object of curiosity, too? Just the other night some guy coming out of a variety store asked Roy about her. Is she well-known here?"

"I couldn't say, Mr. Murphy. Obviously she'd attract a lot of attention if she just walked around in her usual state. But she doesn't. We usually keep a good eye on her."

"I wouldn't call it foolproof. Tonight's the second night she came into my room uninvited."

"Second time?"

"The first time was last night, but she didn't stick around. She left while I was still half asleep."

"I'm sorry about that. But, personally, I don't believe she's in any danger. I don't think anybody's 'after her' despite what she imagines from time to time. She's not sane, as you know."

"Speaking of that, did you ever consider calling a doctor. Anna looks as if she could use some professional help."

"You mean psychiatrists? They'd put her in a ward and pump her full of drugs. She's had her fill of that already. No, Mr. Murphy. I know you think we're ridiculous, but we do try to live our beliefs. And one of our beliefs is that human charity, with the grace of the Lord, is more healing than any psychiatric technique."

"I wouldn't argue with that. But I saw the look in your eye when we came up to the porch. I'd call it desperation, Ira. And I don't blame you one bit. Anna looks as if she's at the end of her rope. At this point she needs more than love. She needs a miracle. That's a tough thing to wait for."

"We have confidence in the Lord."

"Okay. By the way, would you mind coming out back with me? I thought I heard somebody in the bushes."

Dunmoe got a flashlight, and we went out back and made a quick, fruitless search of the greenery. I hadn't really expected anyone to hang around after Anna and I left.

Back in my room I couldn't sleep. I sat on my bed trying to figure out where I was and what my next move should be. I had finally found Anna Lightfoot, a genuine link with Charles's past, and Anna Lightfoot looked as if she were permanently out to lunch. It didn't matter. Even if she were perfectly lucid, I doubt she could have told me much. The only good I had accomplished here was helping out Wolf and Kelly. Now I had to go back to Toronto and face the music. And hope that Peter Hagedorn would eventually prove a more attractive candidate for LeRoy's murder rap than me. Hagedorn was a professional thug, after all. I was a harmless newspaperman.

I tried to get some sleep, but it was useless. There was just too much flowing through the circuit panels. After a couple of hours, I got out of bed and headed out. I just wanted to walk around a bit, clear my head with some early-morning air.

Three or four blocks from the house, on the main highway, I noticed a restaurant open for business. It was a tiny café with a front window covered by a piece of cardboard with crayon lettering, advertising a turkey shoot that was now two weeks old. The café was set in the middle of a gravel lot where a milk truck and a blue van were parked. I opened the screen door and walked inside. There were five or six tables and only one customer, a middle-aged man in a plain white T-shirt leaning his elbows on the chipped Formica surface of his table and mournfully stirring his coffee. He stared at me. Obviously, after hours of watching the painted line on the road, he needed something to look at that moved.

I sat down at the counter. A tall, skinny kid emerged from the kitchen. He had dark hairs growing over his upper lip but none on the rest of his face, which was spotted here and there with little red splotches. The kid was fighting a war with puberty, and puberty, a cruel antagonist, was making sure its eventual triumph was slow and painful. He looked at me as if he weren't sure whether he was supposed to take my order or report to the principal's office. Putting him out of his misery, I gave him my order and he disappeared back into the kitchen.

Yesterday's newspapers were on sale by the door, so I bought a *Clarion* and started reading. A few minutes later the door opened again. The man in the T-shirt and I looked up to see a short, fat man waddle in. He whistled tunelessly and carried his own paper under his arm. There was a hint of a smile on his face as he sat down two seats away from me, unfolded his newspaper with fussy concentration, and started reading. The boy came out again. "Coffee," the fat man said. "Gonna be a cool day today, boy. You can just feel it." The kid mumbled something, filled the man's coffee cup, and went back into the kitchen. He left the door to the kitchen open, and I could hear him scrambling my eggs.

My eyes glanced over the paper, but there was nothing about LeRoy or myself, and I wasn't terribly interested in anything else. I just needed to read something to calm my nerves. As soon as I returned to the house, I planned to get a few more hours of sleep.

"Jeez, that Michael Jackson," the fat man said. "What a weirdo."

I grunted. The grunt said, *I don't want to be rude, but don't talk to me.* The fat man said nothing more and started whistling "The Girl from Ipanema." The man in the white T-shirt, meanwhile, paid for his coffee and left. Five minutes later the boy came out with my bacon and eggs, which were hot and mildly greasy enough to keep the stomach acids occupied for a while. Just as I started to eat, a tall, well-built, blond man walked in. Almost involuntarily I stared at him. A lot of people probably stared at him. He looked like somebody in a light beer commercial — one of those ruggedly handsome linebackers, say, or a center fielder, sitting around a bar. His face was spoiled, however, by eyes that were dull and bad-humored.

It didn't take long to finish my bacon and eggs. I went to the cash register when the boy came out with a pot of coffee for the blond man. He nodded at me. Behind me I heard the screen door slam and, glancing back, I saw a short, wiry young man with black hair parted in the center and a trim little mustache. He was wearing a three-piece blue pinstripe suit and carried an umbrella, although the sky was cloudless.

The newcomer smiled at me and asked, "How's Anna Lightfoot? How's my little girl?"

The two men at the counter turned and looked at me.

"The name's Jimmy Walrath," the man with the umbrella said. "You must be Heywood Murphy." He switched off the lights and turned the OPEN sign on the door around so that it now read SORRY. WE'RE CLOSED. "Why don't you go back to the kitchen, Ron?" he told the kid. "And close the door after you."

Ron did as he was told. The two men at the counter got to their feet. Nobody moved except Walrath, who now and then tried to brush away a fly with a slow, languid movement of his hand. It was as if everybody had become extremely absentminded all of a sudden. I remember thinking vaguely at one point that maybe the man in the T-shirt was still outside in the parking lot and might hear a scream. And then the fat guy suddenly barked, "The man asked you a question. You gonna answer?" He walked up to me and put his hand on my arm, and I whirled around and grabbed his shirtfront with both hands. At that moment I didn't hear but felt the blond man spring at me from behind, and I knew the exact sensation a creature of the fields knows in the instant the hawk descends with its claws. The instant passed. Then a hot, massive blade sliced through my brain, and I saw sparks and bursts of color as I tumbled into a nauseating void.

6

I WAS AWARE that my neck was very stiff, as if I had been pushing a Winnebago uphill with the top of my head. I tried to open my eyes. Slowly. I didn't want anything to stir the waves of pain scalding my brain. As I finally opened my eyes, I saw a man in a three-piece suit stooped inside a van, while a muscular blond fellow squatted with a hypodermic needle in his hand. His other hand was holding my arm. A thought formed in my brain that these men wanted to do something harmful to me, but I couldn't pursue the thought because I couldn't remember who they were, and the waves kept pounding in my head and demanding my attention.

The needle went through the skin of my arm, and the blond man gripped it tighter. Then he withdrew the needle. I stared at the roof of the van. I thought to myself how uncannily it was like the roof of a camper my father once owned when we lived in Robert's Arm, Newfoundland. And then the waves died and I felt myself soaring like a rocket up to that roof, and the blackness came again.

The second blackness lasted a long time. I began to crawl out of it when I heard the click of billiard balls and glimpsed a pool table floating somewhere above me, off to my left. A ball went click and then thud. Click thud. Click thud. I remembered playing pool with Lydia Rothbard. The memory became vivid. I saw myself leaning over to make a shot, I hit the cue ball, the ball rolled across the green felt, and smashed into a yellow ball. The yellow ball went rolling off to the side pocket. I tried to control its speed and direction through my will. The ball was very slow. It rolled up to the side pocket, centimeter by agonizing centimeter, and teetered on the edge of the hole. I held my breath and tried to will it to drop in. Sweat was pouring down my face. The ball was straining to fall, torn between an unbearable desire to do so and its own failing momentum. It strained with every ounce of its being and finally, deliciously, it fell, and I went with it into unconsciousness.

I woke a second time to silence. The pool table was still there, but no one was beside it. There was a wall covered with paneling that vaguely resembled wood, and a tiny window near the ceiling. It was dark outside the window — night had fallen. I wanted to go to the john; my bladder felt as big as a volleyball. But my eyelids started to fall again. A thought wandered into consciousness from some still undamaged center of my brain: *Keep those eyes open. Stay awake. You'll be glad you did.* But the eyelids kept falling, as if they were obeying orders from someone else. And then I heard grunting from across the room. The eyelids stopped, flickered, and went back up a micromillimeter.

I saw Anna Lightfoot sitting on the floor, leaning against the wall, still dressed in her housecoat. Her eyes were closed and she was smiling — the wide, rubbery smile that clowns stretch across their faces. Her face had a curious blue tint. Suddenly her head fell forward, and I could see only her thick black hair. At the same time her hands remained motionless by her side. And then a man put a canvas sack over her face and drew it down over her shoulders and arms. He dragged her away from the wall by her feet so that she was lying on the floor, then pulled the sack over her hips and legs. I thought, *Heywood, you've got to wake up. You've got to get out of here. The next person in a canvas bag is you. The next to be dumped.* And then I thought, *It's all a hallucination,* and my eyelids closed.

It didn't seem long after that I felt hands under my armpits, felt my head rising through the air. I opened my eyes and saw the paneled wall receding. I looked down at my feet, trailing along the floor. Panic washed over me. I tried to move my arms. Somebody had squashed them and then glued them together behind my back.

"Wakey, wakey," said the man whose hands were hauling me by the armpits. "You've had quite a hit of Valium, chief."

I tried to twist my body around, to free myself of those hands, but I could hardly move. I realized now my hands were tied behind my back. We passed through an open door into a furnace room. The man, who turned out to be the muscular blond guy in the diner, pulled me to my feet and turned me around so that I was facing a sink full of water. The fat man was leaning against a corner of the sink and running his tongue over his lower lip. He put his hand on my upper arm and squeezed it.

"It was real nice of you to stop by the diner this morning, pal. Saved us the trouble of grabbing you at the house with all those Jesus jerk-offs. How ya doing?"

I realized, as he spoke, that my old tendency to home in on trouble, as if trouble were a neurochemical substance that made my nerves tingle, had been in perfect working order that morning. He stood on tiptoe and felt my scalp. "Oh, boy, you got a bump all right," he said, as if admiring some piece of handiwork. He leaned back against the sink and smiled. "But at least you're still breathing." He seemed to study my face for a few minutes. "Breathing's nice, isn't it? Inhale, exhale — it's just a hell of a nice process. Take a deep one, Murphy. For auld lang syne."

Then he nodded and the blond man put both his hands against the back of my head and shoved it into the water. I don't know how long my head was submerged — four, five seconds — before I began to feel desperate. It was a desperation in which every part of my body began to scream silently at me, in which I lost all awareness of having a mind, of anything except screams noiselessly reverberating through a tight space. Everything from my feet to my brains dissolved in screams, and I struggled like an animal impaled on a stick, trying to get away from the hand on my neck, to reach air.

And then, almost as a mercy, the screams began to die and I knew, in a curious, detached way, as if I were at last floating above my body, that I was now going to open my mouth and let the water into my lungs.

The hand pulled my head out of the water, and I fell to the concrete floor, gasping. The blond man picked me up by the armpits again and set me on my feet. In the doorway a thin, middle-aged woman in a pantsuit was staring at me. The fat man pinched my arm and said something I couldn't hear, because I was absorbed by the sway and dip of the floor under my feet. I felt as if I were standing in a boat in a rough sea. The other people seemed not to notice the motion of the floor. They all had their sea legs.

"I thought you weren't coming home till tomorrow," the blond man said to the woman in the doorway, who nodded, as if approving what she saw.

"I had a feeling you'd be here," she said. "I just had a feeling. I thought you might have Harvey with you."

"Sorry, Mrs. Henessey," the fat man said.

"You heard anything?"

"We got people watching the New Israel group twenty-four hours a day. We'll find him."

"I thought you might have some news for me," the woman said. It sounded like an accusation. She wrinkled her nose and made a face. "What smells?"

There was a brief silence and then the blond man laughed. "He pissed his pants."

"Is he from New Israel?" she asked.

The fat man shook his head. "Jesus freaks, so-called."

"He looks awful."

"He'll be all right. We'll take care of him."

She shook her head. "I'm sure he'll thank you when it's over."

"For trying to drown me?" I asked. I wasn't being sarcastic. It was a serious question. I was genuinely confused. When you've been hit over the head and knocked unconscious, drugged with enough

Valium to keep you that way for an entire day, and then woken up by somebody who's trying to fill your lungs with tap water, your reasoning powers aren't at their best.

"Just trying to clear your head, chief," the blond man said. "It starts with a little water on the face."

"Where's Walrath?" I asked. I don't know why I asked that. I had no desire to see him.

"He's busy. We're taking care of you," the fat man said. "You're going to be all right."

I remembered Anna, too. That had been no hallucination. She had died here in this basement, with her head in a sink full of water. A chill passed through me, and I felt sick to my stomach. At that moment the floor lurched wildly to starboard and I fell backward against the sink. A bright little voice, the same one that warned me not to fall asleep just before I glimpsed Anna Lightfoot, passed on yet another hint to me: *Soak the rope around your wrist.* I took the hint, leaned back, and lowered my hands and wrists into the water in the sink.

"Hey there, chief," the blond man said, grabbing my shirt collar and pulling me back up.

The fat man smiled. "Yeah, he's not in great shape. But we'll fix him up. We'll get him into shape."

"You're deprogrammers," I said stupidly. Things were becoming clearer to me, but very slowly.

"We specialize in giving people back to themselves."

I had what I thought was a sudden inspiration. "Hey, look, it's all right," I said. "You don't have to convince me. Mrs. Henessey, I . . . I was going to leave that cult, anyway. I'm fed up. I want to see my . . . wife." My wife and I haven't seen each other since we were divorced six years ago, but I couldn't think of anybody else to mention.

Mrs. Henessey looked at me as if my ruse were beneath contempt.

"If we untied him, he'd be out that door in a second," the fat man said. "He'd run right back to the cult. And he'd probably be lost forever. He and the cult would sue us." He shook his head. "It's crazy."

"You listen to them," Mrs. Henessey said. She pointed her forefinger at me. "You'll be so grateful to these men. You'll get down on your knees and you'll bless them for what they did for you."

"We've seen it happen," the fat man said. He didn't crack a smile, either. He looked as if he really meant it. For an insane second I thought maybe I had gotten it all wrong. Maybe these men *were* trying to help me and I should be grateful and get down on my knees and bless them. The second passed. I began moving my wrists as unobtrusively as possible.

"You want me to make some coffee while you get started?" Mrs. Henessey asked.

The fat man shook his head. "You go back to your sister's, Mrs. Henessey. We'll be fine."

"No, please. I want to stay. I won't interfere. My sister's so . . . fretful and worried. I get nervous fits just being near her."

The fat man cleared his throat. "To tell you the truth, ma'am, we were thinking of taking him somewhere else. I'm pretty sure we weren't followed here, but Arnold thinks we may have used your house a little too often. There's a place up in Thornhill we can stay tonight. Better to be on the safe side."

"What he's trying to tell you, Mrs. Henessey," I said, "is they want to kill me without you hanging around."

"Hey, this guy's a laugh a minute," the fat man said. He shook his head. "Paranoia. That's what they feed these guys — paranoia and Popsicles."

I heard myself starting to cry. I was stuck in a nightmare: the old, old, nightmare in which you are sane and the world is psychotic.

The fat man gently put his hand on my cheek. "That's all right, fella. You're going to be all right." He nodded to the blond man. "Let's get moving. The sooner we start work on him the better. Poor son of a bitch. They've really screwed him up. Screwed him up royally."

In an instant the blond man picked me up and held me in his arms like a child. This man was very strong. In response I carried out the most intelligent strategy I could think of at that moment. I started screaming. I kicked and screamed like a kid throwing a tantrum. The fat man picked up a towel, stuffed it in my mouth, and tied it tightly around my head. As soon as he finished, he tapped the blond man on the shoulder and I was carried, followed by the fat man and Mrs. Henessey, into the basement recreation room where I'd first awakened. Then they carted me up the stairs, into the kitchen, and through a door into a garage where an Econoline van was parked. Mrs. Henessey told them to wait for a minute and went back into the house. The fat man opened the rear door of the van, and my bearer dropped me onto the floor inside. I felt as if I were something ready for pickup by the city's sanitation department. Still, I kept moving my wrists. The wet rope was expanding, and I could feel my right hand coming free.

"I told you the broad was coming back," the blond man said. "Good job she didn't come back a little earlier . . . or a little later."

"At least you had your game of pool, didn't you?" the fat man wheezed. "Anyway, I know where we can take care of our friend." He reached into the van and patted my ankle. "We got lots of Valium still?"

"You kidding? We got enough to put out ten more guys."

They both glanced at me as I sat up in the van, my wrists working furiously in the dark. The blond man stretched himself and yawned. He looked fine in his lemon-yellow double-knit sport shirt, beige slacks, and white belt — easy-care fabrics stretched tightly over muscles made larger than normal by heavy workouts, powdered protein drinks, and probably steroids.

Mrs. Henessey came back. "If you see Harvey, you give him this. It's his photo album. You tell him to look at this album. He was such a good photographer. Tell him to look at the pictures he took of his family. Tell him to look at the pictures of Barbados. We used to go there every March break. . . ."

"I'll do that, Mrs. H.," the fat man said. "We'd better get going, Billy."

They shut the rear doors of the van and got into the front seat. "Billy" was the driver. He put on his seat belt, started the car, switched on the radio and, as soon as Mrs. Henessey opened the garage door, backed the van out into the driveway. Simultaneously I noticed for the first time a large canvas bag lying on the floor of the van beside me. Nausea once again oozed out from my stomach walls.

Billy pulled out into the street, and I yanked furiously at my bound wrists, pulled at them with all the strength that rage and fear could lend to the muscles of my arms. One hand began squeezing out from the rope, and in a second it was free.

I slid over to the rear doors, grateful for the sounds of the radio — like all his kind, Billy enjoyed headbanger music — and reached for the handle. I paused for a moment to catch my breath. I heard a shout from the fat man. I scrambled to my feet, pushed open the door, and jumped out. As I landed on the street, I almost fell on my face, but I kept my balance, stumbled forward, and then broke into a run. At the same time I heard the van stop and a door open. My knees seemed to have disappeared, and the faster I tried to run the slower I moved — I hadn't yet escaped from the logic of nightmares. But I saw a couple jogging on the sidewalk a few yards ahead. I ran up to them and almost knocked the man over, holding on to one of his arms. When he yanked it away, he looked more frightened than I was.

I reached behind my head and picked apart the knot in the tea towel while trying to articulate the words "Help me." The couple looked at each other and then glanced at Billy, who had jumped out of the van and was standing in the street, wondering what to do. The man said, "Are you guys fooling around?" Fear made him sound petulant.

"Leave him, Billy!" I heard the fat man shout, leaning out of the open door on the passenger side. "*Leave him!*"

Billy hesitated for another second and then ran back to the van, hopped in the front seat, and started the engine. The fat man closed his door and they drove off. The couple began jogging again at a slightly faster pace than before. They were several yards away when I finally got the towel out of my mouth.

I had no idea where I was, except that it was a suburb, probably in Toronto, although I couldn't be sure. I didn't recognize the neighborhood, but that wasn't surprising. There were large stretches of suburbia that I had never once ventured into as a city dweller and reporter. "News" didn't happen in these areas. The people living there didn't want news happening in their neighborhoods. I walked along the street for a while until I noted a house with a garage door open and the light on. Standing in the light was Mrs. Henessey, with her arms folded and her head bowed. I stopped for a few minutes and watched her as she stood motionless, as if she were deep in thought, and then turned around, went inside the garage, and closed the door after her.

I noted the address of the house and then started walking in the opposite direction. I had no idea if Billy and his friend would call to warn her that I was on the loose, but if they didn't, I wanted to keep her in ignorance of that fact. I walked for about twenty minutes, not knowing where the hell I was going. Eventually I reached a major intersection that gave me my bearings — Sheppard and Victoria Park, definitely Toronto — and spied a Tim Horton doughnut shop nearby. It was now 9:30, according to a clock in the shop. I walked in and ordered a black coffee and a chocolate coconut doughnut. The girl at the counter looked right through me as she handed me the doughnut and coffee. I suddenly remembered that I smelled of urine. I felt desperately embarrassed, but the girl walked to another part of the counter and ignored me. I was just another wasted druggie wandering into the twenty-four-hour doughnut shop after sunset.

As soon as I finished the coffee and doughnut, I went outside to a phone booth. My first call was to Elliston. After several rings, a familiar voice answered.

"Joanna," I said, "it's Heywood."

"What do you want?" The voice was tiny and trembling, like a frightened child's.

"Joanna, listen. I was jumped. Three men attacked me in that restaurant on — "

"Where is Sharon? What have you done with her?" Her voice was louder now, hysterical. "Your friends took her. They took her away screaming."

"Joanna, I know. I saw her. Listen to — "

"You and your friends, you're tools of Satan, all of you. You came here pretending to be a friend. You liar!"

There was a click and then the sound of the dial tone. I stood there for a moment, holding the receiver as if it were a small animal with sharp teeth. Then I flipped through the phone book, found a Malcolm Kelly, and punched in the number. After six or seven rings, a sleepy voice answered. It was the Malcolm Kelly I knew, all right, and when I told him who I was, he became wide awake very fast.

"Where the hell are you, Heywood? Wolf and I have gone crazy looking for you today."

"I found Anna, Malcolm."

7

I SAT UP MOST of the evening in Mose's house telling Malcolm what had happened since I had left for Elliston. Around midnight Malcolm showed me a spare bedroom. When I woke up after a few hours of sleep, Wolf was sitting by the bed. Kelly was standing in the doorway.

"Anna's dead, Wolf."

"Malcolm told me," Wolf said. "You saw her in that basement?"

I nodded.

Wolf closed his eyes and rubbed his forehead with the fingers of his right hand.

"I'm sorry, Wolf."

He continued to rub his forehead. "Anna Lightfoot," he murmured. "I first met her in a group home in Orillia where I was trying to help another kid. She used to keep a notebook. Anybody she met, she took down their names, addresses, phone numbers, notes about what they were like, what they did. She wanted to keep track of everybody. 'You never know when you might need them,' she'd always say."

"Notebooks," Kelly said, staring at the floor.

"Then she started to run away from the group home. At first it was . . . maybe once every few months. She'd run away for a few days, come back, and all the other kids would be excited and ask her what happened. And she'd have stories for them. Mostly true,

I think." Wolf looked at me as if he wanted to make sure I was following his drift. "Mostly true," he repeated. "She learned quick. She learned how to hide underneath seats in the subway after the subway closed so she'd have a place to sleep. Little kids can do that, you know. And she was still pretty little.

"Then she learned other things. She learned about sex." Wolf took another deep breath. "Not that it was hard to find people to give her crash courses. She found them. Every time she ran away, part of the excitement was another escapade she had to talk about. She started to run away more often. It got so the other kids stopped being excited and started getting upset when she came back. And then when she was fifteen she ran away for good. She found a man who lived in the Spadina Hotel, a wonderful man who lost a leg because of frostbite and hung around the hotel drinking beer all day on a disability pension. He took her in, and he shared her with two other men. I don't know why she did it, but she did. Maybe she didn't mind misery. Maybe misery's like a drug, a painkiller for something worse. And it's easy to come by. Very easy to come by. Anyway, she got mad at the guy one day, they had a fight, she pushed him down a stairway, and as he lay there trying to get up, she lit into him with one of his crutches. She smashed his face in."

No one said anything. After a few minutes, Kelly finally spoke up. "What are you going to do now, Heywood?"

"Who the hell knows? Maybe it's time to tell the cops they've got another corpse on their hands. If they can find it."

"You may want to avoid the police for the time being," Wolf said. "I dropped by your place the other day when I was looking for you. I saw them hanging around."

"A friend at the paper told me they'd be coming for me."

Wolf shrugged. "We'll help you. They won't find you."

"That could get you into trouble, Wolf. They have laws that say you should help them, not the people they want to arrest."

"I know the police. Remember what I said about being unpredictable? They're very good at finding people who are predictable. And that's okay, because most guys they want are predictable. I know a guy who used to pass bad checks. He'd always go to Woodbine to spend the money from a score. Never Greenwood, always Woodbine. If the cops got a complaint from somebody, they'd just stand around the windows at Woodbine, waiting for him. But you, you're different. You're an intelligent person."

"Okay. We avoid the cops. But there's another complication here, Wolf." I told Wolf and Kelly about Hagedorn. When I came to the part about Hagedorn's visit to my apartment building, Wolf and Kelly exchanged incredulous glances.

"You make yourself too available to people who want to clobber you," Wolf said. "From now on —" he tapped the side of his head " — clever Indian strategy. We'll give surprises, not receive them."

"That's okay by me. Anyway, the point is what my friend at the paper dug up about Hagedorn." I then related the conversation with De Luca.

"So it looks like you'd be better off nosing around Hagedorn," Kelly said.

"Maybe I'd be better off turning myself in and letting the police or my lawyer look into it. But I can't exactly forget about Anna and Walrath, either. Among other things, I'd love to pop into that house where I was just entertained."

"Ah, revenge," Wolf said. "Something us redskins understand very well. We can certainly arrange that, Heywood. Tell you what. We'll drop in on LeRoy's apartment building and see if this Hagedorn character still lives there. If not, we'll visit this Mrs. . . ."

"Henessey. Wolf, how come you want to help me? Is it because of Anna?"

"You were dumped on me. I had no choice."

"Sure you have a choice. You could turn me in if you wanted. You might even get a good citizen's award."

"No, I had no choice. I couldn't ignore all the signs. Like Jerome."

"Jerome?"

"Jerome is magical. Anybody he attacks or insults when I'm around is always somebody I need to listen to. Without fail."

"Is this supposed to be a logical explanation?"

"I'm a child of the wilderness, deeply versed in the ways of Mother Earth, who hasn't mastered the science of logic. Let's have something to eat. Then we'll do our visiting."

In the kitchen I said hello to Mose, and to a young giant of an Indian named Farley, who wore jeans, a faded shirt of no particular color, and a cowboy hat. They were sitting around a kitchen table, talking about a baseball game they had once seen on the reservation at Wikwemikong, in the tones of old men who remember some heartbreaking and splendid game they had seen Ruth and Gehrig play.

"Morning friend," Mose said. "How you feeling after your adventures?"

"Reasonably okay. Good enough to make some social calls today."

"Mind if Farley and I come along?"

"Sure. You can be the muscle."

Mose served some pancakes, but what I wanted more than anything else was a Scotch on the rocks. For one thing, I could hardly hold a fork in my hand. A Scotch would relax me, ease my jumpiness, help me push aside that image of Anna Lightfoot in a canvas bag. It might even give me an appetite for breakfast.

"Just try to breathe, Heywood," Wolf said.

"You reading my mind?"

"First of all, we don't have any booze in this house. Second, you can get through this without it."

I put my elbows on the table and buried my face in my hands.

"Don't feel sorry for yourself, either."

"Wolf," I said, looking up at him, "there was a time when I swore a few drinks did wonders. Helped me do my job. I could call the mother of that child who had just fallen twenty stories from an apartment balcony and get a good quote from her. Maybe even visit the apartment and walk out with a photo of the deceased toddler. A color photo. So our grateful city editor could put it right there on the front page, top of the fold. Just a few drinks, Wolf, and I'd be alert as ever, but ready to do anything."

"What would you do if you were like that now?"

"I'd walk right up to F. Wilson Staigue in a manly and self-confident way and talk him out of arresting me. Persuade him to let me help him in his investigation to find the real killer."

Everybody in the room roared. They knew police, and they knew what it was like to persuade them to do anything they didn't want to do.

"You can see why we don't keep booze in the house," Mose said.

I sighed. "It'd be no use, anyway. I lost the knack of achieving that blessed alcoholic state a few years ago. Just before I dried out, it seems I'd drink and drink and still feel lousy, and before I knew it I was falling-down drunk."

After breakfast we all got into Malcolm's car, a green Buick LeSabre. It was eight years old and had more than 200,000 miles on the odometer. Inside, on the floor, there was a brown carpet. From the rearview mirror hung a rosary.

Mose, Wolf, and Farley got into the back seat. Mose and Wolf looked very serious. Farley, however, was grinning as he sat there with his hat in his lap. Something amusing had occurred to him. I had the feeling it had to do with the baseball game.

When we stopped for a traffic light at Bloor and Sherbourne, a police car pulled up beside us. At first I didn't notice. Then the air in our car suddenly became a bit harder to breathe. I turned around. The cop in the passenger seat was staring at Farley, as if the big Indian's height were cause itself for suspicion. Then he looked at all of us. We had all become instant suspects; the five of us radiated dubious lifestyles, particularly the four who belonged to an ethnic group "known" to have trouble being good citizens. I knew what was going on in the cops' minds: What the hell were these guys doing driving around the city before sunup? "Take it easy, Heywood,"

Wolf said softly. Finally the light changed, and Malcolm drove on. With relief I watched the cop car pull ahead and continue on its way.

At LeRoy's apartment building I studied the names on the directory. No Hagedorn. "Let's leave it for now," I said to Wolf. "On to Mrs. Henessey's."

It took us half an hour to get to the address, by which time the sun had risen. Malcolm pulled to the side of the road and I got out.

"I'll go alone," I said. "But keep an eye on me."

I didn't want the residents of this nice suburb to see my gang and maybe start thinking some band had jumped the reservation and was about to burn and scalp and carry off bags of their garden fertilizer. So I walked to the house and told myself to calm down. The bile and fear inside my body, first stirred by the sight of the cop car, was bubbling away at insane temperatures. The only thing that steadied me was the reflection that Walrath and friends must be a long way from this house by now. The only question was whether they had alerted Mrs. Henessey.

I pressed the doorbell. Seconds passed. I pushed it again. I stepped back from the door and looked the house over, but I realized I couldn't really afford the chance some neighbor would see me crawling into a window, supposing I found one that would open. And then Mrs. Henessey opened the front door in her housecoat. Her mouth tightened, but otherwise she kept good control of herself. She looked like any other housewife confronting a door-to-door salesman. No surprise. No fear. Just annoyance. Walrath had run across one tough lady.

"Morning, Mrs. Henessey. Guess what? I'm deprogrammed. Now I'm looking for those two fellows who had me in your basement last night. I want to thank them for what they did to me."

"Get out of here or I'll call the police."

"Call them. But remember, you're an accessory to what happened yesterday. I think they refer to it in the Criminal Code as 'forcible confinement.' Believe me, I'll do my best to see that charges are laid." I pushed the door open and she stepped aside.

"Nobody's here."

"Where'd they go?" I demanded.

She shook her head again. "You're from New Israel, aren't you? Don't say you're not. I know you are." Her voice quavered with indignation.

I waved to the car. Malcolm got out and came up to the front door. I told him to come in, then said, "I'm going to check the house quickly. Why don't you stay with this lady?"

Then I went on a tour of the first floor of the house. It was very tidy. There was a sofa with a rosewood coffee table, and a piano that looked as if it had been recently polished but hadn't been played in ten years. I went down to the basement. Squeaky clean, too. Even the billiard balls were neatly placed inside the wooden triangle on the pool table. I checked the furnace room. The sink was still full of water. I pulled the plug and emptied it and then went upstairs. Malcolm and the woman were still standing by the doorway.

"What are you people going to do?" she demanded. "You've got my son. What more do you want?"

"Look, Mrs. Henessey, we're not members of New Israel. We're not members of any cult."

A glint darted from her eyes, which looked as hard as cobalt. "Mr. Hainesworth told me you'd say that. He said you'd lie through your teeth. You'd act as if you'd never heard of New Israel. Apparently you people believe it's all right to lie to other people, as long as they're not members of your group. Well, you can't lie to me."

"Who is Mr. Hainesworth, Mrs. Henessey?"

The woman practically spat at me. "They're always being threatened by people like you. They'll keep their whereabouts a good secret, believe you me."

"Would he be kind of short, with dark hair and a nice mustache?"

"He's a little man with a big heart."

"Right. Good day, Mrs. Henessey. Malcolm, we might as well go." We started to leave when I heard a choking sound.

"Where's my son?" I turned and faced her. Tears were in her eyes. She grabbed my arm. "Did you know he got straight A's from the School of Engineering at the University of Toronto? Did you? He was at the head of his class until you got your filthy hands on him. Where is he now? Where's Harvey?"

"I'm sorry, Mrs. Henessey. I haven't seen him."

"He never hated his parents before you got hold of him. He never hated his own mother. Never. Where in the Bible does it teach you to hate your own parents? Where? You tell me that."

"Mrs. Henessey, I don't know your son."

"Was it you who taught him to write vile, filthy letters to us?" She went to a drawer in the kitchen and pulled out some sheets of paper and held them out in front of us. "And his father with a heart condition. Does he want to kill his father with these letters?"

"Good day, Mrs. Henessey."

We walked out the door, but she followed us, the tears flowing now and a low, barely audible moan in her voice. "Please," she begged. "Please tell me where my son is."

"Mrs. Henessey, I'm sorry. I'm not a member of New Israel. I've never met your son."

"Please tell me where he is. Please."

Malcolm and I stood in silence while she covered her face and sobbed. Then we walked back to the car. "Let's get out of here. Fast," I said. But Malcolm wasn't fast enough. Mrs. Henessey came running up to the car, her eyes still wet.

"Now you tell Harvey that his father is sorry. He's sorry about the argument. We both realize he's big enough to decide for himself about . . . about what they were arguing about. You tell him that. Tell him his father is sorry."

"Yes, Mrs. Henessey. I will."

"His father realized he made a mistake," she cried as we drove away.

"Where next?" Malcolm asked. "Elliston?"

I shook my head. "The public library. I think I know who this character Hainesworth is — Canada's very own professional deprogrammer. And I'll bet there's a file of newspaper clippings on him."

There wasn't. But I remembered a features writer on the paper who had done a story on Hainesworth's group. I phoned her from the library and got her at home. She had only the vaguest memories of Hainesworth and his colleagues, but she was at least able to tell me the month and year she'd written the story. I went up to the section where they had newspapers on microfiche and eventually found the article. The lead was a little story about an anonymous young lady from a loving family, with a normal personality, well liked by friends, et cetera, lured by a pal to a week-long outing with the Moonies. She ended up cracking during that week and became a fanatical cult member through lack of sleep, poor diet, and constant psychological pressure. The anonymous young lady then spent a year as a willing slave of Reverend Moon's cult until she was "kidnapped." The reporter had put quotation marks around the word. After that she was deprogrammed by a team including one Arnold Hainesworth, thirty-eight, one Herbert Mellon, thirty-four, and one William Shrule, twenty-seven, members of an organization called CAB, Council Against Brainwashing. There was a photograph of Mellon — the fat man. He was quoted as saying, "It churns your guts to see what these guys do to human beings, to sane, healthy kids. Our methods of deprogramming might seem harsh to some people, but they're nothing compared to what these cults do."

The article raised more questions than it answered, such as where Hainesworth, Mellon, and Shrule had come from and who financed what sounded like a very sophisticated operation. It was a start, though. I flipped through a phone book and spotted a listing for William Shrule. There couldn't be two men in the city with that name. I jotted down the address and then rejoined my four companions in the foyer of the library. They were deep in conversation with a wino.

"Heywood, this is Hank," Wolf said. With his long gray hair and toothless smile, Hank looked like a malevolent old woman out of a fairy tale. "We've been catching up on some mutual acquaintances," Wolf continued. "I bet Hank would love a fin so he could get a cup of coffee and a doughnut. Wouldn't you, Hank?"

"Coffee's bad for you," the old guy wheezed. "I'm quitting. No smokes, no booze, nothing but health foods. Lots of tofu. Starting next week."

I gave him a five-dollar bill, which he studied, then pocketed. We said goodbye, and the five of us walked to our car. I told them what I'd found and suggested we pay Shrule a visit. "I do believe Mr. Hainesworth is our friend Jimmy Walrath. No positive identification yet, as they say, but it looks pretty certain to me."

"Murphy, none of this is solving your problems," Kelly said.

"To hell with my problems. This is interesting. You might say my reporter's instincts are being aroused."

This was true. I wanted to get back at Walrath now almost as bad as I wanted to find LeRoy's killer. But the truth was also that I didn't want to face up yet to some difficult decisions, such as whether I should turn myself in to the police or, if not, whether I should try to find some way to reach Theresa Hagedorn without setting off alarm bells all over City Hall.

Shrule's address turned out to be a Cabbagetown street in the heartland of scrubbed brick and new Gyproc. The house itself was a typical reno, porchless, with the address in big brass numbers. A middle-aged man with a mustache and a receding hairline opened the door. He was wearing sandals, white shorts, and a white strap-style undershirt.

"Is Billy Shrule around?" I asked.

The man smiled nervously. "You're about three months too late. I don't know where William is. He's moved. What do you want with him?"

"I just want to give him a friendly warning. If he keeps assaulting people, he's going to be in big trouble."

"Don't I know. Between you and me, friend, Billy could use a few more folds in the front part of his brain. It's a pity, because there's nothing wrong with the rest of him."

"Do you know where he works?"

The man restrained himself from smiling, then shrugged.

"What's so funny?"

"Oh, nothing. When he lived here, he was employed as a masseur."

"Is it possible he's gotten into a rather unusual form of employment since then? Like deprogramming former members of cults?"

This time the man had no trouble refraining from smiling.

"It's true, isn't it?" I said. "Who does he work for?"

"Ever heard of Arnold Hainesworth?"

"Yeah."

"Well, find Hainesworth and you'll find Billy. I don't recommend it, though. I've met Hainesworth. He's a little thug in a three-piece suit. Used to be a pimp downtown. He'd sit in Fran's all night sipping soft drinks and looking so fine. They called him the Pepsi-Cola pimp. It wasn't meant as a compliment."

"I didn't think so."

"Now he's a big 'deprogrammer.' And he's got more money than he had when he was running thirteen-year-old hookers in the city. Somebody's bankrolling him. And somebody's protecting him, too. Don't ask me who, but I know they've done some things that are quite illegal. And nobody ever touches them. They've beaten up people, too. I mean, really bad. Billy told me so himself. Billy may be stupid, but he doesn't lie. He lacks the requisite imagination. And I'll tell you something else. He's quite capable of beating people up." He gave me a long look. "I guess you know that."

"Yes, I do. How did Billy meet Hainesworth?"

"Billy gets around. He leads a very active social life."

"Popular fellow, is he?"

"He's probably handled more naked men than a Russian army doctor."

"How did you meet Hainesworth?"

"Billy brought him home one day for dinner. Can you believe it? He was introduced to me as Mr. Arnold Hainesworth, but I knew who Super Fly was. I didn't spend a few years on Yonge Street without getting to know some of the landmarks. You know, the Eaton Centre, Simpsons, and Jimmy Walrath of Detroit. We had a great evening of let's-pretend that night. Now you tell me, what's your interest in this? I haven't been interrogated so much in years, I swear."

"Your friend Shrule may have tried kidnapping once too often. Do you have any idea where I can find Hainesworth?"

He shook his head emphatically. "Sorry. I try to avoid knowing as much as possible about him or Billy. Besides, they travel all over the province now. A regular dog-and-pony show for the Rotary Club. Except when they go into action. It's not so funny then. Anyway, I don't know any address. Honest, I'd tell you if I knew."

"You haven't heard from Billy lately, then?"

"Not for a month. I hope that period of noncontact extends for a long time, like the rest of my life."

"Did he ever mention the names Anna Lightfoot or Charles LeRoy?"

He thought for a moment, then shook his head again. "Sorry, they don't ring any bells. Are they friends of Billy's, too? If they are, I'm not surprised I don't remember. When it comes to people who know Billy, you're talking about a list the size of the Toronto phone book."

"Thanks anyway."

"Let me tell you something, friend. If I were you, I'd forget all about Billy. It's not worth the pain. Take my word for it. I learned the hard way."

From the smile on his face I knew he wasn't kidding.

Back in the car I discussed the situation with my companions. Both Billy's "friend" and Mrs. Henessey had made it plain that Walrath's policy was to keep out of sight. And after my close call yesterday, I was pretty sure Walrath would be even harder to find.

"I have an idea, brother," Wolf said. "Let's look up Tony Barzula. I found out where he lives."

"He wasn't too helpful the last time, as I recall."

"He was lying last time. Don't you think he'd know his old friend had become a deprogrammer? It's not the usual career for a pimp, is it? Barzula wouldn't let that get by him."

"So why would he open up now?"

Wolf didn't answer. Nor did he change his expression in the slightest. But I looked at each man and found myself nodding. Yes, Barzula just might open up this time.

He lived in an area not far from the poolroom where we had first met. It was a street of bungalows with angelstone facades and wrought-iron porches. On these porches teenagers with nothing to do sat beside enormous radios tuned to local rock stations. The kids stared with sullen curiosity at our car as we passed; stifled energy smoldered in their eyes like the heat from gears grinding against each other. No one, however, was sitting on Barzula's porch as we got out of the car and went up a walkway bordered by small round rocks painted in bright colors that made them look like shiny pieces of candy. All of us went this time; small groups of men hanging around weren't such an unusual sight in this neighborhood.

I walked up the stairs to the front door by myself, however, and pressed the doorbell. A girl of about fourteen in pedal pushers and a sleeveless jersey answered. "Is Tony in?" I asked her.

She turned around and hollered his name without noticeable affection. Then wearily she said, "Come in," as if calling her brother had sapped every ounce of her strength.

I followed her into the kitchen off the hallway, where she sat down at a table and focused her attention on drinking a glass of ginger ale as she propped her chair against the wall beneath a reproduction of Da Vinci's *The Last Supper*. In the center of the kitchen a fat, middled-aged woman held a baby in the air, shrieking words of endearment to it. The baby looked stunned. All three of them completely ignored me.

Finally Barzula appeared. The key chain hung from his belt as usual, but now he had a T-shirt on as well as a jacket. "What are you doing here?"

"Come outside, Tony. I want to talk to you."

We went out onto the porch.

"Hey, man," he said, closing the door behind him, "don't ever come to my house. *Ever.*"

"Tony, you lied last time. You tell the truth this time and I'll be happy to respect the privacy of your home life."

Barzula was about to reply when he saw my four companions sitting on the porch. "What the fuck's going on?" His voice quieted significantly. "It looks like the whole tribe's here."

"Hello, Tony," Wolf said.

"We just want to ask you about Walrath again," I said. "Where can we find him?"

Tony stared at Farley, who was leaning against a wooden railing. Part of it began to wobble under his weight. Farley straightened and smiled apologetically at Barzula. The smile gave Barzula courage. "You think I'm scared of you guys? Or that big shithead? Get outta here."

"Farley, did you break that railing?" Mose asked with a smile. "Show Mr. Barzula where it broke."

Farley walked over to Barzula, put a massive arm around his shoulder, and guided him to the railing. When he resisted, Farley took hold of his neck and put his face a few inches from the railing. "Is this broken?"

"No, it's fine. It's terrific."

"Mose, he's got something in his jacket pocket," Farley said.

Mose reached into it and pulled out a gun.

"Okay, don't anybody sweat it," Barzula said. "It's not loaded. And would you put it away someplace, please? People see everything in this fucking neighborhood."

Mose showed the gun to Kelly. "A starter's pistol. You can buy one at most sporting goods stores. See the cylinder? He's got it drilled out so he can fire .22s." Mose turned to Barzula. "You carry this piece of shit to impress people?"

Barzula squirmed away from Farley's grip and then tried to smile at us, one man of the world to other men of the world. "Hey, you'd be surprised. The sight of that thing cools out a lot of people."

"I knew a guy at Millhaven who blew somebody away with a gun like that," Farley said. "A little Korean fellow in a variety store tried to take the gun away from him." He shook his head. "Why don't people realize a guy does almost as much time for armed robbery as for killing somebody? A guy's got nothing to lose."

Mose handed the gun to Wolf. "This is a dangerous toy. Too dangerous for kids to play with."

Wolf put the gun in his pocket.

"Hey," Barzula cried, "that's personal property."

"Forget it, Tony," I said. "Some people might consider the fact that you carried a concealed weapon in their presence an unfriendly act. Some people might react strongly to that. But we forgive you. We just want to ask you a few questions. And I want good answers this time. It's too late for bullshit. Number one, where's Walrath?"

"Go to the Four Seasons Hotel tonight at eight. He'll be giving a talk there. Only his name ain't Walrath anymore. And his talk won't be on the subject of teenage pussy, which is what he knows best."

"His name is Arnold Hainesworth and he'll be talking about deprogramming."

"Hey, you guys are way ahead of me. Where'd you find out?"

"Who's in the audience?"

"The Ontario Psychologists Association. Pretty good, eh? I always said to be a pimp you got to know psychology. Now he's talking to the brains. Fuck, you got to admire that guy."

"You should have told me this the first time, Tony. You could have saved me a lot of time."

"I told you nothing. I told you nothing the first time and I told you nothing this time. You understand? You read it in the papers. You heard it somewhere else. I hope your friends understand that."

"They understand."

"They better. I'm told Jimmy's very happy being Arnold Hainesworth these days. Anybody who starts reminding people he used to be a pimp named Walrath might end up losing his kneecaps."

"Where's he live?"

"Don't know. He's all over the goddamn place. It's not like the old days where you could always walk into some video place on Yonge Street and half the guys there had seen him around. It's a brand-new scam. It's big league. I just hear the tidbits."

"Who's paying Walrath?"

Barzula sighed. "Hey, I wish I knew. Somebody who's got money to burn, that's for sure. I could use an employer like that myself."

"All right. You know anything about Billy Shrule or Herb Mellon?"

"Mellon's a one hundred percent certified gearbox. He used to be a fence down in Riverdale, knew all the thieves out there from way back because he grew up with them. I'm not sure, but I think he sold Walrath a leather coat for about a third of the price, and that's how they got to be friends. No kidding. You want to get on Jimmy's good side, that's the way to do it. Shrule's a faggot, too, but he's a heavyweight faggot, and Walrath can always use somebody like that. I don't know how they met. Somebody told me Shrule used to work in a hospital emptying bedpans. Christ, who knows where Jimmy finds these goofs?"

"Okay, Tony. One more question. I asked you before, but maybe your memory's improved since our last talk. What's the connection between Walrath and Anna Lightfoot and Charles LeRoy?"

Barzula shook his head. "Lightfoot, I told you. She worked for him. LeRoy, I don't know. I never heard of him. He must have been before my time."

I let out a sigh of discouragement. "Thanks, Tony."

"See you later, okay?" Barzula said as he edged his way back into the house. "You want to see me again, come to Carafa's. Don't come here." He glanced at Farley briefly, his face full of woe and resentment, and then shut the door behind him.

This time we went back to Mose's house, where he heated up some soup and Farley made some salami sandwiches. I didn't want to be rude, but I couldn't eat.

"What's the matter?" Mose asked. "You feel sick? You didn't finish your pancakes, either." He sounded hurt.

"Can't blame him for feeling sick," Wolf said. "Not after yesterday."

"Miss anything from your place?" Kelly asked.

I shook my head. I had no ties to my apartment except for my books. I've never kept houseplants or cats; they need you too much, and I don't like the thought of something dying in my apartment because I've been away too long.

"I want to attend Walrath's lecture," I said. "I'm looking forward to it."

Wolf broke up a cracker and sprinkled it over his soup. "Heywood," he said slowly, like a teacher driving home a point to a dumb pupil, "is that good strategy?"

I rolled my eyes.

"We should use good strategy," he continued. "To confront Walrath head-on sounds like dumb strategy."

"Okay. You're suggesting I make myself invisible. Keep an eye on him and tail him after the lecture."

"That sounds a little more intelligent."

"Except the only car we have is the Buick. It's a lovely car, Malcolm, but I like to tail somebody in a car that doesn't look like something you drive at a Mafia funeral. Does anybody have a nice Honda Civic? Something that doesn't look so conspicuous in a rearview mirror?"

"This is no good," Wolf said. "It's a public meeting. He'll be on his guard. He knows you're looking for him." Wolf absentmindedly crumbled another cracker into his soup, then shook his head. "It doesn't make sense. We're trying to smoke this guy out. But it feels as if he's trying to smoke *us* out."

I knew what Wolf was talking about, but I felt if I could just manage to corner Walrath and rip his heart out, I might obtain relief from all my troubles. I guess that was what Wolf meant by "dumb strategy." Before we could pursue the topic, however, Wolf was called away to the phone. He looked very serious when he returned.

"Heywood, I'm going to have to go. Some elders are in town this afternoon and they want to talk to me. I'll be back in a few hours at the latest. Why don't you just relax and stay here for the afternoon?"

"I can't stay, Wolf. I've got to do something."

Wolf put both his hands on my shoulders, as if he wanted to force me physically to sit still in my chair. "Stay here, brother. You're a wanted man. And don't forget, we act together now."

"You play hearts?" Mose asked me.

I sighed. "Yes."

"Stay here," Wolf said. "Play a few hands of cards. Malcolm and I will be back soon."

After they left, I called De Luca to find out if a warrant for my arrest had been issued. He wasn't at his desk. I tried another friend named Blaine Walters who was a copy editor in the city department. Blaine seemed quite pleased to hear from me.

"How ya doing, Heywood?" he asked. "How's work in the magazine world?"

"Terrific. Blaine, has the paper run any stories in the past few days about the LeRoy murder? I've missed a few issues."

"You mean you don't read your *Clarion* every day? I'm shocked. There hasn't been any recent story, Heywood. I don't think so, anyway. We just ran that story the day after."

"The one that mentioned me."

"Yeah. How'd that work out, anyway? Was he really a friend of yours?"

"Yeah, he was a friend. You sure there's been no story in the past day or two?"

"Here, let me check. I can get the library computer on my terminal." I heard keys clacking over the phone, and a minute or two of silence. Then his voice came back on the line. "Nope, not a thing."

"Thanks, Blaine."

Well, that was interesting. Maybe the cops weren't ready to arrest me quite yet. Maybe they just wanted me for questioning or were afraid I really had disappeared somewhere. On the other hand, maybe they did have that warrant out, only some *Clarion* reporter had fallen asleep in the penalty box and missed the story. That had happened before.

Meanwhile, Farley, Mose, and I sat at a card table in the living room. The room had lots of pictures, the biggest being an oil painting of an Indian warrior facing an eagle. It was bold and colorful and not very good. There was also a table cluttered with the most incredible assortment of knickknacks, plastic Mounties, and souvenir coffee mugs. In the most prominent position was a trophy with a bronze baseball pitcher on top. The inscription read: "MVP, Sudbury Industrial Softball League, 1973, Mose Latouche." Someone who had never known a home had been determined to mark this room, claim it with the artifacts of a life. The artifacts insisted that the life had significance.

Mose shuffled the deck. "You deal," he said to Farley. "I'm going to get some ginger ale. Who wants one?"

Farley raised his hand.

"Heywood?"

"No thanks."

Mose went to the kitchen and came back with a couple of glasses of ginger ale and we started playing. The things I held in my hand looked strange to me. It was as if I had never seen playing cards before.

"You do time in Millhaven, Farley?" I asked.

He shrugged. "One year out of a three-year sentence for driving cars down to Massachusetts."

"Oh?"

"I was working for a bunch of guys in Toronto. They'd buy some smashed-up car from a junkyard and take the serial number off it. Then they'd steal the same model car, same color, and everything and switch the serial numbers, in case the car ever got checked. Then I drove it down to Massachusetts. They don't license auto body shops there. It's great."

Farley took a swig of his ginger ale, half-embarrassed that he'd talked so much in front of someone he hardly knew. I noticed his right arm as he lifted the bottle to his lips. Even with the shirt on you could tell he had biceps like bowling pins.

The last hand was played and we added up our scores. "Hey, you got a shitload of hearts there," Mose said to me. "You feeling okay?"

"Yeah, I'm all right. I wouldn't mind going out for a second, though, just to get a breath of fresh air."

I stepped out to the backyard, climbed over a wooden fence, and walked past a neighbor's house to the street. A streetcar came along presently, and I took it. I wanted to be by myself, and I had an idea I could clear my head a bit if I took a ferry to the Toronto Islands.

The islands, just offshore, were public parks, although a few hundred people still lived on them. They weren't exactly primeval, but at least when you were there you didn't feel as if you were risking black lung disease every time you inhaled deeply. I took the ferry, along with some young men and women with mountain bikes, to Hanlan's Point. When the ferry landed, I started walking aimlessly, trying to think.

I thought first of LeRoy the drifter. He wasn't so unique. It seemed to me that every year the number of these drifters in Toronto increased. You met them all the time. There was X who was now "producing" a Canadian movie, among other things, riding the crest of a wave of successful dope deals, flying down to St. Lucia two or three times a winter to recharge his batteries. There was Y, who had made a killing as part-owner of a string of chic hamburger and spinach salad restaurants, but who had also made a few dubious moves and come back to his town house one night to find a bomb had gone off in his garage. Now he was driving a taxi. They carried out their scams not because they really wanted to be rich or coveted the things money bought, but because money was the symbol of power. It was proof they could manipulate other people.

The question was: what move had LeRoy made that backfired? Did it have anything at all to do with Walrath or Anna Lightfoot? Perhaps he had found out about Walrath's Hainesworth scam and made a move to blackmail him. Barzula's words came back to me: *Jimmy's very happy being Arnold Hainesworth these days.* Blackmail was a possibility, but that didn't figure, either. There must have been an awful lot of people who knew about Walrath's new identity, Barzula and Billy's boyfriend included. If Walrath wanted his past kept secret, it would have been hopeless. Too obviously hopeless for him to react with such desperation to one guy who tried to cash in on the secret.

Blackmail, improbable in Walrath's case, struck a chord when I thought of the Rothbards and the Lusks. Two families who had nothing in common with each other except for the fact that they were very rich. Two families who, unlike LeRoy, had a lot to lose. When you have a lot to lose, it can be very difficult not to lie once in a while. It could have been very difficult for Ivan Lusk, for example, with his Filipino maid and his ring that just happened to end up in LeRoy's footlocker. And then there was Lydia Rothbard. Charming Lydia, who also could easily have been lying to me. Perhaps she did know LeRoy, after all. It wasn't something a "powerhouse of the community" would advertise.

But the likeliest possibility was still the simplest one: LeRoy's connection with all these people was pure coincidence, but his connection with Peter Hagedorn had to be more than that.

It was early evening by the time I finally took the ferry back to the mainland and then the subway uptown. Shortly before eight I walked into the Four Seasons and asked where the OPA meeting was. I knew I shouldn't be here. I knew Wolf was right. But for the life of me I couldn't stay away.

The receptionist directed me to the second floor, the first door on the right. I opened that door and saw a man in a green plaid jacket speaking from a lectern with the name of an insurance company emblazoned on it. "That's what separates the giants in the field from the ordinary Joes," he shouted in an East Texas accent. "They don't think, I am going to become. They think, I am! It's always present tense. They know there is no down the road." I closed the door. Bad directions.

The middle set of doors had a card that read: ONTARIO PSYCHOLOGISTS ASSOCIATION. I opened it. There were round tables, each with seven or eight people sitting around them, a dais at one end of the room, a baby grand in the corner. Waiters were taking away plates from the tables. Seated at the dais, near the center, was Jimmy Walrath, deep in conversation with the man seated beside him.

I entered the room. A table near the doors had an empty chair, so I strolled over just as a bearded man leaned back in his chair, convulsed with laughter.

"Mind if I sit down?" I asked no one in particular at the table, and took the seat. There were three couples sitting at this table. I looked at the couple to my left. The man, a round-faced, pink-cheeked gentleman, was staring at me through thick glasses, his mouth half-open. He had the look of someone who was brilliant with slides and petri dishes but was baffled and frightened by anything that could talk back to him. Obviously no one had ever taught him any social graces. Now he was a psychologist.

A woman I took to be his wife, who looked as if she were suffering from anorexia nervosa, had a pair of glasses attached to a cord around her neck. She spoke up. "This is an OPA dinner." The woman enunciated these words the same way an outraged three-year-old would say, "This is my sandbox."

I smiled. "I'm a friend of Arnold's." I said.

"Any friend of Arnold's is a friend of mine," her husband said with exaggerated heartiness, reaching out to shake hands with me. I think he wanted to annoy the thin woman. He looked three-fifths drunk, anyway. "Lloyd's the name."

His wife smiled at me. A name tag pinned to the lapel of her jacket told me her name was Vicki Ross. "Do you work with Arnold Hainesworth?" she asked me pleasantly.

I shrugged. "I've been involved in some of his deprogramming."

"It's so interesting having a man like Mr. Hainesworth speak. I think it's a terribly important issue, don't you? We get so used to hearing just from academics talking about things that, well, are certainly important, but this is closer to where people are really at. *I* think, anyway."

"Who's that up on the dais there, besides Arnold?"

"Well, there's Dr. —" She blushed. "Oh, I forget his name. Can you imagine? The president of the OPA. He's in the middle. And then there's his wife to the right, and then Paul Hornak . . ."

Chubby Paul Hornak sat in a dark blue suit, his elbows on the table and his fingertips pressed together. He was listening politely to something the OPA's president's wife was saying, his baby face tilted slightly her way. At that moment the OPA president stood and cleared his throat. "Ladies and gentlemen, it's my pleasure tonight . . ."

"He's such a little guy, isn't he?" Mrs. Ross whispered to me.

"It's a real treat to be here tonight," Hainesworth began, following his introduction. "Although I have to say it's also a little intimidating. I'm not trying to flatter anybody, but I know what kind of audience I'm talking to, and I know what caliber of people you are. So I hope you'll excuse me if I seem a bit nervous. And also if I talk to you tonight in a kind of straight-ahead way, because I'm no university professor and I'm no scientist and I sure as hell am no psychological wizard. What I learned about psychology I learned on the streets the hard way.

"I guess I'm still pretty ignorant about what makes human beings tick, but I will say this, I'm learning all the time. And some of what I've learned over the past few years, ladies and gentlemen, I tell you, it's enough to make you think. Money explains a lot, I know — don't I know — but still it's horrifying to see what cults and so-called therapeutic organizations are doing to people. Particularly to young people, the most vulnerable of all. I know what I'm talking about, my friends. I've seen the results. I've seen young people with their minds twisted, their personalities warped, their very lives almost totally destroyed. Not a pretty sight. And the sad thing is, I'm seeing it more all the time."

Walrath then told his audience he had slides of an indoctrination center used by a cult called New Israel. Somebody set up a slide projector in the middle of the room, and Walrath pulled down a screen behind the dais. The lights went off and a slide appeared on the screen. It showed a fat man surrounded by a circle of people sitting on a floor. He looked as if he were dancing the hornpipe. The audience laughed.

"Looks kind of funny, doesn't it?" Walrath said. "In New Israel this is called Dancing in the Spirit."

Out of a corner of my eye I saw somebody leave the dais and walk out the door. I had no idea who it was, but the action suddenly made me nervous. The full realization that what I was doing was very stupid sunk in. Quickly I stood, walked out of the room, and took the escalator down to the lobby. As I left the hotel, I heard a commotion in the lobby. Turning to see what was going on, I spied two policemen walking up the escalator. They were accompanied by Herbert Mellon.

8

WOLF AND KELLY were waiting for me outside the hotel. I wasn't surprised to see them there. Wolf shook his head sadly, as if extremely disappointed in me, but all he said was that I had been rude to Uncle Mose and had "made a mockery of his hospitality."

"I'll apologize."

"You'd better. Then we're going up north."

"North?"

"Little Current, on Manitoulin Island. Lightfoot's father's been up there for a couple of months, since he got out of Stony Mountain on parole."

"What's he got to tell us?"

"One of those girls from that house in Elliston paid him a visit earlier today, according to my sources. Does that make you feel curious?"

"She probably wanted to talk about Anna's kidnapping," I suggested. "Maybe she figured he could help out somehow."

"Yeah, maybe so. Anyway, *I'm* curious. And it wouldn't do any harm to get you out of town for a while the way you've been behaving."

The next morning Wolf and I drove north in Kelly's Buick. We traveled through a landscape of granite outcroppings and dead-looking ponds surrounded by firs, and oaks and maples that were

≈ *Philip Marchand*

just beginning to turn color. Late in the afternoon we turned off the Trans-Canada and crossed a series of bridges until we were on the island.

After driving down a gravel road and an old logging trail, we stopped at a tiny house covered with Insulbrick. On one side was a metal cistern for collecting rainwater, and a pile of scrap wood, including old doors. In front of the house plastic lawn furniture lay in shreds and tatters. We went to the front door and knocked. There was no sound except for voices talking on television. Wolf opened the front door. Inside we could see a man wearing blue jeans with the cuffs rolled up and a white T-shirt. He was lying on a sofa facedown.

Wolf walked over and gently shook the man's shoulder. I glanced at the television set, which was hooked up to a portable generator. There was a commercial on for a breakfast cereal. A small child was sitting at a table making a face and refusing to eat something. I turned off the set.

"Lawrence," Wolf said. "Lawrence, wake up."

Little noises emerged from Lawrence's throat as he rolled over and opened his eyes. The corneas of those eyes were yellow. Lawrence appeared to be in his sixties, but I had the feeling he could be twenty years younger.

"It's Wolf, Lawrence. Remember me? Saw you at Stony Mountain five years ago. We were doing a performance for you guys."

Lawrence stared at us for a few minutes before he sat up. "You want a beer?" he whispered. Wolf and I shook our heads. Lawrence walked to the kitchen stiffly, leaning forward as if his spine were permanently bent in its socket. In the kitchen he took out a bottle of beer from a Styrofoam cooler full of ice and opened it with the handle of a drawer. He whispered something from the kitchen.

"What?" Wolf asked.

"You said you was Wolf. Who's your friend?"

I introduced myself. Lawrence glanced at me on his return to the living room and then sat down on the sofa. There were no other chairs in the living room, so we remained standing.

"You come about Anna?" he asked after a moment of silence.

I nodded.

"Thought so."

"How's that?"

"Why else would you come?" His eyes tried their best to take us in. There was no bitterness in his raspy voice, no irony, no curiosity. He was stating the obvious. "You boys drive up from Toronto?"

Again we nodded.

"Thought so. You come a long way. Must be important business." A corner of his mouth lifted slightly in what I gathered was a smile. "The cops told me Anna might be dead, you know. What was she, sixteen? Last time I saw her she was a little baby. And now they tell me she might be dead." He took another swallow of beer. Again his voice was devoid of bitterness. He was merely mentioning a fact.

"You never took her out on the trap line?" I asked, remembering Anna that night in the backyard of the house in Elliston.

He frowned. "Someone else did that. I've been a guest of the federal government for the last fourteen years." He scratched the top of his head. "You guys know what happened to Anna?"

I shook my head. It seemed less complicated than telling the truth.

"Kids like her shouldn't go to Toronto. They should stay up here where they belong. Can you boys lend me some money?"

I handed him a twenty. He hardly glanced at it, put it in the back pocket of his jeans, then set the beer on the floor. "Excuse me, fellas. I got to take a leak." He went out the front door with that stiff walk of his, was gone for a few minutes, and then returned and sat on the sofa.

"She ever write to you at Stony Mountain?" I asked.

Lawrence shook his head and finished his beer.

"Ever visit?"

"Why'd she want to do that? You ever been to Stony Mountain?"

"No."

"It's where they dispose of the garbage. It's a garbage dump. Why'd she want to go there?"

"To visit her father."

"I ain't her father."

"Who was her father, Lawrence?" Wolf asked.

Lightfoot looked up at me. "Get me another beer, will ya?"

When I returned with the beer, his head was bowed and he was running his fingers through his hair. I handed him the beer.

"Ask her mother," he said to Wolf.

"Her mother's dead."

Lawrence grinned. "Yeah, I forgot. I killed her. You better not ask her." He took a swallow of beer and mentally disappeared somewhere. After a moment, he came back. "Her mother was a little crazy in the head. They told me Anna was crazy like that, too. You ever hear that?"

"Who told you she was crazy?"

"This nice little white girl came up yesterday. Said she was a friend of Anna's. I never heard nothing like it. Said Jesus would take care of Anna." Lawrence didn't laugh or smile. "I told her it was nice of her to say that. I said, 'If Jesus takes care of her, he's one fine fellow.'" He turned to Wolf and shook his head. "Don't believe it, though. Do you?"

Wolf just sighed.

"I told her it was nice of her to say that."

"She said Anna was crazy?" I asked.

Lawrence shrugged. "She gave me this long story about devils and demons and shit like that. From the sound of it, she was crazy enough. You boys know Anna? Was she crazy?"

"A little bit," Wolf said.

"A little bit? Everybody's crazy a little bit. That don't tell me nothing. What you boys want?"

"We're looking for another friend of Anna's," Wolf said.

The corners of Lawrence's mouth went up again. "Sounds like she had *lots* of friends, for all the good it did her. Anyway, you boys better go back where you came from. No friend of Anna's ever looked *me* up. Except that nice girl."

"What's her name?"

"I think it was Joan."

"Joanna?"

"Yeah, Joanna. Hell of a nice girl. You think she really was a friend of Anna's?"

"Yes."

Lawrence made another one of his disappearances somewhere behind his eyebrows. "Anna's mother was a nice girl, too," he said finally. "When I think of it, she was a nice girl, too." Something seemed to occur to him. "I saw a friend of Anna's a while back. He asked me about her mother. Came to Stony Mountain all the way from Toronto."

"How long ago?" I asked.

Lawrence grinned. "I forget the date. Don't ask me to remember, sonny. When you do time, you forget things. Time just rolls up into this big ball and swallows you up."

"Who was it?"

"I forget his name, too. A Jewish boy, I think."

I remembered the name Anna had mentioned to me. "Reuben?"

"Could have been. Like I say, I can't remember."

"What did he ask you about?"

"Anna's mother. Wanted to know all about her — what she did before we got married, who she fucked, you know. One thing I told him, and I'll tell you, too. She was no whore. She was no cheap, fucking, two-dollar whore."

"Why'd he ask you those questions?"

"'Cause he's like you. Nosy." Lawrence cackled.

"He give any reasons for seeing you?"

"He probably did. I forget 'em. They were all bullshit, anyway. The same as if you gave me reasons for coming up. They'd be bullshit, too. And I forget 'em just as quick. Maybe quicker, 'cause I'm older and what's left of my brain is going fast."

I decided to change the subject. "What else did Joanna say to you?"

"She left a scrapbook of Anna's. Said I should have it. Said it belonged to me because I'm her father." He snorted. "Her *father*."

"Can we see it?"

"It's on the kitchen counter."

I went and fetched it. It was the book Joanna had shown me, all right. I opened it and flipped through the pages. There were a lot of sketches, pen-and-ink drawings, and comments like the one I had read in Elliston. And then I saw a drawing of LeRoy. It was unmistakable. He had the same sardonic smile I remembered from Willow Crest, the same expression wavering between amusement and contempt. Anna must have been a hell of a good draftswoman. Underneath his portrait, in swirly letters decorated with flowers and butterflies, was the message, "For the mitey Reuben, from his girl freind forever, Anna."

I heard a whisper from the living room. Lawrence was getting impatient.

When I returned with the book, he pursed his lips. "That's my book. She gave it to me." As he felt the book in his hands, he relaxed. "Come all the way up here to give it to me. 'What the hell good's it to me?' I asked her. She said you could read Anna's soul in this book. Can you beat that? You can read her soul, right in this book. Just look at some of these drawings." He spread the book on his lap and thumbed through the pages. Occasionally he lingered over a page and admired a drawing. "I knew a fellow at Stony Mountain could draw almost as good as this, but he was a mean son of a bitch." Then he stared at a drawing of the sun bursting through some clouds. "Look at that." He shook his head. "Ever see anything like it? These drawings are worth money, I bet. Look at this, a deer. Look at the antlers. Isn't that something? Little Indian girl drawing like that."

When he got to the page with LeRoy's picture, I asked him if that was the man who had visited him years ago. He looked at it for a minute.

"Could be. I'm not sure, but it could be. What's it say here?" Lawrence moved his lips as he read Anna's inscription. "She was way too young for that girlfriend stuff. Guys like this — what's his name? — Reuben, they just took advantage. You knew him?"

"Yes."

"What kind of a no-good white scumbag was he?"

"He didn't harm her, if that's what you're asking."

Lawrence looked at me for a moment and then turned away. No use getting worked up now, his face said. No use at all. Wolf said something to him in Ojibway.

"Why should I give you the book?"

"Just overnight. We'll bring it back tomorrow morning."

Lawrence's face broke into a delighted smile, his eyes closed, and he thrust his tongue out for a second. Then he opened his eyes again. "Who you talking to? A little boy? I'll tell you who you're talking to. You're talking to Lawrence Lightfoot, jailbird. The wise old con. Nobody bullshits the wise old con, especially with *that* kind of bullshit."

"No bullshit, Lawrence," Wolf said.

"You're damn right. No bullshit. This book stays with me."

Wolf and I headed for the door; it was obvious we wouldn't get any more information from the man. Lawrence put the book down on the sofa and got up to follow us. At the doorway he shook hands with us. A troubled look passed over his face. "If she's dead, she's better off. Look at me, boys. I died, oh, about fourteen years ago. It's not bad. I died and they buried me. They rolled a stone over my body and said a few prayers and laid me to rest. Goodbye, Lawrence, it was nice knowing you." He grinned. "Then it got crowded there and they had to dig me up. They had to throw some of the garbage out. So it was goodbye, Lawrence, park your carcass somewhere else. And here I am, boys. Moving my bones around just like a living person."

"See you later, Lawrence," Wolf said.

We got into the car and drove a few miles to the house of an

Ojibway family where Wolf had arranged to spend the night. En route I told Wolf about my discovery in Anna's book. It wasn't only confirmation that LeRoy had been close to Anna, but suggested — if "Reuben" was more than just another nickname he had picked up — that he had at one point assumed virtually a different identity. Reuben. I felt as if I had a glimpse into a whole new landscape with this discovery, with a new cast of characters. It probably wasn't a pleasant landscape, but then the other landscapes I'd been wandering in recently hadn't been very nice, either.

After dinner Wolf told our hosts about my quest for Anna Lightfoot. He didn't give them all the details about why I had been looking for her, of course, just enough to let them know I was serious. The man had little to say, but his wife, Lois, had lots. She had known Anna's mother, Evelyn Lightfoot — née Laframboise — very well, which is why Wolf had decided to spend the night here. Lois was a tough old bird, plump and bright-eyed, someone who had cheerfully battled for decades with employers, loan officers, car dealers, and unemployment insurance counselors.

She had an inexhaustible store of anecdotes about Evelyn, but only one seemed useful to me. It came out toward the end of the evening when the four of us, she and her husband, Wolf and I, had long since finished our coffee and there was a small mound of cigarette butts in her ashtray. She leaned forward in her armchair, with the last cigarette of the day between her fingers.

"Evelyn used to say to me, 'Just between the two of us and the doorpost, Lois, my girl is something special. If I told you about her real dad, it would knock your socks off.'"

"What did she mean by that?" I asked.

Lois shrugged. "She never said. I never pushed it, either. I figured she was either talking to make herself feel good or else there was something to it, and if there was something to it, she'd tell me when she felt like it. Unfortunately she got her head bashed in before that happened."

"You had no idea who her real father was?"

"Near as I could figure out, it was somebody she met while she was down at that Bible college in Toronto. Anna was born a few months after she came back from there."

"Did she mean Anna's father was famous, or some kind of big shot?"

Again Lois shrugged. "Maybe. Or maybe she meant he was one of those UFO aliens who get earthlings pregnant. It was hard to say with Evelyn. She wasn't quite right in the head by that time."

The next morning I made a few phone calls to Toronto and discovered that Evelyn Laframboise's Bible college had moved to a town north of Toronto. The college archives were at this new location. I figured, since the college was on our way back to the city, we might as well stop and check them out. It wasn't top priority — what I found in Anna's scrapbook had that distinction — but it would be easy enough and, to tell the truth, intriguing to poke around in the college archives. Those reporter's instincts again — the instincts, in other words, of a snoop and a gossip. Maybe one of Evelyn's classmates really was a famous person. Maybe that famous person really was Anna's real father. And just maybe, although I had serious doubts on this point, that famous person had something to tell us about Anna, or even Anna and Reuben.

Over the phone I told the college librarian I was researching a magazine article about the tragedy of Lawrence Lightfoot — the all-too-typical story of a wasted Indian life, et cetera — and was interested in checking the dates when his murdered wife had attended the college. She let us have the run of the archives when we arrived. I took a look not only at Laframboise's own class list, but the lists of several classes before and after hers, just to make sure I didn't miss any likely, now famous Bible student who might have planted his seed where he shouldn't have. In the list of the class two years ahead of Laframboise, I found the one name I recognized. Bennett Kellogg, a well-known preacher who headed the Ontario equivalent of the Moral Majority, an intrepid foe of homosexual militants, English teachers who taught naughty literature, and secular humanists. Evelyn would certainly have knocked the socks off a lot of people if she had revealed that he was the father of her child.

I mentioned to the librarian my agreeable surprise that the well-known Bennett Kellogg was an alumnus of her institution, and she told me Kellogg was speaking at a suburban Toronto church that same evening. If we hurried, we could get there in time for his appearance. Once again I thought, why not? It was on our way. Wolf agreed, and we pulled into the church parking lot, after driving all afternoon, about five minutes before Kellogg's scheduled talk.

The ushers at the church smiled at us and helped us to a pew at the back. The church was built like an auditorium, with the pulpit on a stage in front of a curtain. Almost exactly on cue a man in a three-piece suit introduced Kellogg to the congregation. Kellogg was tall and robust, with a powder-blue suit that complemented his gray eyes and curly gray hair.

"My friends," he began, "I could start off by saying that ever since I made the decision to commit my life to Christ I've never felt discouraged or confused." He paused slightly. "Then again I could also tell you it's just great to be a fan of the Toronto Argonauts." A small, thin wave of chuckling from the audience lapped at his feet. He paused again and grinned. "Let's see, what other lies can I tell you?"

Then he launched into his address, which wasn't on anything controversial but had to do, I gathered, with missionary efforts. Something about a boat full of missionaries off the coast of South America that was a great "soul winner," and then something about a poor, dogged missionary in India who had been living in a village of mud huts for twenty years and hadn't made a single convert. Even speaking about discouragement and failure, Kellogg was vibrant and dynamic. In his line of work you had to be.

After he finished, and after he had answered some questions from the floor, we waited patiently while various members of the congregation chatted with him, patted him on the arm, soaked in a little dynamism and vibrancy. Eventually the crowd of admirers thinned out, and I introduced myself, giving him the line about my doing an article on Lawrence Lightfoot. He looked at his watch and told me he could give me five or ten minutes. We went to a small office just outside the auditorium.

"What magazine did you say you were with?" he asked me.

"*Toronto Life,*" I lied.

"You're writing this and you hope to sell it to them?"

"I don't live on hopes, Mr. Kellogg. It's commissioned."

"I see." He nodded. "Well, I can't say as I understand what you're trying to do, but go ahead and ask your questions."

It was clear he was giving me his Total Attention. Close up I found myself wishing he would dim his personal dynamism just a bit.

"Did you know Evelyn Laframboise?"

"Evie . . . Evie Laframboise." He pronounced the last syllable of her name as if it were the capital of Idaho. "A very nice girl, but I didn't know her very well. I just saw her in the halls, that sort of thing."

"Did she have a lot of friends?"

"Oh, yes." He nodded and looked me straight in the eye. "At least I think so. Very nice girl." He looked at the ceiling. "Yes, I think she was very well liked."

"Any close friends?"

"Wouldn't know. Sorry."

"Any boyfriends?"

The gray eyes gave me more Total Attention than ever, but not quite so friendly this time. "Again Mr. — I'm sorry, I've forgotten your name."

"Murphy."

"I wouldn't know, Mr. Murphy. I only had eyes for a student in my own year. My wife, Charmaine."

"Well, Laframboise became pregnant while she was at the college. She must have had at least one close friend."

"If you're asking me who the father was, I haven't the faintest idea. Honest to goodness, Mr. Murphy, what are these questions all about?"

I muttered something about trying to understand what had happened to her, et cetera. Kellogg stood up. The interview was over.

"You know, I like to make myself accessible to the media. I find it pays to be as straight as you can. What you fellows do with what I say is your business. You have your job and I have mine. But I'm not big on personal gossip."

Then he smiled again and offered me his hand as we left the office. I thanked him for his time.

That night Wolf and I stayed at Mose's house. I dreamed about LeRoy again, and when I woke up, I spent a long time thinking about him. Sad memories of the past came and went, memories of Willow Crest, memories of our curious friendship. I thought of him, and Pete Dalzell, too, men whose deaths had been logical outcomes of some terrible refusal to break a silence that dogged them. I knew for certain, for example, that if Dalzell had allowed himself a howl of pain, words for his outrage, he would be alive today. And as for LeRoy, there must have been something he could have told me, some secret, old or new, that might have broken the spell of his isolation. Perhaps the night I saw him for the last time he was ready to tell me. And I had put him off, fatally.

Eventually I drifted back to sleep. When I awoke, it was midmorning. I decided it was time to call Shelley Rheingold and find out if she knew anything about my current legal status. It was a Sunday and I caught her at home, and from the sound of her voice she hadn't been out of bed much longer than I had. Over the phone I heard her boyfriend Norman coughing in the background. Norman was an engineer who was so socially conscious he recommended I read Mikhail Sholokhov's *And Quiet Flows the Don,* his idea of great socially conscious literature. I found the novel about as exciting as a new hydroelectric dam. But I forgave Shelley for loving a socially conscious engineer. She was a good lawyer and could be forgiven a great deal, especially by a client in my circumstances.

"You wouldn't happen to know if there's a warrant out for my arrest?" I asked.

She took the question in stride. "Not that I'm aware of, Heywood. But hadn't you better start explaining to me why you think there would be a warrant for your arrest?"

I explained. It took a while, but I think I told most of the story in a reasonably coherent and unemotional fashion. I was getting pretty good at it by now. When I got to the part about discovering LeRoy's body, she was incredulous and cross-examined me about every conceivable detail. When I told her about my conversation with Staigue, she was plainly put out.

"You know, Heywood, lawyers were invented for things like this. Talking to the police without one is dumb."

"I realize," I said contritely.

"And you further realize you're going to need a lawyer from here on, don't you? If there's no warrant for your arrest right now, there'll probably be one very soon." She sighed in exasperation. "Fortunately there's probably not a lot of pressure on the cops for this one. Just be glad you're not a suspect in the rape and murder of a child, or some bright young female university student. You know, pretty, vivacious, great future ahead of her, et cetera. Your friend LeRoy sounds like some guy nobody gives a damn about. Or no city editors or TV news producers, which is what we're really talking about."

"Lucky me. By the way, I found out recently LeRoy used to have another name, which might make him more interesting. He used to call himself Reuben."

"Reuben? Was that a first or last name?"

"Don't know." There was a long pause at the other end of the line. "Shelley? You there?"

"Tell you what, Heywood. Want to meet me at my office this afternoon?"

We made an appointment for three o'clock. I informed my friends, of course, and then called a cab when the time came. On the way I kept turning around and looking out the back window of the taxi, as if somebody were following me. I didn't know what was getting into me. Nervous breakdown or paranoia. But then I remembered I had accused LeRoy of the same thing. And whatever he had been feeling, it wasn't paranoia. There was his corpse to prove it.

Shelley's office was in an old four-story building on Spadina Avenue near King Street. On the first floor was a store selling the kind of hats with narrow brims that old men wear to racetracks. Shelley's office on the second floor came with creaking wooden floors and high plaster ceilings with water stains. You could be sure, walking into this office, that you weren't about to deal with a lawyer soiled with fees from corporations that polluted the environment or oppressed Guatemalan peasants.

When I walked into Shelley's office, she handed me a yearbook from a private school whose name I happened to recognize. I also happened to know it specialized in educating two categories of adolescents. The first consisted of kids from Hong Kong, carrying suitcases full of dollar bills en route to permanent residence in Canada. The second consisted of problem adolescents — kids who would likely be in much less pleasant institutions if their families didn't happen to be very rich.

"Look up Salinger in the senior class photos," she said.

I did. And there he was. Charles LeRoy. Only his name in this photo was Reuben David Salinger. Class nickname, "Ruby." Extracurricular activities, none. Favorite saying, "But, Teach, didn't you get my paper? I put it right there on your desk this morning." I don't know how long I stared at that photograph, but I didn't look up until Shelley asked, "Is that your man?"

"Yes. How'd you find him?"

"You remember when you mentioned the Rothbards to me? I couldn't get over that. It stuck in my mind. I kept asking myself what somebody like Heywood Murphy, no offense, could be doing with that crew. When you mentioned the name Reuben to me, it clicked."

"What?"

"Guess who Reuben David Salinger's sister is?"

"Lydia Rothbard."

"You got it, kid. Lydia Rothbard, née Salinger. I knew both of them when they were kids." She took a deep breath. "You're a suspect in the murder of Solomon Rothbard's brother-in-law."

"Except nobody seems to know that except you and me."

"I was thinking before you came, Heywood, that if your friend LeRoy did turn out to be the Reuben I remember, our next step might be to call the Rothbards."

"I can't believe this is Sol Rothbard's brother-in-law. LeRoy was a rat from the sewer compared to Rothbard. They just weren't on the same planets."

She shrugged. "The Salingers are almost as loaded as the Rothbards. They just produced a son who was bent way out of shape. It happens."

"Well, give Sol and Lydia a call. I can't think of anything better to do."

Unfortunately I'd left the sheet of paper with their phone number at my apartment, and I didn't dare go back for it. Shelley, however, knew a friend of her mother's who worshiped at the same synagogue as the Rothbards and was also friendly with them. She got hold of him and gave him a line about legal matters connected with Beth Yehuda. She did it very convincingly. Lawyers, even my dear Shelley, seem to have a knack for sliding around untruths.

After she hung up, she did a little drumroll with her fingertips on the surface of her desk, took a deep breath, and then punched out the number. I walked out of her office and sat down in a chair in the waiting room next to a glass case containing five volumes of *Wigmore on Evidence*. I flipped through a copy of a magazine on a nearby table — obviously a socially conscious journal, judging by the picture on the cover, which looked like a crude woodprint of a woman being devoured by an oil refinery. I heard her say, "Mr. Rothbard? This is Shelley Rheingold." And then she lowered her voice. Ten minutes later she emerged from the office.

"They want to meet us right away." She gave me a critical look. "I hate to say this, Heywood, but do you think you could lay your hands on a freshly ironed shirt?"

She was touching a sore spot. As a reporter, I had accepted the dress code of the newsroom, which was the more casual and rumpled the look the better. Only the music and dance critic wore blazers and wool pants with a sharp crease, and he was fussy about everything. At one point, post-Willow Crest, I got the idea my self-improvement program might include an upgrading of my wardrobe, and I began by buying a pair of Bass Weejuns at a price I couldn't afford because I remembered somebody telling me that maître d's always judged customers by their footwear. But I hadn't gotten much further in my sartorial ambitions when LeRoy was murdered, and now I was back to wearing jeans, a green corduroy jacket, white athletic socks, and a scuffed pair of black loafers that were starting to come apart on me.

We did manage to get to a men's clothing store and buy a new shirt for me, however, before we drove to our rendezvous, an office building in the north end of Toronto. The building was an ordinary thirty-story office tower in the middle of an industrial park. Rothbard had told Shelley he wanted to meet us in this building, perhaps because it was vacant and would be deader than a mausoleum.

"What exactly did you tell Rothbard?" I asked Shelley as we approached the building.

"Only that we have information about Reuben."

Inside the lobby of the building a security guard sat behind a table. Shelley signed the book in front of him and told him the two of us would wait in the lobby for Mr. Rothbard. The guard said nothing. He was old and fat and had watery blue eyes that weren't too happy with what they saw. Shelley and I waited for about five minutes until Rothbard showed up in a cab. He stepped into the lobby, with his dark blue suit, white shirt and tie, his brisk and yet slightly weary air. "How are you doing, Jerry?" he asked the guard softly as he signed the book.

Jerry cleared his dusty throat, coughed, and replied in an even softer voice, "Not bad, Mr. Rothbard."

The three of us ascended in the elevator to the top floor. When we got out of the elevator, Rothbard led us to a nearby office. It was almost empty except for a desk, a few chairs, a bookshelf with stacks of empty looseleaf binders, and a painting on the wall of some circles and rhomboids in bilious shades of pink, orange, and blue. Rothbard sat behind the desk, eyed the painting, and shook his head. "Didn't know that was still here."

"One of your Russian avant-gardes?" I asked.

"That," he said with a sigh, "is an early Rothbard, circa 1966." He smiled. "There are no middle or late Rothbards. The painter realized very quickly he was not destined to become the Canadian Malevich or Rodchenko."

"Why those painters, Mr. Rothbard?" Shelley asked.

"Physics."

"Physics?"

"Particle physics . . . cosmology . . ." He shrugged. "An interest of mine. I found the same kind of interest — the same dynamics of space and relation of forces — in their work."

"Nothing to do with the Russian Revolution?" Shelley asked.

I could tell she wanted to get the real story on Rothbard's radicalism. Solving a murder had its place in the scheme of things, and so did gossip.

"For a few months, when I was fifteen, I was enchanted by Trotsky's theory of permanent revolution," he said. "Then a cousin told me to read Karl Popper. The perfect antidote to totalitarian dreams of grandeur, he said, and he was right."

"Nice to know the Monarch of Malls isn't a raving Bolshevik," I said.

Rothbard rubbed his face with his hands and then sat back in his chair. "Miss Rheingold, I'm sorry to say I never met your late father, but I was aware of his excellent business and personal reputation."

"Where's Mrs. Rothbard?" I asked.

"I will deal with this, Mr. Murphy."

"The information concerns Mrs. Rothbard. She should be here."

"I said I will deal with this. I will decide whether or not she should be here."

Shelley put a hand on my arm. "Hal, why don't you just ask Mr. Rothbard what we came to ask?"

"All right. Lydia's brother — do you know where he is, Mr. Rothbard?"

Rothbard stared at me. There was anger and unhappiness in his stare, and returning it was making my corneas hurt. He didn't make a move; indeed, he seemed to stop breathing. But he was thinking hard. This was a man who probably didn't stop thinking hard until five minutes after he was asleep.

"No, Mr. Murphy, I don't."

"Does Lydia know?"

He shook his head.

"When was the last time either of you heard from him?"

"I thought Miss Rheingold said you were the ones who were going to provide information."

"Just this question, please. I want to make sure of something."

"Lydia last heard from him about eighteen months ago."

I looked at Shelley, and she handed me her attaché case. I opened it, took out the yearbook, and flipped the pages. "They tell me you graduated from Forest Hill Collegiate shortly after the war. One of our fine public high schools. Is that true, Mr. Rothbard?" I asked as I thumbed through the yearbook.

Rothbard said nothing.

"If it's true, then there's a handy way to check up on you. Suppose, for example, the CIA wants to make sure you're really Solomon Rothbard and not some international drug baron using the name as a cover. They'd just look up your old Forest Hill yearbook. It's the kind of record that can't be falsified. That's how we got hold of your brother-in-law's yearbook. Of course, this particular institution doesn't always put out yearbooks because the students are too busy with cocaine and reckless driving, but we got lucky. The year your brother-in-law graduated they had one."

I showed Rothbard the page with Salinger's photograph. He was grinning in the photograph. He looked smart and confident and ready to do anything and go anywhere. Rothbard glanced at it, then looked up at me, puzzled and wary. "Where is Reuben?"

"He's dead, Mr. Rothbard. At the time of his death he was living in Toronto under the name of Charles LeRoy."

"How do you know this?"

"I remember that time I was in your house. There was a framed photograph in the second-floor study. One of the people in that photo was wearing a hat. I didn't study that photo, but enough of it stayed in my memory, and part of what stayed was that hat. I later made the connection. It was just like the hat LeRoy used to wear. If I had actually looked closely at the photo in your house, I'm sure I would have recognized LeRoy."

"I'm not following you, Mr. Murphy."

"I made the connection after Shelley showed me this yearbook. Reuben David Salinger is the same man I knew who had been living and working in Toronto under the name of Charles LeRoy. I have no doubt whatsoever." I paused, not for effect, but because I suddenly realized, in a strange way, the significance of what I was about to say. "He ended up murdered in his apartment more than a week ago."

"You're sure about this? Absolutely?"

"That's what I said."

"Who killed him? And why?"

"I don't know. And neither do the police."

Rothbard leaned forward and covered his face with his hands.

He was silent for a moment, then he straightened and stared at me. "How did you meet her brother?"

"It's a long story. We met at Willow Crest a few months ago. That's a clinic for alcoholics, Mr. Rothbard. I was an unemployed newspaperman and he was a clerk at City Hall on sabbatical. He was trying to take the cure, like the rest of us. We became friends. We got together a few times afterward. One night a couple of weekends ago I went to his apartment to see him. I discovered his body." I saw no reason to go into certain complications of the evening.

"Was it a gun?" Rothbard asked.

I swallowed. "Knife."

Rothbard took in a sudden breath of air.

"I'm sorry. I'm very, very sorry," I said to the circles and rhomboids.

Rothbard shook his head. "The police would have discovered his identity by now. They would have found out the name LeRoy was an alias."

"Why would they have found out? His body was identified by myself and Theresa, his girlfriend. He may even have had a birth certificate in his wallet when he died."

"That's what I mean," Rothbard said, his voice tightly wound now. "The police would have found out it was a false ID."

"No, they wouldn't. Because the man who originally belonged to that ID has probably vanished." This was the man whose family history Dr. Glinsk had read to me, the man Chris Lang had told me about, the man who Anna thought had gone back to New Brunswick. He had been a street hustler who cast no shadows, made no friends — a vacant identity ready for Reuben Salinger to step into. All the more ready since the two men must have been about the same height, the same build, the same hair and eye color.

"Who was the real Charles LeRoy?" Rothbard asked.

"All I know is that he was born in New Brunswick, came to Toronto sometime in his early teens, hung around Yonge Street, did a few hustles, and disappeared some time ago. His existence can be documented. The place and date of his birth, some vital statistics, his residence at certain foster homes, attendance at various schools in Toronto and New Brunswick. But after the age of sixteen, zip. No school, no fixed address, no known employment."

"All they'd have to do is check dental records."

"Why would they bother? There was no reason to assume he was anybody but the guy he was identified as."

"I still can't believe it."

Silence came over the room. Rothbard said he didn't believe what I was telling him, but he knew it was possible. I had the feeling he knew anything was possible with his late brother-in-law.

"I've told you about as much as I know about the true and false LeRoy. You'll have to tell me something about your brother-in-law, Mr. Rothbard."

He picked up a letter opener on the desk and began to play with it. "Mrs. Rothbard would be a better source of information. But I can tell you all you need to know. He was nasty a good deal of the time and charming at other times. He could hurt you a lot if you trusted him, and some people did trust him — girls, women. He was very persuasive, you see." He smiled. "He could have done all right in my business. For a while. But he just couldn't stop himself from hurting people." He pointed the letter opener at me. "Would you say this was true of your . . . friend LeRoy?"

"Yes."

"I see. Anyway, my brother-in-law, among other curious ideas he entertained, truly believed that no one had a right to stop him from doing what he wanted to do. He could drive a car over someone's lawn, smash windows, do far worse things, and nobody had the right to touch him. And usually nobody did touch him."

"Who did he run with?"

"The most unfortunate young people imaginable. Prostitutes, junior dope dealers, and con artists." He smiled again. "Do you know Reuben once showed me how you persuade a cashier to give you the wrong change? I mean, so you end up with ten or twenty dollars more than you should?" He shook his head. "It's quite something. I think they call it flimflamming."

"Street kids."

"Yes. Every half-grown child who had nothing to live on but his wits. Reuben and these ... adolescents had the same way of looking at things. Only Reuben had money. Which made him, of course, much more of a danger to himself and others. He once hired a thug to beat up a teacher who failed him. He had the money to do it. Do you understand what that does to a thirteen-year-old kid who doesn't have much conscience to start with?"

I understood. I also understood that there was a part of Reuben, a tiny part maybe, that recognized and respected the good in people. The part that sometimes drew pictures of those people. Like the picture he had drawn of me showing a spiritual quality I had never had but wanted to get, and a picture of Terri showing a quality she had lost but wanted to keep.

"Did Reuben have friends in his own social level? Classmates and so on?"

"Oh, yes. He had friends on 'his own social level,' as you put it. Other children without principles, without direction, without conscience." He shrugged. "Children brought up, let's say, by a dozen or so nannies, who evidently failed in their duties."

"Was Ivan Lusk one of them?"

Rothbard gave me a sharp glance. He seemed incapable of appearing nervous, but I had the feeling the mention of Lusk's name had just done funny things to his metabolism.

"What brings his name up?"

"LeRoy had something that belonged to Lusk when he died."

"What?"

"A ring."

"Are you sure it was Lusk's?"

"Lusk identified it himself."

Rothbard thought this one over for a moment.

"Does Lusk know anything about LeRoy's . . . real identity?"

"I don't believe so."

Rothbard went back to toying with the letter opener for a minute or so. Finally he spoke in a soft, almost inaudible voice.

"I suppose you'll find out for yourself. Ivan did know Reuben. They had a very strange relationship. Ivan was the fat kid who got beaten up by kids like Reuben. The fact that he was reading Gibbon's *Decline and Fall of the Roman Empire* at the age of fifteen was sufficient reason."

"What was Reuben's interest in Ivan?"

Rothbard paused again before answering. "Reuben delighted in . . . I suppose you might say, corrupting Ivan."

"How?"

"I don't know the details. I don't think it was drugs or alcohol or cruising on the highway at more than a hundred miles an hour. Ivan had much more of an instinct for self-preservation than that. And, of course, he wasn't interested in money."

"That leaves just about one other area."

Rothbard nodded. "I think Reuben introduced Ivan to some . . . female companions. Girls who came from the street."

Yes, I thought. Young girls. Some of them very young. Twelve, thirteen years old. Girls like Anna Lightfoot, who in the slow collapse and crumbling of her sanity clung to fragments of memories, dreams of love made a long time ago on tennis courts with a young man of charm and wealth and a confident grin.

"Did Reuben ever mention someone named Anna Lightfoot?"

Rothbard shook his head.

"Jimmy Walrath?"

"A pimp?"

"Yes. I'm surprised, Rothbard. You must know a fair bit about Reuben."

"Lydia knew. And she has been communicative."

"What did she say about Walrath?"

"Nothing much. Apparently Reuben admired this gentleman.

And Reuben admired very few people, believe me. But Walrath exceeded even Reuben in vicious and outrageous behavior, and so, in a manner of speaking, extorted admiration from Reuben."

"Did Ivan know Walrath, too?"

"I doubt it. I think Walrath would have been a bit too much for Ivan."

"What about a man named Peter Hagedorn?"

Rothbard thought for a moment, then shook his head.

"So what was Reuben doing eighteen months ago?"

"He left home with an American Express Gold Card in his wallet. He said he wanted to travel for a few months. Many of us, I'm sorry to say, were rather pleased at the prospect."

"Did he go alone?"

"As far as I know."

"Where was he going?"

"South America. He started out in Mexico and worked his way down."

"Where was the last place you heard from him?"

"Brazil. Lydia got a couple of postcards from Manaus three months after he left."

"Do you remember what they said?"

"If I remember correctly, he said in one that he thought Brazil was 'another greaseball-and-jigaboo haven.' His words, of course. He said he liked the Amazon, though. He liked to go for boat rides and look for piranha. He was joking, I think."

"Did your brother-in-law have an interest in things like umbanda, macumba, voodoo, et cetera?"

Rothbard groaned. "What is *that* about? No, don't tell me. I don't want to know. That sort of amusement was one thing I thought he was innocent of."

I shrugged. "He might have been. I'm just asking."

"So tell me, what's your next area of inquiry?"

"That's it, Mr. Rothbard. For the moment, anyway."

Nobody said anything for a few minutes. Unspoken sorrows lay heavy in the room like sour humidity. Out of the weight of this humidity Rothbard's voice spoke again. "And what do you think happened to Reuben?"

Both he and Shelley looked at me as if I knew the answer.

"I don't know. I have a few ideas. I think somewhere in his travels he met the real Charles LeRoy. I think they knew each other before, although I guess, from what you told me, he never mentioned his name to you or Lydia."

"Not that I can recall."

"Anyway, it's possible they set out together, or maybe they just bumped into each other. At some point they traveled together. And at some point LeRoy died. Or disappeared. It's easy to do in those countries. North American drifters are particularly vulnerable. They look rich to the natives and nobody misses them for a long time. After LeRoy made his exit, your brother was left with his passport, his ID. It must have intrigued him. Except for the passport photo, the identification could just as well fit him as LeRoy. Maybe it gave him an idea. He could return to Toronto, but as a different person. Start a life where nobody knew him. He didn't have to worry about running into LeRoy's old buddies. LeRoy didn't have any. As for his own buddies, Reuben probably had a pretty good idea how to avoid them. Plus a change of hairstyle, dress — it wouldn't have been hard for him to melt back into the city."

"Why would he want to do that?" Rothbard asked.

"That's what I don't know. It might depend on why he left Toronto in the first place. Was he in trouble?"

"Reuben was always in trouble. That didn't bother him. He always got out of it."

"I mean big trouble. Do you remember what state he was in before he left? Any special agitation?"

"I can't say. If I try to remember, I seem to recall he may have been a little agitated, but that might be my imagination. It's hard to tell. It's been a while. And he was very good at not revealing what he felt. What trouble do you think he was in?"

"I think something very bad happened. Very bad." I stood up. I had the feeling now that very little could be accomplished anymore in this office. "I'm sorry about your brother-in-law, Mr. Rothbard. We became friends in the short time I knew him. At least I think I became as good a friend as he would have allowed anyone to become. We liked each other. It seemed to me he'd gone through a lot. He'd changed. The feeling that no one had a right to touch him had gone." I paused for a moment, remembering the man I knew as Charles LeRoy in his room at Willow Crest. "He knew people could touch him."

"Now what shall we do, Miss Rheingold?" Rothbard asked.

"Nothing for the time being."

Rothbard got up from behind the desk, a little smile on his face. "Sounds like the advice I usually get. Most of the time it's quite sound." Rothbard then looked at me. His voice was dry. Certain emotions within him had been successfully banked. What was left was a mind exquisitely tuned to weighing and calculating the ponderables of life. In most cases that mind gave him a clear superiority over other mortals he encountered in this vale of tears. I think he was content now simply to fall back on that instrument of superiority.

"I want to be kept in touch with what happens. Closely in touch. Do you understand me? I won't call the police. But I will be informed."

"Yes, of course," I said.

"I've been forthcoming here. In return I want information, as well, since this affects my family intimately."

"We understand," Shelley said.

"Good. Shall we go now?"

We left the office and took the elevator to the first floor. In the lobby we heard a light snore from the guard, who was slumped in his chair. As we were about to step out the front door, Rothbard stopped. "This umbanda business you mentioned."

"Yes?"

"Reuben did write something on a postcard — I forget where, but it was probably Brazil — about 'cuttin' up chickens and shakin' all over.' I think that's what he wrote. Does that sound like your umbanda?"

"Sort of."

"What does it mean? That he really engaged in that kind of practice?"

"I don't know. But I think so."

Rothbard shook his head. "Merciful Lord help us all."

9

SHELLEY DROPPED me off downtown after I assured her that I had a safe and comfortable place to stay, with my friends Wolf and Malcolm Kelly. But I didn't go back to my friends. Instead, I hailed a cab and headed for Lusk's house. I had an almost physical craving for information at this point: information on why LeRoy, or Salinger, had left Toronto. Lusk might not be the right man to ask these questions, but he seemed an awfully good candidate. And although I had promised Wolf we would act in concert from now on, there was no way I could bring Wolf to Lusk's house. If Lusk was going to tell me anything, he would only tell it to me alone.

The maid answered the door. I gave my name and she went off somewhere and returned in five minutes. "Mr. Lusk says he's occupied at the moment. Call his secretary tomorrow and you can set up a meeting at a more appropriate time."

Behind her I heard someone say, "Adele? What's happening?" Mrs. Lusk appeared, wearing tight-fitting black wool slacks and a silver-blue blouse with a pearl necklace. As soon as she recognized me, she gave me a look of pure loathing.

"What do you want?" she demanded.

"I want to speak to your husband, Mrs. Lusk."

"You're intruding. Get out."

"Mrs. Lusk, just tell Mr. Lusk that a Mr. Murphy has —"

"I know who you are."

"That a Mr. Murphy has information about the murder of Reuben Salinger. I'm sure your husband will be very interested in discussing it."

Mrs. Lusk didn't even blink. She stood there with her spine as straight as a rifle barrel. It made me nervous, but I knew I damn well better not show it. This woman was merciless. Weakness and insecurity were like bad smells as far as she was concerned, and her nose was in perfect order. So we stood there in front of each other, two human bodies working on obscure but powerful principles. Finally she said, "Wait here. I'll talk to Mr. Lusk," and closed the door.

I waited a long time. It was an unpleasant wait because this time I had more reason to think the Lusks might simply call the police, and more reason to fear the results if they did. But she reappeared after a while and told me to follow her. The hallway led directly to a stairway. At the top of the stairway we went down a hall to a room at the end that turned out to be Lusk's study. It was a long room, lit with soft lights behind mahogany valence boards, and it was lined with books on all four sides, from the floor to the ceiling. They weren't Book-of-the-Month Club selections, either — the shelves were crawling with red morocco.

In the center of the room was a heavy rosewood table beneath a skylight. The table had curved lion's paw legs and would have looked at home in the boardroom of an august capitalist institution from the past century. On top of it were some metal battleships of World War II vintage, scale models with elaborate and meticulous detail, down to the hatches and railings on the ladders. At the end of the table there was a bottle of Scotch and an open book. In front of these sat Lusk, who looked at me balefully as I entered the room.

Mrs. Lusk didn't say a word or enter the room; she just closed the door after me. Lusk didn't rise. He took a sip from his glass of Scotch, as if mildly pleased to hear the ice cubes clink, and looked at the open book. "Thucydides," he said, glancing up at me with expressionless eyes. "I was just reading the part where the Athenians discuss the fate of the Mityleneans." He sighed and closed the book. "They knew how to argue a point, the Athenians did. Wonderful political intellects."

"I'm sure."

"You're sure." He took another sip from his glass. "Of course, your colleagues probably think Thucydides is a new form of sexually transmitted disease. But you haven't come here to discuss Athenian history, have you?"

"No. A less edifying subject."

"The murder of Reuben Salinger. What an entrance, Mr. Murphy. It must give you great pleasure to come here flourishing this dramatic piece of news."

"Yeah, I haven't had so much fun since the police interrogated me. You should try discovering a dead body, Lusk. You'll never be at a loss for interesting conversation."

"And just what have you discovered about Salinger?"

"He was living in the city under the name of Charles LeRoy, the very same man I once asked you about. Since then I've found out the most amazing things."

"Oh? Has your friend been using his pipe again?"

"No. This is the kind of information they use in court cases when they're trying to put somebody in prison."

"I see. And you've found out — to your amazement — that Salinger and I used to be friends."

"Yes, indeed." That fact established, I wondered what else Lusk might be able to tell me. I knew that at one point Salinger and Walrath had been friends. But then, at another point, according to Anna, they had become enemies. So I had a suspect. Sort of. Walrath, at some time and for some unknown reason, had come to hate Reuben Salinger. It didn't have to be a big reason. It could have been Salinger making fun of his wardrobe. In any case, Walrath hated the man. And when Walrath hated somebody, he probably felt that was grounds right there for that man to die. I would also bet money that Lusk had an idea why Salinger and Walrath had fallen out. Rothbard's words came back to me. Salinger delighted in Lusk's corruption, too. So there would have been unspoken agreements between the two men, knowledge that implicated and entangled, and yes, I'd bet even more cash that Lusk knew why Salinger had suddenly felt like becoming a tourist.

"Before you get into this, who else knows about this LeRoy business?" Lusk asked, filling his glass again.

"Mr. and Mrs. Rothbard."

Lusk thought that over for a minute. It was obvious the thought gave him no pleasure. "So tell me," he asked, "why did Reuben go to all the trouble of putting on that ludicrous disguise of a City Hall clerk?"

"He was having a little joke. A joke on all his old friends."

"But working at City Hall? For *months*? That's not a joke. That's cruel and unusual punishment. Especially for a man like Reuben."

"All right. It wasn't a joke. There was a reason for it. Let's say Reuben wanted to assume a new identity — maybe because he had big problems with his old one. You were a friend of his. You should have some ideas about that."

"Oh, come now. Reuben's problems were no secret. He was a very bad boy. I confess I found him charming, though."

"Because of his problems, or despite them?"

"Both, I guess."

"That's very interesting. Some of his problems, as I'm sure you know, weren't so charming."

"Which problems?"

"His occasional habit of procuring the sexual services of teenage girls. Also known as pimping."

Lusk looked at me for a moment and then took a drink from his glass. Not a sip this time, a drink. "What do you want, Murphy?" he asked. "Do you want me to tell you all the sordid details about Reuben so you can carry on your personal investigation, which, as far as I can see, has been requested by nobody in particular? Sorry, Murphy. That period of my life is over with, and it's nobody's business now, least of all yourself and your Indian friend with his conduit to the spiritual realm. I haven't seen Salinger since he left, and that's all I have to say. Any other information you might want from me is impertinence."

"Was there a particular reason, by the way, for his leaving? Other than to catch up on some sight-seeing?"

Lusk shrugged. "Reuben didn't have reasons for what he did. That was partly the source of his charm."

"Everybody has reasons for what he does. Some people just hide them better, that's all."

"Reuben hid his exceptionally well. But I said these questions were impertinence and I meant it. You're outwearing your welcome."

"That's one of the risks of trying to pursue nasty subjects, like the question of who wanted to kill Reuben Salinger. You're right, Lusk. Nobody asked me to do this. It sort of fell into my lap. But now I find more and more people are getting interested. I think it's because Salinger did things to people, and they can't forget about it. Usually he had the money or the connections or the gall to get away with what he did, but at one point he just went too far. And then he couldn't buy his way out of it. Or charm his way out of it."

"Oh? And what is 'it'?"

"I was thinking of asking Walrath about that."

"And just who is Walrath?"

"Another pimp you used to know."

Lusk played with his glass some more, filling the silence with the noise of the ice cubes. A slight belch rose from his chest and caused him to pull in his chin, "Whatever it is you're looking for, Walrath won't tell you anything. He's a man of remarkable aplomb. One of the most capable liars I've ever met."

"Coming from you, that's quite a compliment. But it doesn't matter. Walrath is smart enough to know when it's in his interest to tell the truth for a change. Like when it might take the pressure off him — and put it on someone else."

Lusk raised an eyebrow. "Is this an oblique reference to myself?"

"Not necessarily. But it's very strange, this whole business of Salinger taking off like that."

"I'll give you a little clue. One time I saw Walrath and Salinger argue about the point spread in the 1989 Super Bowl. Salinger turned out to be right — amazing memory for some things, that man — and poor Mr. Walrath wasn't gracious in conceding defeat. The language he used — he was positively vituperative. If it had been a hot day in the summer, there could have been bloodshed, for all I know." Lusk shrugged. "So they had a falling out. And possibly Salinger for once in his life was afraid of somebody."

There was a knock on the door. The sound made Lusk look even less happy. "Yes?"

Mrs. Lusk opened the door. She frowned at her husband. It was a very deep frown. She wanted to make absolutely sure her husband wasn't under the impression she was happy, either. "Ivan, tell him to leave."

"Are you worried?" Lusk asked with a tiny hint of amusement.

"Of course I am. Ivan, this is my *house*."

"I've been in houses before, Mrs. Lusk. I'm not going to spit on your carpet or swipe the silverware."

Lusk stood and gave his wife a brief kiss on her forehead. "Murphy, would you excuse us for a moment? I want a word in private with my wife. Wait outside."

I did as I was told. There was nothing else to do. Fifteen minutes later Lusk called me back into the room.

"I agree with my wife, Murphy. You've outworn your welcome. Shall I see you to the door?"

I sighed. There was no point in pushing Lusk further. If he had more information, I wasn't getting it tonight. Not with his wife around.

"How are the renovations going?" I asked on the stairway.

"Splendidly," Lusk said dryly. "I have only one stipulation. No changes to the study." Lusk opened the door to his house and, to my surprise, followed me out. "I want to show you something," he said. "In the garage."

There was nothing in the garage except two cars — a Lincoln and an Oldsmobile. He opened the trunk of the Oldsmobile. There was a spare tire and a jack, and that was it. Lusk cleared his throat. I turned and saw a Smith & Wesson .38 in front of my face.

"I could kill you with this right here, Murphy, if I had the inclination. I could kill you and, I assure you, the consequences for myself would be absolutely minimal. Imagine the scenario. A murder suspect —"

"How do you know I'm a murder suspect?"

"A murder suspect barges into my house, threatens me, et cetera. I tell him to leave, he tries to take a gun out of my hand, I shoot him dead."

"I hope you've had enough Scotch, Ivan. Shooting somebody takes a better set of nerves than you've got wired to your brain stem." I don't know why, but I wasn't particularly frightened of Lusk. I was a little jumpy, mind you. Anybody with functioning hand muscles holding a gun in my direction makes me jumpy. But I couldn't believe Lusk would pull that trigger. I stepped up to him and brushed aside the gun with the back of my hand. I did it slowly and deliberately. Lusk's face went the color of wet Polyfilla, but he didn't resist. "Please put that gun away," I said. "Put it away or I'll break your neck."

Lusk put the gun in his jacket pocket and backed away from me. Suddenly I felt my heart beating. It wasn't beating; it was bouncing up and down inside my chest. But that was okay. My sphincter was tight, my hands were calm, and I wasn't looking at the funny end of a gun anymore. I started to breathe again.

"The gun is a little joke," Lusk said. "I'm sure you realize that."

"Yeah, I could tell by the smile on your face. You're quite a sketch, Ivan."

Cynthia appeared in the garage entrance. Wherever Ivan went, it seemed, she was sure to follow.

"Give me the gun, Ivan," she said. With amazing speed she reached into his pocket, snatched the gun, and aimed it at me. She held it the way some housewives hold bottles of Windex. I was the stain she was going to remove. She didn't even look at her husband. "Get in that trunk."

"I beg your pardon?"

"*Get* in that trunk."

"Mrs. Lusk, I have a brand-new shirt on."

She walked up to me and I examined the set of her mouth, and then her eyes, and then I looked at the gun again and I turned and climbed into the trunk. Lusk jumped forward and pressed the top down on me.

I inhaled a stench of rubber and vinyl, an overwhelming smell of oil and inorganic matter. Someone opened and closed one of the car doors. After a few seconds, another door opened and closed, the engine started, and the car began to move. It kept moving for a long time. The trunk was hardly airtight, so I didn't fear suffocation, but after the first half hour, I had a splitting headache and the muscles in my back and legs tormented me to the point where I began to moan softly for relief. I also picked at the rubber sealant around the edges of the trunk with the jack handle and one free arm, not sure what I was trying to do. The idea, I guess, was to prevent panic with some physical movement.

Two hours later the Oldsmobile stopped and I heard doors open and close. Fifteen minutes later the trunk opened. Walrath stood over me, giggling, holding Lusk's .38. "I didn't think they could pile that much shit into the trunk of an Olds."

Lusk stood by his side, looking miserable. I struggled to get out of the trunk, but my arms and legs felt as if they didn't belong to me anymore. They were stiff, numb appendages that hurt every time they obeyed an order to move. Still, as I managed to climb out, I almost cried for relief. It was a relief that belonged to my body alone. My mind was busy taking in the fact of Walrath and the .38.

Night had fallen, and we were in a gravel parking lot next to a two-story cottage. Obviously it was Lusk's. A chimney stuck out from the roof like a megalith, and there was a veranda in front with wicker chairs overlooking a lake. The waters were quiet under the cool night sky; the woods were an impenetrable darkness, full of living creatures trying to keep as still as possible. Floodlights beneath the roof of the cottage lit up a freshly mowed semicircle of grass in front.

Walrath herded us inside into a living room with a fireplace, cedar walls, and a bar covered in leather, behind which stood Herbert Mellon, a happy grin plastered on his face. Walrath sat on a chair with an adjustable backrest pushed as far as it would go so that he was almost horizontal. His right arm touched the floor near an empty cardboard box with a greasy patch on the top. The box was from a fried chicken take-out place. Walrath wore a green-and-white-striped seersucker suit, a deep blue shirt, and a tie the color of banana cream pie. He seemed to be very relaxed. "Sit down, folks," he said. "Make yourself comfortable."

"Like a drink, Mrs. Lusk?" Mellon asked. "Mr. Lusk?"

Cynthia shook her head,

"Scotch on the rocks," Ivan said.

Mellon handed him the glass, and Lusk moved toward the door. "I'll see you all later. I'm going to —"

"Now don't you go anywhere." Walrath said, sitting bolt upright. "I want Mr. Murphy to hear *all* sides of the story."

Lusk smiled involuntarily. "I'm sure you're perfectly capable of —"

"Come on, sit down. Mrs. Lusk, take a chair, please."

Mrs. Lusk obeyed, sitting on a sofa. Lusk hesitated, then sat beside her.

"You, too, Murphy. Lusk tells me you want to know about Salinger. Is that true now?" he asked the ceiling. "What exactly do you want to know about Reuben Salinger? Just ask Mr. Walrath. He knows everything."

"Why did Salinger decide to go on his South American tour?" I asked. I felt dizzy, hardly able to concentrate on what was happening. Still, I managed to speak. "Did you two have another argument about the Super Bowl?"

"Didn't my girl Annie tell you that? Annie knows."

"She said you wanted to kill him."

"Of course I wanted to kill him. I did, too. I got his blood all over one of my best suits. Remember that suit I bought in New York, Herb? Just ruined it."

"You're putting us on, aren't you?" Lusk said.

"Why wouldn't I want to kill him? He took away my best little girl. She was no skanky whore, either. Fuck, no, she was young stuff. She wasn't mouthy, she did what she was told, and she kept herself clean and presentable. And besides that, I was in love with her. And then that crazy asshole — excuse me, Mrs. Lusk — tried to hide her on me." Walrath sat up in the chair and pointed a finger at me. "I'd say that was cause for serious action. I'd say that meant it was time to break faces. My ladies look up to me, Murphy. Don't you smile, asshole. Somebody works for me, I look after them. When I was in business, I *meant* business." He lay back in his chair. "Old Ivan here said I shouldn't take it personally. But I do take things personally. I'm a person, ain't I? Aren't I? Ivan said he'd make it up to me. I said, 'Lusk, you . . . callous individual, who do you think I am? You think that girl is nothing to me but a negotiable asset? That's a human being you're talking about.' Same's true of all my girls. They're trash, but they're *my* trash, and every one of them loves me, and I take care of them. Which is more than I can say for you, Lusk." He shook his head. "Jesus Christ, I got a call at four in the morning from the Lusk residence. There's Debbie lying on his living room floor, having goddamn convulsions. I still haven't figured out what you and Salinger gave her."

"Salinger gave her, please," Lusk said. "I gave her nothing." He gave a little smile. "I still can't tell the difference between amphetamines and barbiturates. One is supposed to be an 'upper,' and the other is a 'downer,' isn't it? Anyway, I was very upset about it all. But the girl did have an appetite for drugs."

"I got news for you," Walrath said, still looking up at the ceiling. "I didn't allow my girls to do that kind of shit. They get skinny and their teeth and hair go all to shit and then you got nothing but a little buzzbox on your hands. Debbie did grass, and that's it. So don't give me that shit about her appetite for drugs. You'd have an appetite for drugs, too, if you had to blow slopes in underground parking garages. But I never allowed them to do the stuff Salinger handed out. Never."

"Who was Debbie?" I asked.

"A friend and colleague of Miss Lightfoot," Walrath replied. "Mind you, Debbie wasn't the same as Annie. No way. Debbie *was* trash. She used to say, 'Jimmy, I'm not putting out. I'll give head, I'll jerk those guys off, but I'm not putting out.' I said, 'I can't believe you. Are you in this business, or are you not in this business? Sweetheart, you can't afford to specialize like that. You just ain't that good. There's too much competition out there.'"

Suddenly Walrath straightened and looked at me. "Okay, she didn't like screwing, so fuck, she should've been a waitress. Jesus Christ. That night I went to Lusk's I saved her life. I'm a regular — what do you call it? — paramedic. I saved her fucking life. And then I took her home, and what do I find in her purse? A necklace. A very expensive little necklace."

Lusk and his wife looked at each other. I knew then that Salinger hadn't gotten his ring from any Filipino maid.

"Yeah, that's right," Walrath continued, leaning back in his chair. "She'd been going to your house with Annie for your little fun and games and boosting stuff. So next morning I tie her up and start asking questions. First off, Mr. Lusk is a valued friend of mine. Second, I set her up, I introduce the lady to my friend, so where does she get off making extra profit out of the deal? Third, she's been pissing me off in general. So I said to her, 'You've been going to his place four or five times. What other shit you take? What did you do with it?' And you know what? She got stubborn on me. Me, the guy who saved her life." He sighed heavily, as if still upset over her ingratitude.

No one said anything. After a few minutes of silence, Lusk turned to his wife. "Cynthia, why don't you go upstairs? I'll join you in a —"

She shook her head fiercely. She wanted to stay. She wanted to know everything.

"What did you do to her, Walrath?" I asked.

"Ha! You don't want to know the details, Murphy. They're pretty gruesome. You see, I had this knife, and I used it on her. See, I don't like stubbornness. I just hate it. And she just got more and more stubborn, and I said, 'Debbie, you're a bad girl. I'm going to punish you until you start to be a good girl. I'm going to cut that stubbornness right out of you.'"

"Is that what happened when you saw Salinger last week?" I asked.

Walrath grinned. "You got it, boy."

"I think this is in the nature of a leg pull," Lusk said. "Mr. Walrath enjoys doing that a great deal." I don't know why Lusk kept pretending Walrath was kidding us all. Probably so he could deny something later on, I guessed. Maybe even deny it to himself.

"One of my girls saw him at the Red Lantern," Walrath explained. "It didn't take me long to find out where he lived."

"Why'd you bother?" I asked.

"I had my reasons. A lot of reasons. Herbie, a rum and Coke, please. You want a drink, Mr. Lusk? Mrs. Lusk?"

Mrs. Lusk shook her head again. Lusk looked at his empty glass, sneaked a glance at his wife, and then nodded almost imperceptibly. Mellon brought the drinks. "Shall we give this guy the water treatment?" he asked, looking at me and wiggling his eyebrows. "Cool him out in the sink?"

"Don't interrupt, Mellon." Walrath ordered, giving Mellon a sour look. The fat man retreated behind the bar.

"I told you he tried to hide Annie on me," Walrath continued. "Just because she got scared. Which was reasonable, I admit. Helping me take Debbie out to this farm kind of spooked her. See, I had Debbie wrapped in a bedsheet and then we planted her in a cesspool." He grinned at me. "Aids the process of decomposition. Anyway, she ran off to her good friend Mr. Salinger, the Jew prick with lots of money. And he hid her. My friend Mr. Shrule almost cornered him one night with a tire iron, but he got away." Walrath turned to me. "Just like you did, Murphy. Billy's strong, but he sure ain't bright. Anyway, Salinger got the message. He disappeared. And then Annie, well, she popped up here and there after he left, and then she tried to disappear, too, with that bunch of religious nuts. Not to mention some of my money. Neither of them were smart enough to stay disappeared."

He took another drink and then stared at the fried chicken box on the floor. "Salinger, he should've known better than to ever set foot again in Toronto. He knew I was permanently pissed off with him. Not to mention I knew damn well Annie told him where we dumped Debbie. He would have asked her what happened. He wasn't stupid. And you just can't trust him. No way. When I found out where he lived, I put a little bug in his apartment. A tiny little thing we use all the time in my deprogramming business. So after you left that night, I went to see him." He shook his head. "I didn't want to kill him. I just wanted to persuade him to go back to Brazil, or wherever the fuck he went to. But it was no good. He just kept carrying on like the asshole I always knew he was. And I just got so mad." He scratched the back of his head. "I wish I hadn't gotten so crazy. I really didn't want to kill him. It just complicates things."

"That's quite a tale, Mr. Walrath," Lusk said. "Quite a tale." He looked thoughtful for a moment. Then he gave me a rueful smile. "I'm well aware that some people love to imagine men like myself oozing with sexual corruption. Nasty sins of the flesh to compound our oppression of the people. High-priced whores and champagne and all that nonsense. Well, go ahead and feel superior to me if you want to."

"Are you saying you're actually concerned what I think about you?" I asked.

Lusk stared at me and then sighed. "I regret my friendship with Reuben, deeply regret it, but I'm sure that makes no difference to you." He shook his head. "Reuben was so . . . interesting. And he seemed to like me." He paused, as if to reflect for a moment on that rather odd fact. "I don't make friends easily and I have a keen appreciation of people — especially smart people — who are friendly without being deliberately ingratiating. And Reuben was smart. He was smart and he knew how to have a good time, which is something, Mr. Murphy, that was inexplicably left out of my own education. You get tired of always being the best boy in the class. Unfortunately Reuben's way of having a good time wears on the nerves after a while. Two years was long enough."

"You had yourself quite a time for those two years," Walrath said. "Not just partying with my lady friends, but getting even with all those people who were mean to you." He grinned at me. "There was one fellow who gave Mr. Lusk here a hard time. I forget why. But Reuben helped him get even with baseball bats. The two of them beat the guy up so bad he ended up in a hospital. In a wheelchair, as a matter of fact."

Lusk cleared his throat. "Anyway, when Reuben left the country for reasons I never understood, I was extremely relieved. I hoped I'd never see him again."

"You got your wish," I said.

"So I understand."

"You're saying this is all new to you?"

Walrath giggled. "I told you, Mr. Lusk, that I removed Mr. Salinger from consideration. You just didn't want to believe me. But you were relieved just the same, weren't you?"

"So you did know Salinger was back," I said.

"I had an idea," Lusk said. "I *felt* he was back." He smiled. "I'm psychic."

Walrath snorted.

"Psychic enough to know when somebody's wishing me ill, anyway. You may not believe this, Murphy, but a certain . . . psychic sensitivity isn't a bad trait to cultivate in the financial world."

"Are you serious?"

"Let's just say I had bad dreams, and then later Walrath corroborated my feeling about Salinger's return."

Bad dreams. Ill wishing. It was possible Salinger had indeed picked up some weird habits in Brazil.

"My husband has never acted with the intention to harm anybody," Mrs. Lusk said. She said it to me apparently, although she wasn't looking at anybody in particular. "That incident with baseball bats was almost entirely Salinger's doing. He was a disgusting man. He tried to drag Ivan down to the gutter with him. Anyway, Ivan had nothing to do with what happened to him."

No one responded to her outburst. Walrath just smiled. Then he shook his head. "All right, folks. Let's not worry about it. Mr. Salinger is dead. Let the dead bury the dead, as the Bible says. No reason to get upset about anything. One thing for sure, he's not going to flap his lips anymore. I say that's a real comfort for most of us here."

"What about Anna Lightfoot?" I asked.

"What about her?"

"Why did you kill her? Why did you try to kill me?"

"I told you nobody runs away from me. *Nobody*. Besides, she'd flipped out of her tiny mind. No telling what she would have raved about to some goddamn psychiatrist. And then there was the money. I don't like my whores stealing from me."

"You killed Anna?" Lusk blurted.

"Not me personally. My friends. Hey, Ivan, don't be shocked." He winked at Mrs. Lusk. "You don't need that little girl now, Ivan."

"You're lying."

Walrath bared his teeth. "Yeah, I'm lying. I'm making it all up."

"Murphy, I didn't mean . . . I . . ." Lusk swallowed and tried to pull himself together, but his words came out in a mumble. "I never meant for that girl to come to harm. I'm sorry I had anything to do with her. I was sick, I admit that. I was in a state of emotional dysfunction. I had to learn I . . . I didn't have to be afraid of mature women. I could relate to them . . . emotionally and . . . sexually . . ." His voice trailed off.

"Sure, Mr. Lusk," Walrath said. "You got yourself a good woman. You stick with her and forget the young stuff. I mean," he added with a leer in Mrs. Lusk's direction, "I mean, *real* young stuff."

"I told you Walrath was a bit of a storyteller," Lusk said to me with the desperation of a child. "You can't trust a word he says."

"That's right, Mr. Lusk. I'm just a big fibber." Walrath made a face as if he were an indulgent father. "You better go home, Mr. Lusk. You better go back to Toronto. You just leave this man to me. I'll take care of him."

Mrs. Lusk stood and bent over her husband. "Come on, Ivan," she whispered. "Take me home."

Lusk looked up at her, slightly dazed. He lifted his glass of Scotch, but the melted ice cubes were all that were left in it.

"Come on, Ivan. Take me home."

Slowly he put his glass on the table in front of him and rose from the sofa. "Goodbye," he said to no one in particular.

"Now you drive safely, okay?" Walrath said. "And you have a pleasant ride, Mrs. Lusk." He reached for her hand, kissed it, and held it for a few seconds too long.

Mrs. Lusk withdrew her hand and gave him a pained smile. "Goodbye, Mr. Walrath."

She took her husband by the arm, and the two of them walked out of the room. We could hear Lusk's heavy tread on the wooden stairway outside.

"He set you up, didn't he?" I said to Walrath. "In your new job."

"He sure did. That man talks too much, but he comes through when it counts with good money. And influence. When he farts in Toronto, they smell it in Ottawa. And to look at him you'd think he was just some fat kid who won't take gym because he doesn't want to shower with the rest of the boys."

"Nice of him to be so generous."

"Mr. Lusk is always interested in rehabilitation. Helping people like me find socially useful occupations. How'd you like his missus? A little doll, isn't she? She must have shown him things even my girls couldn't, though I can't see how that's humanly fucking possible." Walrath cackled at the thought of Mrs. Lusk outdoing his girls. "Hey, bartender, another rum and Coke." He sat down in his chair and stretched himself noisily. Then he sighed with contentment. Outside I heard Lusk's car engine start.

"You know she was a psychiatric nurse in a private clinic when he met her?" he asked. "Yes, indeedy. The strain of all that carrying on in his own house." He shook his head. "It was just terrible. So he went into a clinic for rich fuck-ups. Old Cynthia, she knew the right job to get. A nurse in a clinic for rich unmarried fuck-ups." He cackled again, and I could hear Lusk's Oldsmobile moving off in the distance. Walrath turned to Mellon. "Is Billy still watching TV?"

Mellon nodded.

"Well, get him out here. Time for you two to do some work for a change."

Mellon disappeared into another room.

"So, Murphy," Walrath said, "no hard feelings, eh?" He winked at me. "How do you feel about cesspools? They're not as nice as the marble orchard, but what the fuck will you care?" He put the safety on and aimed the .38 at me, squeezing the trigger over and over, as if the action gave him sensual pleasure.

Mellon and Shrule came into the room.

"Okay, Herbie," Walrath said, "you and Billy take that piece of garbage out to the boathouse."

Mellon and Shrule came over to my chair, and I got up. Mellon took out his .38 and pressed it against my spine in the small of my back. "Follow Mr. Muscle," the fat man ordered. "Walk slow and just keep your hands hanging loose. If you need to pick your nose or scratch yourself, let me know in advance. Otherwise I'll pull the trigger and you'll have to crawl to the boathouse."

Billy led us out of the living room the same way Lusk had left. He opened a door, and we stepped out onto the stairway on the side of the house near the driveway. Now there was a familiar van parked there. As I climbed down the stairway behind Billy, I heard frogs calling to one another in the night, while crickets kept up an incessant chatter in the grass.

The boathouse was on the opposite side of the cottage from the driveway. When we got there, Shrule put a key in the padlock on the door, opened it, and switched on a light inside. Something tiny and black scurried across the dirt floor and disappeared under the shelter of an overturned canoe. Except for the canoe the boathouse was empty. Shrule shoved me inside and then closed the door behind the three of us.

I barely saw his first punch. He hit me somewhere below the stomach, and the impact was like a bad electrical shock through the middle of my body. After the shock came the sickening realization that I had almost no air left in my lungs. He hit me a second time below my right eye. My knees buckled and I sank to the floor.

"You didn't get the nose," Mellon said. "I didn't hear the snap."

"He's got good reflexes," Shrule said. "But he'll slow down. We got all night, don't we?"

"No we don't got all night. I want some sleep. It's not as much fun for me as it is for you. Take half an hour, but that's it."

Shrule squatted beside me. I was doubled up on the floor, my hands over my abdomen and my forehead in the dirt. My face throbbed with pain and I was still gasping.

"You're going to wish that old broad never showed up when we had you in the sink," he said in a tone of voice that indicated he was in excellent humor. "This is going to be a lot slower and a lot worse."

He pulled me to my feet and then danced around me playfully, jabbing his fists in the air. I tried to step back, and something came shooting through the air and hit my nose. My eyes closed and I forgot where I was. Then my eyes opened and I discovered my knees had dissolved again. I staggered backward, fell against the side of the canoe, and slid to the ground. My head seemed to be moving in circles, lurching in an orbit around the part of me that was bursting with pain, which was my nose. A warm liquid seeped over my upper lip.

Shrule pressed his lips against the knuckles of his fist. "Shit, that hurt."

Just then the door of the boathouse opened and Mose Latouche stuck his head in. He looked at me for a moment, then shook his head. "Jeez, Murphy, he really pasted you."

He walked in, and I noticed that Farley, Kelly, and Wolf were behind him. I didn't see or hear clearly what happened next — I was trying to pull my head out of its insane orbit — but I know there was a scuffle involving somebody and Mellon, who shouted something, then began whining. Shrule remained strangely passive, standing there as if he were an innocent onlooker. No telling who might be packing what, he was probably telling himself.

Farley came over to me with a handkerchief and held it under my nose. I saw it turn scarlet. This happened to two or three handkerchiefs. I didn't know there was that much blood in my head.

"Better get him some ice," Mose said at one point after I had been absorbed for a long time in the spectacle of my nosebleed. "His head's going to swell up like a balloon."

"Before I forget, Mose, thanks for interrupting that beating. They were going to kill me. Slowly."

"Hell, it was fun following you around."

"You guys followed me?"

"Wolf said there was no way we were going to let you out of our sight when you left for that lawyer's. Not the way you look for trouble. So we tailed you."

It was nice to know my paranoia in the taxi wasn't paranoia.

"Where'd everybody go?" I asked.

"We put your two friends in their van for safekeeping," he said. "Wolf and Kelly went to see Walrath."

I got up. "I want to go, too."

Mose and Farley helped me stagger to the cottage, where I found Walrath sitting in his chair in the living room, facing Wolf and Kelly and rolling his eyes in mock exasperation.

"So Mellon and Shrule fucked up again, eh?" he said. "You just can't get good help anymore."

"You and your boys are coming back with us, Walrath," Wolf said. "You're going to talk to the police about Anna Lightfoot. And Reuben Salinger."

Walrath grinned. "Sure, I'll go back with you." He lifted his right hand to scratch his chest. As he did, Wolf's hand darted into a pocket of his jacket and pulled out the starter's pistol Mose had taken from Tony Barzula. The pistol appeared a fraction of a second before Walrath's revolver emerged from a pocket inside the pimp's jacket. Wolf squeezed the pistol's trigger and, instantaneously with the noise of the firing, I saw a circle of red appear on the blue shirt where Walrath's finger had scratched. Walrath looked surprised. He peered at Wolf and then at the gun in his hand and then at the red spot on his blue shirt. The arm holding his gun dropped to his side. He kept gazing at Wolf for a moment. And then, absentmindedly, as if he had forgotten why he had taken the revolver out, he put it back in the pocket. He leaned back in the chair and looked up at the ceiling. We could hear his breathing now; it was coming in hard, short bursts.

"Jesus Christ," he said. "I should have gotten rid of Salinger years ago. All this wouldn't have happened. I could have done it hundreds of times and nobody would have given sweet bugger all. Even with his hot Porsche and all the bad stuff he gave my girls and his little rich boy charm. Little rich boy shit!"

Walrath looked at us now as if we were about to give him an argument. I heard Kelly on the phone calling an ambulance.

"He abused my friendship," Walrath continued, a plaintive note in his voice for the first time. "I offered him my sincere friendship. I don't do that very often. Lots of guys around town say, 'Jimmy Walrath's my friend. Jimmy and me are tight.' But it's all bullshit. Except for Salinger. I offered him my *sincere* friendship."

"Take it easy," Wolf said.

A fit of coughing seized him, and the blood came up in spurts. He tried to wipe it off his chin with his fingers. Then he stared at us, one blood-smeared hand held in front of him and a new look of surprise on his face. He realized he was going to die, which evidently struck him as quite odd.

10

T HERE WAS A HALF SMILE on Inspector Staigue's face. He wasn't very happy, but something was amusing him. "That's a hell of a story, Murphy. There's only one problem."

"What's that?"

"Since when has a pimp ever told the truth under any circumstances? They're not like you and me, Murphy. Guys like us can tell the truth once in a while. Pimps can't. It has something to do with the chemicals in their brain that turn them into pimps in the first place."

"What would he have to gain by lying, telling me in front of Mr. and Mrs. Lusk that he killed Salinger?"

"He was bragging in front of the lady, Murphy. Three murders he was bragging about. Okay, the first two he probably did — Debbie and Lightfoot. But in his eyes they were trash to begin with, so they don't count. Salinger was different. Carving him up would have been something. So he took the credit. You got to understand, Murphy. Pimps are like everybody else. They're not satisfied being who they are. They usually dream of being hit men. That's their idea of class."

"What makes you so sure he lied?" Shelley asked.

"The night Salinger was murdered we had Walrath — then known as Arnold Hainesworth — under surveillance. I won't go into the details, but we knew this Hainesworth deprogramming outfit was bogus and we had an idea they might do something out of line that night. As it happened, they all went to an Arnold Schwarzenegger movie. Nice, eh? Walrath didn't go anywhere near Salinger's apartment."

"How come you didn't have him under surveillance in Elliston the day he took me and Lightfoot?"

"Don't be so bitter, Murphy. We've got plenty on your friends Shrule and Mellon. Murder one, kidnapping, forcible confinement, assault, the whole ball of wax."

"Thank you. Will you also charge Mr. and Mrs. Lusk with forcible confinement?"

His half smile faded. "That was real dumb of them. They definitely shouldn't have done that." Then he took a deep breath, reached for his pen and started bouncing it off his front teeth. "In the meantime you're still our best candidate for the Salinger murder."

"You don't have any real evidence against Hal, Inspector," Shelley said. "And besides, now that you know who your victim really was, which you can thank Hal for, by the way, that should give you something new to think about."

Staigue grinned. "Thanks for all your help, Murphy. As a matter of fact, however, we have sent up guys for murder one in this province on less evidence than we got on your client, Miss Rheingold."

"Staigue, what about Peter Hagedorn?" I asked. "Number one, he's a thug. Number two, I got the strong impression he hated Salinger, or LeRoy, from the few words he uttered over my supine body that day he nearly took out my kidneys. Number three, he lived in the same building as LeRoy, which would indicate —"

"Yeah, yeah, I hear you. It might surprise you, Murphy, but we have investigated Hagedorn thoroughly. We know he's a thug. We know he used to live in LeRoy's building. That's how LeRoy met Theresa, as a matter of fact. He and Hagedorn used to swim a lot in the pool there. They started off as pals, but when LeRoy began two-timing Hagedorn's sister, he wanted to beat the shit out of him."

"So what's the catch? Was Hagedorn at a Jean-Claude Van Damme movie the night of the murder?"

"Well, he does have an alibi, kind of. But the main thing is, we have no evidence. None. We went over Hagedorn's place with a fine-tooth comb, we looked at his clothes, we found nothing. No bloodstains, no hairs that belonged to LeRoy, no fibers from the scene of the crime. Nothing."

The three of us sat in silence for a while after that last speech. Staigue and I kept glancing at each other and then shifting our eyes away. Now that his grin had vanished he looked depressed enough to have a good session of electroshock therapy. I wasn't feeling much better myself after his news about Walrath. I didn't care for shock treatment, but I sure could have used a drink. The fact was, we were both back at square one.

"Let me tell you something, Murphy. You're not very popular right now in the Crown Attorney's Office. For starters, you made yourself inaccessible at an inconvenient time. And then you helped instigate the killing of Walrath — Don't open your mouth. Let me finish. You helped instigate the killing of Walrath in the country residence, no less, of Mr. Ivan Lusk. That last fact isn't public knowledge yet, but if reporters start sniffing around, there's no way we can bury it. Apparently lawyers for Lusk, even as we speak, are busy concocting some story in case it does become public knowledge. Like Walrath was breaking and entering at the time or something. And meanwhile we may end up with nobody to hang a rap on except for something chickenshit like illegal possession of fire arms with your friend Wolf, or maybe manslaughter."

"Manslaughter?"

"All right, illegal possession of firearms. The point I'm trying to make, Murphy, is that right now you're still of great interest to me and my colleagues in Homicide. I wish you weren't." He finally looked me in the eye. "Fortunately for you, regarding the late Mr. Salinger, we do have a witness the night he was killed. Sort of."

"What do you mean, 'sort of'?" I asked.

"A kid saw somebody in Salinger's building wearing a shirt soaked with blood. He's not exactly sure when, but it could have been around the time of the murder. Whoever this guy was, he wasn't you, Murphy. The kid said he wore a three-piece suit and looked on the porky side. But there's a little problem with the witness. Before he got on that elevator he'd smoked enough dope to get an elephant high. Plus he had his Walkman on full blast and could barely find his way out of the elevator when the doors opened. Any testimony he gives in court will be worth an ounce of dog shit."

"What's his name, Inspector?" Shelley asked.

"Get real, Miss Rheingold."

I promised Staigue I wouldn't make it hard for the police to find me anymore, and we left on reasonably good terms. The question I kept bumping up against now was the old question of why Salinger had left Toronto. Walrath had given me an answer to that question, of course. He'd told me he'd threatened Salinger for taking Anna away from him and also for knowing about Debbie's murder. All this might be true. Nobody can lie *all* the time. It takes too much neurological energy. But I could no longer take it as an explanation, or the only explanation, for Salinger's departure.

So I ended up calling on Reuben's sister again. Nobody had any better ideas. I phoned her on a Thursday afternoon, and she invited me to drop by right away. The same maid opened the door, looked at me with considerable interest, and led the way to the room with the pool table where I had first met Lydia. True to form, she was in the middle of making a fairly spectacular shot off the side of the table when I entered. She looked up at me and then glanced at the maid. "Thanks, Riva." The maid left reluctantly, and Lydia nodded at the table. "Reuben taught me."

"He did a great job."

"I got lessons from a master. He could have taught me a lot of things — how to study a racing form, how to bet two pair in a poker game — but this was enough. I wanted to leave time for my trigonometry homework. And canvassing for the United Jewish Appeal, and all the other stuff that comes with being the good child in the family."

"Were you the good child?"

"Listen, Heywood, I married Solomon Rothbard. That's not being a good child. That's being a fantastic child." She got off a hard shot at the green ball at the end of the table. It rattled around for a while but went nowhere in particular, on purpose.

"Why'd your brother leave Toronto?" I asked suddenly.

"Still haven't figured that out, eh? Well, I can't figure it out, either. Honest, I just don't know. Want a game?"

I shook my head.

"Sol found out from your lawyer all about Walrath and Lusk and that crew. What a story, eh? I always thought Lusk was a creep. According to Ms. Rheingold, Walrath told you he killed my brother. But the cops said he couldn't have."

"That's right."

Lydia rubbed her eyes and took a deep breath. I wanted to apologize to her for something, but I wasn't quite sure what. Then she straightened her back and studied the pool table. "I broke the news to Dad. We talked about Reuben a little. He says he cut Reuben off without a cent months before he left the country. Wouldn't pay his American Express bills or anything. I didn't know that. I didn't think the old man had it in him."

"Did he have any reason for cutting him off?"

"Are you talking reason, as in rational? You've got the wrong address, Heywood. I guess Dad just had enough, that's all. Something clicked, like maybe the realization that Reuben was going to hit middle age without ever having gone to the Harvard School of Business. Or doing anything worthwhile. Meanwhile his cash reserves were getting seriously depleted by his son's carefree lifestyle. Maybe Dad was experiencing a personal liquidity crisis because of Reuben. You can ask him yourself."

She started to cry. It lasted a few seconds. Then she went for a Kleenex and returned more or less composed.

"Apparently one of the delightful things Reuben used to do was borrow money from people on the basis that his brother-in-law was Solomon Rothbard. These people would occasionally get in touch with my husband." She sighed. "Poor Sol. He's had to put up with so much."

We stood in awkward silence for a moment.

"But you don't want to hear all this dreary soap opera stuff. How about a game?" She nudged my rib cage with the cue. "Come on, coward. Afraid a woman will beat you?"

She beat me all right. We played three games and she won all of them. Then I said goodbye to her.

"Who taught *you* to play pool?" she asked. "Your maternal grandmother?" She gave me a polite kiss on the cheek. "Goodbye, Heywood. Good luck to you."

"Good luck to you, Lydia."

She shrugged, as if good luck were something she had risen above or sunk beneath but wasn't sure which.

Later that day, after I had taken a cab back to my apartment, I got a phone call.

"Heywood? You're a hard man to get a hold of."

The voice was unmistakable. It was Paul Hornak's.

"Oh, I've been out and about. What's up, Paul?"

"Thought we might get together for a drink, if you've got some time this week."

"I'd be delighted."

"Terrific. How about tomorrow night? Around eight? The rooftop bar at the Park Plaza?"

"Sure."

"Great. I'll look forward to seeing you."

"Wait a minute, Paul. I don't mean to be inquisitive, but what exactly do you have in mind?"

"It's been a long time. We've missed you in the press gallery."

"Glad to hear it. I'd still like to know what you have in mind."

There was a pause on the other end of the line.

"I was talking to Bennett Kellogg."

"Oh?"

"He said you told him you were doing an article for *Toronto Life,* about an Indian girl. But when he checked with the magazine, they told him they didn't know a thing about it."

"And what, may I ask, does that have to do with you?"

He cleared his throat. "Look, Heywood, why don't we talk about this over a drink? Tomorrow night."

"Okay. Park Plaza at eight."

As soon as I hung up, I had the feeling all reporters experience when they have a big interview coming up. I realized I damn well better prepare for it and know the right questions to ask. In fact, I knew I'd better have the right answers to them, too. At this moment, however, I could only guess. Was a friend of Hornak's the man who dated Anna Lightfoot's mother, who fathered her child? Was it Hornak himself? None of the woman's classmates at the Bible college had any political connections from what I could tell, but that didn't mean much. I was no expert on the politics of Ontario, even in the days when I had covered them as a reporter. So I needed an informant. And the name that kept occurring to me was Lusk.

When I parked the borrowed Buick LeSabre at the Lusks' house later that night, I knew immediately they had followed Cardinal Moone's advice and gotten some security, or at least beefed it up. As I walked up the driveway, a young man built like a linebacker came around a corner of the house and stopped me. "Can I help you?"

"I'm here to see Mr. and Mrs. Lusk."

"They're out of town. You can leave a message with me."

"Tell them Heywood Murphy dropped by."

He took out a notebook. "How do you spell that?"

I spelled it for him. "Look, why don't you go in and drop that note off? Like right now. I'll be in my car for a few minutes in case the, uh, maid or the butler has some word for me."

We stared at each other silently for a few seconds. I had kept my tone as far away from smart-alecky as I could. He didn't look as if he was ready to kid around, or do anybody any favors, for that matter.

"Can't hurt, and your employers might be grateful." I added.

"I wouldn't wait too long in that car if I were you."

I went back, turned the car's dome light on, and opened a book about the Toronto Blue Jays farm system. I hadn't read more than a few pages when the security man came into view and gestured with his head in the direction of the house. He led me back up the driveway to the front door, and when he opened it, I saw Mrs. Lusk waiting for me in the hallway. She nodded to the man, who muttered, "You know where you can find me, Mrs. Lusk." Then she led me to a room on the first floor. The walls of the room were blue and were covered with black-and-white engravings of Venice. I guessed it was Venice, because there were boats floating between the buildings. The room also contained vases filled with roses, and sofas and chairs covered in chintz that looked as if you weren't supposed to sit on them.

Mrs. Lusk actually smiled at me, however, and invited me to have a seat. "What can I do for you, Heywood?"

"Your husband around, Mrs. Lusk?"

"Cynthia, please. No, Ivan's not around. He's in New York on business."

"I see."

"He wouldn't see you, anyway, I'm afraid. He's very upset at all the talk that's happened since that . . . horrible man died. Ivan blames you for the scandal."

"That's too bad. If Walrath had killed me, like you wanted, he would have been spared the scandal. Tough break for your husband."

She pretended she hadn't heard me. "I said to him, 'Ivan, be grateful. He got rid of him for you. What you didn't have the ... resolve to do, he did. He got rid of that pimp once and for all.'" She shook her head, as if in disgust, and then looked me in the eye again. "Can I get you anything? Coffee, tea, a drink?"

"No thanks."

"What do you want to see Ivan for, Heywood?"

"Information."

"More information? Seems to me you got quite an earful the other night. What else could you possibly want to know?" She leaned forward in her chair. "I know we treated you badly, Heywood, and I'm sorry about that. I really am. I was desperate. Ivan can't handle these things, and I just didn't know what to do. Anyway, we can make it up to you." She smiled again. "I mean that."

I glanced around the room. Yes, she could make it up to me. "Even though your husband won't see me?"

"Yes."

She said it as if she meant it.

"That's nice of you to offer, Mrs. — Cynthia. But I still —"

"Excuse me, I'm going to have a glass of wine. Sure you won't join me?"

I shook my head. She went over to a liquor cabinet and poured herself something from a decanter. There were a lot of splendid things in this room, but nothing looked quite as gorgeous to me as what was inside that cut-glass bottle.

"On second thought, Cynthia, I'll have some soda water, if you've got some."

"Sure. What were you saying?"

"I still entertain fears for my personal safety when I'm around you, Cynthia. That's kind of standing in the way of our budding friendship."

She sat down again after handing me the soda water, then spread her arms a bit, as if inviting me to frisk her. "No more firearms. We have security people now who take care of that end of things. And no more friends like Mr. Walrath. So we can put our relationship on a new footing." She chuckled. "You're as safe with me as if you were in church. Now, what's this information you want?"

"Paul Hornak called me up tonight." I paused. There was no hint of any change of expression in her face. "He wants to talk to me tomorrow night," I continued. "Something about Anna Lightfoot, I gather. I thought I might get your husband to brief me before the meeting."

"On what?"

"On what Hornak's after. He's after something very bad. He wouldn't have called me otherwise."

Mrs. Lusk arched an eyebrow. The arch meant she was going to say something interesting. Maybe drag somebody else's name through the mud. Her husband wouldn't be alone.

"You know about Anna Lightfoot's mother, don't you?" I asked.

"You mean the woman who went to Bible college?"

"Yes."

"Indeed I do. She was a very nice young Indian girl, I understand. She wanted to study the Bible, and so she came to the big city and went to Bible college and met all sorts of very nice people. And one of those very nice people wasn't a student in the college, but he was active in his church and hung around the college a lot."

She got up and filled her glass again from the decanter. "And wouldn't you know it," she continued, "despite their high moral standards, they ended up in bed and she got pregnant. Abortion was out of the question, with their high moral standards. Marriage was out of the question, too. The young man was very ambitious. He had a career in politics all mapped out. And having a squaw for a wife in Ontario will never do. Especially as this girl was kind of . . . rustic. Cocktail parties with Cabinet ministers and their wives would have been too much for her. So although she was very, very nice, the nice young man who knocked her up strongly suggested she go back to her reserve. Which she did. And she immediately married a young Indian man who I understand wasn't so nice because he killed her."

As she reflected for a moment on that last fact, I thought I could make out the faint traces of a smirk on her face. "Anyway, our nice young man back in Toronto felt he was off the hook when he read about it in the newspapers. He was now the father of a baby daughter, but as far as he knew, nobody knew about it. So he continued his career in provincial politics and got to be very well-known."

She looked at me hard over her wineglass. "I'm not talking about Hornak, by the way. Or my husband. I'm talking about somebody who is very well-known. Anyway, about thirteen years later, your friend Mr. Salinger, who'd become well acquainted with this famous man's daughter, somehow ran across something — I believe it was a photograph — that clued him in."

I remembered, when she said this, the photocopy of the photograph I had found in Salinger's trunk, the one I had in my pocket. The one I never could quite make out. I also remembered Anna's remark about her "mommy's photograph."

"He realized who her father was," she continued, "but he didn't tell anybody right away. This famous man's daughter now worked as a teenage hooker. What she used to do to earn money was go to parties and make the acquaintance of certain gentlemen there. And some of those gentlemen were quite important people, as you know. Want some more soda water?"

I shook my head.

"Anyway, this Salinger character took his time. One night he took her to a party where a lot of big politicians were present. And Salinger went up to one very big politician and whispered in his ear that he had just the girl for him. A girl who would give him a bigger thrill even than making speeches and getting his picture in the paper. Needless to say, that would have to be quite some girl. So the very big politician was interested. By then he'd come a long way from hanging around Bible colleges." She paused. "But he still had a taste for squaws."

She examined the wine in her glass for a moment. "So Mr. Salinger proved to be very clever. After that evening, he got in touch with Mr. Hornak and told him the whole story. Told him the very big politician was now in very big trouble. He had proof this man had done something that was quite beyond the pale. And Salinger just might get in touch with whatever branch of the police that investigates these nasty offenses. Quite a story, isn't it? So Mr. Hornak, who is very ingenious, told Mr. Salinger that it was all quite unnecessary."

She pronounced Hornak's name as if it were an embarrassing disease. "Hornak arranged for Salinger to take a trip outside the country. He arranged for someone else to send him funds on a regular basis so Salinger could enjoy his trip to the fullest. Salinger wasn't used to economy class, even though he was broke at the time."

"Was that someone else your husband?"

"Ivan never misses a chance to do favors for this very big politician. Besides, he had his own reasons for wanting Salinger to go away. Stupid reasons, in my opinion. After I found out about it, I insisted he stop the payments. Funding 'Arnold Hainesworth' was bad enough. How much does somebody have to pay for past sins?"

"It depends, Cynthia. So Salinger stopped getting his money, and then he came back for more."

"I guess so. But he didn't get any more. Walrath took care of that, as you know. Ivan had nothing to do with it."

"Walrath didn't take care of it."

She looked up sharply from her glass. "What are you talking about?"

"The cops had Walrath under surveillance the night of Salinger's murder. He didn't touch Salinger."

Cynthia continued to stare at me, then laughed suddenly. "You did do it, after all, you bad man. I didn't think you had it in you."

"I don't."

"You don't." She shrugged. "Well, so you're still behind the eight ball."

"No. The cops have another suspect. Somebody else who hated Salinger. Someone who had nothing to do with Lightfoot or Walrath or anybody."

I was lying, but she seemed to believe me. She shrugged again. "So that's all over with. Are you satisfied with your information?"

"Yes." I pulled myself out of the chair. "Thank you very much."

She put her glass down and rose. We faced each other for a moment.

"Yes, you'd better go. Security will get nervous. I think they realize you're not an ordinary guest. I have my own telephone number, by the way. Have you got a pen?" I gave her one, and she took my hand and wrote the number on the palm. "Can you read that?" she asked, still holding my hand in hers.

"Perfectly."

She gave the hand a slight squeeze. "Remember what I said tonight? About making up for previous rudeness? I'm not naturally a dangerous woman."

"I'm not so sure about that."

She dropped my hand and laughed. "Nothing you can't handle, Mr. Murphy."

Now it was her turn to lie. The most frightening thing for me was that I was beginning to believe her, to think maybe I could handle her.

Later that evening I called Sue Spurdle. I figured it was time to get in touch with Theresa again despite what the police had told me.

For some reason I couldn't fathom, when Spurdle answered, she was a lot friendlier than the last time I'd spoken to her. But she wasn't any more helpful. She told me Theresa had taken a three-month leave of absence from City Hall and was staying with a cousin in Calgary, trying to repair the damage done to her nervous system by recent events. Spurdle claimed she didn't have the cousin's phone number, or even the name.

"By the way, Sue, you never told me about Theresa's brother," I said.

"Peter? What do you want with that creep?"

"You know him?"

"A little. He came around a few days ago and told me not to talk to you or I'd be sorry."

"Did you believe him?"

"Nah. He's got his own problems."

"Such as?"

"Like, he'd better watch out he doesn't get beaten up himself."

"By whom?"

"By guys who are even bigger creeps than he is. Don't ask me for details."

"Sue, this could be important —"

"It's been nice talking to you, Mr. Murphy. Maybe someday we'll have a drink or something."

She hung up. That was interesting, I thought. I hadn't gotten any information from her I could make sense of, but she certainly aroused my curiosity. And I realized one thing for sure. The police might have investigated Peter Hagedorn thoroughly, as Staigue assured me, but they hadn't been thorough enough.

The following evening at eight I sat at a table in the Park Plaza's rooftop bar with a glass of Perrier water in front of me. Wolf, who was waiting for me in the lobby, had driven me there in yet another car he had managed to borrow — a relatively new Toyota Corolla. Five minutes after the waiter brought my drink, Hornak entered the room, saw me, and smiled. "You're looking well," he said when we shook hands.

I returned the compliment. There was a brightness in his eyes, a crisp energy in his movements, that I hadn't noticed in the past. He'd never looked sleepy before, but he now seemed braced like a tennis player forever waiting to return a serve.

"Last time I saw you, you were walking out of an OPA dinner in the middle of an interesting talk."

"I had an appointment."

"With the police?"

"I don't make appointments with the police. Lately they've been glad to see me anytime."

"And how is life treating you otherwise?"

"It's been a difficult couple of weeks, Paul, what with one murder after another."

"That's too bad. May I ask you a question before we proceed any further? Are you wired?"

I guffawed.

"Why don't we go to the john for a minute?"

"Sure, Paul."

Inside the men's room a young man with a white shirt, narrow tie, and Mohawk haircut stood over the urinal and watched Hornak frisk me. The young man finished, did up his fly, and walked out with a grin on his face; he was going to enjoy telling his friends at the table about this one. Hornak satisfied himself that I had no tape recorder on me and gave me a pat on the arm. "Just making sure we weren't having any of your journalistic pranks, Murphy. Now we can talk freely and frankly."

Back at the table I noticed the young man and his girlfriend glancing at us from a table across the room. Hornak ignored them.

"So, Hal, what on earth is this Bennett Kellogg business all about?"

"You answer first. What's it to you?"

"Kellogg is worried about a smear. As you know, he's not popular with the media, and he's afraid people like you are trying to set him up as Canada's version of Jimmy Swaggart or Jim Bakker." He smiled. "Not that he's got anything to hide, or that you would be unscrupulous, but, since he happens to be a friend of mine and knows I've had lots of experience with the media, he came to me and I told him I'd talk to you."

"Don't lie to me, Paul."

"I beg your pardon?"

"You're not worried about Kellogg. You know I was barking up the wrong tree. And you know who I was really after."

"Good God, what *have* we been smoking?"

"Your friend in politics, Paul. Not Kellogg."

Hornak shook his head, leaned forward, and placed his hands on the table. His alertness was a force radiating from his body — a steady, quiet force that penetrated my skin.

"Your friend who was being blackmailed by Reuben Salinger," I added.

"Where did you hear about this?"

At that second I knew. The way he placed his hands on the table told me, or maybe it was the three-piece suit he was wearing, the suit that must have been very like the one he'd worn the night he'd killed Salinger. I grabbed his shirtfront. "Goddamn you, Hornak," I whispered. "You did do it, you son of a bitch."

The couple who had been glancing at us were now staring, along with a few others. I released Hornak's shirtfront and leaned back in my chair. Neither of us said anything for a moment. Then the waiter appeared. "How are we doing, Mr. Hornak?" he asked softly.

"Just fine, Ralph, just fine. I'll have another Scotch." Hornak looked at me. "Another Perrier, Hal?"

I shook my head. The waiter gave me a look and then left.

"To go back to where we were, Hal, before you assaulted me. Where *did* you hear this story about Salinger blackmailing somebody?

"Mrs. Lusk."

"Now why would she tell you a story like that?"

I leaned forward again, my face inches from his, ready to shout at him, but he held out his hand before I could open my mouth. "One thing at a time. Why *would* she tell you a story like that?"

I slumped back in my chair. "She's annoyed that her husband's getting all the flak about Walrath and teenage hookers. Or she happens to be in the mood for gossip and she's never going to have better dirt than this. Or she can't stand you. You tell me. All I know is what she said is true."

"Oh, come now, Hal —"

"Stop it. I don't care about your friend who was being blackmailed. I don't even care that you killed Salinger. Just stop lying to me."

"All right. She was telling the truth. But she's also being less than completely candid with you, my friend."

"Oh?"

"She's paying me back. I know all sorts of amusing things about her past." He mentioned a well-known political figure who had died of a stroke a few years ago. "Do you know *where* he died?"

I shook my head.

"In a Jacuzzi with dear Cynthia. They were attempting some interesting acrobatics at the time." He laughed. "She had a job at a clinic frequented by wealthy patients, and she certainly made the most of it."

"I can tell there's no love lost between you two."

"Oh, I assure you, the woman despises me." He cleared his throat. "I hope you realize she'll never back up this story."

"It doesn't matter."

"It does matter. If she doesn't back it up, it's just what you said — gossip. Worthy of no credence from right-minded people."

"Right. But it's true."

"Truth is what can be substantiated, Heywood. I realize lack of substantiation never stopped a newspaper from printing anything, but even our fearless Toronto media won't touch this one, believe me. No one will stand behind the story. No one. Not even the ineffable Mrs. Lusk. Therefore it's not true. It's a grotesque ... lie. Anybody should be ashamed to repeat it." He leaned back in his chair. "So much for my motivation. Do you have any other evidence that I killed Salinger?"

"I'll find more."

"I doubt it. I was very lucky that night."

Ralph returned with Hornak's Scotch, then left.

"Foolish, but lucky." Hornak's eyes glittered. I suddenly had an idea why he was looking so good. Killing Salinger had proved to be a tonic for his nerves and muscles. It had sharpened an already acute intellect, improved his circulation, heightened his senses.

"Tell me about it, Paul."

"You're still a suspect in Salinger's murder, aren't you? From what I hear they have a real case against you."

"Not enough to get by a jury."

"I see. Maybe your best policy, Hal, is to forget all about Salinger's murder. And hope everyone else does, too."

"Don't keep me in suspense, Paul. Tell me about that night."

Hornak wanted to tell me. I could see that. It was an unusual event in his life, I'm sure, committing murder. People like to talk about unusual events in their lives. To somebody, anyway. To somebody who can understand. So why shouldn't he talk to me? He had nothing to fear from me, not even that I would spread stories about him. The stories would always remain "unsubstantiated." Even if some people believed them, or half believed them, they would only provide him with a whispered reputation for wickedness. In Hornak's business a suspected reputation for wickedness was a bonus.

He sat back in his chair and yawned, not altogether convincingly. Then he leaned forward again. "Here's a story for you, Hal. Once upon a time Paul Hornak paid a visit to your friend Reuben Salinger. He wanted to talk about Salinger's peculiar ideas for obtaining a guaranteed life income." Hornak looked me straight in the eye. He was mischievous now, like a boy accepting a dare. "So this is what happened," he continued. "That night no one answers the door when Hornak knocks, so he lets himself in through a devious means we won't go into now. And Hornak discovers Salinger lying fast asleep in his bed. Hornak looks around the apartment and gets lucky. He finds some money in the vegetable bin of Salinger's refrigerator. Blackmail money. But he wants more. He wants a certain photograph of one of Hornak's associates, the object of the blackmail. This photograph shows the associate — let's call him a distinguished Ontario statesman — in his younger days with a certain Indian woman. The distinguished Ontario statesman has written something on the back of the photograph that is surprisingly indiscreet.

"Hornak has the idea this photograph is in Salinger's bedroom. He goes into the bedroom, carrying — for protection, for intimidation? — a carving knife from the kitchen. He looks around the bedroom. He looks in a chest of drawers, in a closet. Then he has an idea. He lifts the corner of Salinger's pillow and finds the photograph." Hornak smiled. "A photograph that no longer exists, needless to say. Anyway, Hornak is very, very happy. He's found what he's been looking for. Salinger will no longer be a problem. And at that moment Salinger opens his eyes and sees Hornak with the photo."

Hornak paused for dramatic effect. "You can imagine what Hornak's reaction is," he said. "From happiness and relief, bordering on the euphoric, to anger and dismay. And then Salinger, who instantly realizes what's happening, gives Hornak a most disgusting smile."

Hornak sat back in his chair and looked at me almost in defiance. "That smile makes Hornak very, very angry. And besides, he doesn't want to give up that photo."

"So you killed him."

Hornak shrugged. "It was a split-second decision. Another second or two and Salinger would have been sufficiently awake to put up a struggle. Hornak had to decide instantly whether to take up arms against a sea of troubles, and by opposing, end them, or to put up with that prime asshole for an indefinite future. He let his emotions decide. And that's why your friend Salinger ended up with a knife in his chest." Hornak giggled. "Now what would your friends at the *Clarion* think about that story?"

"I wouldn't tell them."

"Why not? It's a marvelous story."

"I'm saving it for the boys in Homicide."

"They don't have much time for such fanciful tales, Hal. Especially from dubious characters like yourself."

"Maybe I could persuade them to go over Salinger's apartment again, Paul. Who knows what you left there — fingerprints, hair —"

"Don't be such an idiot, Hal. Look, I wouldn't dream of threatening you, but you should keep certain things in perspective. Remember, I can make much more trouble for you than you can possibly make for me. The fact I'm talking to you with this kind of frankness is a small indication of that."

"I suppose so."

"You know so. I certainly don't want to cause you trouble. It gets tiresome doing the dirty work for the distinguished Ontario statesman."

Hornak looked at me as though he fully expected agreement. I said nothing. His "confession" seemed curiously anticlimactic, and I was getting tired of the conversation. Hornak now struck me as nothing more than a Billy Shrule with brains and a membership in the Albany Club. Talking to the original Billy Shrule hadn't been any fun, either.

"What did Edmund Burke say — 'Kings are naturally lovers of low company'?" Hornak continued. "Well so, alas, are some of our distinguished Ontario statesmen. It can't be helped. And the consequences have to be faced. *C'est tout.*" He put a credit card on the table and signaled to Ralph for the bill. "Anything else you have to ask me?"

"No, I think I've heard enough. See you later, Hornak."

I got up and took the elevator to the hotel lobby. In the elevator I remembered LeRoy suddenly confessing to me that he was "losing it," and the feeling of bewilderment and panic he had radiated. That feeling, I now knew, wasn't caused by his fear of Hagedorn, or Walrath, or anyone really. It was a feeling, I suspected, caused by his awareness that something inside him was burning up and disappearing. Some weird energy, some nervous fuel that had propelled him, that drove him on his cruel and careless way, was at its end. Perhaps it happened to all sociopaths in the end. A natural process nobody could understand.

On the other hand, I thought, maybe it was simpler. Maybe he was afraid Hornak was really going to pull the plug on him, take away a source of income he had been counting on. Maybe he was afraid he would have to go back on the street and start over again, with not even a crummy job at City Hall to fall back on.

Wolf was sitting in a chair in the lobby near the elevator door. He was reading a book — *The Guide for the Perplexed* by Moses Maimonides.

"You really are serious about becoming a Jew, aren't you?"

"This guy's great, Heywood. I wish I'd read this ten years ago. How'd your talk with Hornak go?"

We left the hotel, got into his car, and drove back to Uncle Mose's house. On the way I told him everything about the meeting. After I finished, we were both silent. Five minutes passed before either of us said anything.

"What are you going to do now?" Wolf finally asked.

"I don't know. Maybe call on Mrs. Lusk."

Wolf looked at me.

"Keep your eyes on the road! You almost killed that pedestrian. She told me last night she'd make up for the way she treated me the night at the cottage."

"What does she mean by that?"

"Come on, look where you're driving. She means . . . I don't know . . . various things."

"You can't be serious about taking up with this woman? She's bad news."

"Yes, she is. But she's also filthy rich. Hey, Wolf, if you don't pay attention to your driving, I'm getting out. She's rich and I'm broke. So why not 'take up' with Mrs. Lusk, as you put it? It'll pay a hell of a lot better than journalism."

Wolf tapped the book on the front seat with his index finger. "Read Maimonides. He'll give you wisdom and inspiration."

"Oh, bullshit!"

Wolf smiled. "Read Maimonides and come up north with me and Malcolm and relax for a while. We'll give you wild rice and moose meat, real Indian stuff."

"What about your illegal possession charge?"

"I'll worry about that later. I don't know much about white man's justice, but I think I see a suspended sentence in my future."

"Anyway, you're right. I'm not really serious about Mrs. Lusk. I'd rather breed rattlesnakes for a living than cozy up to her. It's just that if somebody offers you wads of money for breeding rattlesnakes, you tend to at least think about the proposition."

I decided then that maybe I would go up north. Take a laptop with me. If bringing Hornak to justice through conventional means was no longer a possibility, perhaps there were other ways of obtaining satisfaction, like writing an account of my recent adventures. A full and frank account. Yes, I thought, that might be the ticket. A true story that would end with this evening's conversation at the Park Plaza. And begin years ago when Anna Lightfoot and Reuben Salinger walked the streets of Toronto, looking for interesting chances to take.